MW00529327

Ghost Dance

A SEQUEL TO GASTON LEROUX'S
THE PHANTOM OF THE OPERA

CHRISTINE POPE

This is a work of fiction. Names, characters, places, and incidents are either the product of the author's imagination or are used fictitiously. Any resemblance to actual events, places, organizations, or persons, whether living or dead, is entirely coincidental.

GHOST DANCE: A SEQUEL TO GASTON LEROUX'S THE PHANTOM OF THE OPERA

Copyright © 2020 by Christine Pope

ISBN: 978-1-946435-37-8

Published by Dark Valentine Press

Cover design by MiblArt

All rights reserved. No part of this book may be reproduced in any form or by any electronic or mechanical means, including information storage and retrieval systems—except in the case of brief quotations embodied in critical articles or reviews—without permission in writing from its publisher, Dark Valentine Press.

CHAPTER 1

Uneasy Ghosts

The Paris *Presse* sat in its usual place at the breakfast table, awaiting Raoul's return from his morning ride. The paper was several days old, of course; even the Comte de Chagny could not expect to receive a Paris paper on the day it was published when his estate was located several hundred miles away from the capital.

What made Christine pause to glance down at the paper, she would never know, although perhaps she thought there might be some news of her old friend Meg in the society column; the announcement of Meg Giry's engagement to the

Baron de Castelo-Barbezac had immediately catapulted the erstwhile opera dancer into the ranks of the Third Republic's highest society. Otherwise, there was very little other incentive for Christine to read the paper, as the endless parliamentary bickering and internecine squabbles between the various ministers and undersecretaries of the current government held absolutely no interest for her. Tucked away here on the Chagny estate in the Loire Valley, she felt very far away from Paris...and thank goodness for that.

The very last thing she had expected when she glanced at the newspaper was the headline that screamed at her in large type even from a foot away: *Murders in the Rue Scribe!*

Christine knew the Rue Scribe well, of course—a narrow but busy lane that bordered the Paris Opera to the west. With a shiver, she recalled the hidden door that opened to the street, and the dim passageway to the bowels of the Palais Garnier it concealed. At once, it seemed as if her nostrils were filled with the dank smell of water that had been trapped down there in the dark for years, the air heavy with damp and secrets too long kept. For a moment, the sunlit room in the Chagny chateau spun crazily around her, and she had to reach out and grip the back of a heavy carved oak chair to steady herself.

That was a very long time ago, she told herself in what she hoped were bracing inner tones, *in another world*.

Taking a breath, she forced her attention back to the paper. It had been more than two years since she fled the opera house, after all. She couldn't—no, she *wouldn't*—allow herself to be consumed by those memories once more, not when she had worked so hard to thrust them away into a hidden corner of her mind so they would no longer haunt her thoughts.

Her resolve lasted only a few seconds, however. As she read further, her knees began to tremble underneath their concealing layers of multiple petticoats and the draped swags of her fine wool bustle gown, and she pulled out the chair she held and collapsed onto it, fearing her legs might not support her any longer if she remained standing.

Her eyes flashed over the words, and her heart started to pound in quick, breathless strokes. Unfortunately, the mounting distress within her did nothing to change the contents of the article.

This reporter is pained to relay the information that another hapless victim has met his end in the dark recesses of the Rue Scribe. The Sûreté will not release any details, but those first on the scene have reported that the second victim, like Monsieur Charles, whose body was discovered only three days ago, was found with livid marks about the throat, marks that would indicate a garrote of some kind was used. The manner of execution brings to mind the events of several years past, when the Opera Ghost unleashed a reign of terror at the Palais Garnier and dispatched several victims in the same way. The authorities are refusing to speculate on the similarities between these two new cases and the events of two years ago. This reporter, however, cannot help but be struck by the parallels. Are we now facing another onslaught by the notorious Phantom of the Opera?

Christine closed her eyes. It couldn't be true. He was dead; the announcement in *L'Epoque* had said so in three brief words — *Erik is dead* — and Meg had faithfully sent the clipping to Christine at the direction she had left, a charming little hostel in Copenhagen where she and Raoul had first stayed on their honeymoon. They had only been married for a week then, and Raoul had been most concerned when he returned to their rooms from a quick errand to find his new bride crying there alone. Of course, Christine had never been able to tell him the real reason why she wept — she had made up some nonsense about women's sensibilities and he, dear boy, had believed her. After all, a woman on her honeymoon could not very well confess her feelings for a man everyone else thought a monster.

After all that, why could she still hear the Opera Ghost's voice in her mind? *You must love me, Christine*, he had said, voice urgent, pleading, and then those terrible tears had rolled down his savagely sunken cheeks. Oh, the horror of it all, of a face that could have been dredged from the depths of her darkest nightmares, and yet—

And yet she still dreamed of him, still sometimes recalled how those coldly elegant fingers had touched her with a moth-light brush against her throat, against her hair, awakening emotions she had never wanted to acknowledge. She had grown accustomed to the sad reality that she often rose in the morning after hearing Erik's and not Raoul's voice in her dreams. More than once, she had told herself it was just a form of mesmerism, only the last lingering shreds of the hold the Opera Ghost once had on her mind. She wouldn't allow those dreams to mean anything.

But that was why they had returned to Raoul's homeland as soon as they did, even though the night they'd fled from the Opera

House, they had assured one another that they would never again set foot in France. True, the family's solicitors had been most pressing— Raoul was cleared of any wrongdoing in the death of his older brother, but once the matter of his culpability had been set aside, naturally, he was expected to come home to manage the family estate. Still, that particular duty wouldn't have been enough on its own to compel his return; Raoul most likely would have put off family business for as long as necessary if it had pleased Christine, but she had been overcome by a desire to leave Scandinavia almost as soon as she'd seen the solicitor's telegram. Raoul had simply thought she was being considerate, that she was thinking only of his duty to his name and his estate, and she let him believe that.

How could she have ever told him the truth?

I went home to Scandinavia thinking I would rediscover the sound of my father's music, and yet I heard only him. Where she should have heard the echoes of the folk tunes her father had loved so much, instead her mind was filled with the seductive whispers of Erik's voice, the haunting strains of "The Resurrection of Lazarus," which she had once heard him play on the violin. No, fleeing France and returning to her childhood haunts had not solved anything. If possible, her new surroundings had made the situation even worse. She had not been to Sweden for more than ten years, and she found it had become foreign to her. Even recalling the words and phrases of her native tongue had been painful as she fumbled to remember the correct syntax, so different from the French she had lived and breathed and dreamed in for so long.

And so they had returned to France, but not to Paris. The Chagny estates were located in the lower reaches of the Loire Valley and were famed for their excellent Chenin blancs and sweet dessert wines. It was there that she found her first measure of peace in a long while; at Chagny, as the estate was simply called, she was finally able to turn her back on the past. It was almost possible to forget the terror of her last days in Paris in the sunlit calm of Chagny.

But now—she pressed her palms against the pale gray fabric of her morning gown, willing herself to be calm. Surely, the article could only be the sensational fabrication of a reporter seeking fame—what better way to stir the public's imagination than to recall the ghost who had once haunted the Paris Opera and then blame him for these new, completely unrelated crimes? Too well she recalled the lurid stories that had been published about her—fortune hunter, loose woman, adventuress—when her relationship with Raoul couldn't be hidden any longer. It did not require a great leap of the imagination to infer that the same sort of yellow journalism might be involved in this particular matter as well.

Then she heard Raoul call her name as he came in from his daily ride through the vineyards. Without thinking, she gathered up the paper and shoved it under her chair; it would be well hidden there under her cascading, ruffled skirts.

Raoul entered the room, still wearing his high riding boots and close-fitting breeches. He looked particularly well that morning; although the sun was out, the air still had the early spring chill of March, and the brisk ride had brought a flush to his cheeks.

As usual, she lifted her face for his customary kiss, this time hoping he wouldn't notice anything unusual in her expression.

His lips brushed her cheek, and he smiled. "My darling," he said, and as always, his tone was warm, indulgent. "It really is a glorious day outside. Perhaps we might walk in the gardens later?"

"Certainly," she replied, relieved that at least she sounded fairly calm, as though nothing had occurred to disturb the quiet fragility of her world. "Berthe wanted me to look at the hangings in the drawing room after breakfast, but—"

"After that, then," he said, then paused, as if truly focusing on her face for the first time. "Are you quite well? You look rather pale." And there it was, the quickest darting of his gaze toward her midsection, the unspoken question forming once again.

Dear lord, how she hated that. She knew Raoul longed for a child, and she thought she did as well, but it had been more than two years since their wedding night, and still there was no sign of an heir to the Chagny line. Raoul had made light of the matter, pointing to the more than fifteen years which had separated him from his two sisters, but Christine knew that her continued inability to conceive disturbed him, as indeed, it did her as well. That would be the ultimate irony, she thought, for Raoul to have fought so hard for a barren wife. Doctor Lambert, the Chagny family physician, proclaimed her to be completely healthy and saw no reason why she shouldn't have a nursery full of children by the time she was done. But every passing month put the lie to the good doctor's words, and every month, she didn't know whether to feel regret or relief.

"Everything is fine," she said at length, smiling even as she gave the smallest shake of her head to put an end to his wordless speculation. "It's just —"

He looked at her, obviously concerned.

The lie came to her lips almost before she knew what she was saying. "I've had a letter from Meg, and she'd very much like me to come up to Paris early. She says that Monsieur Worth is throwing tantrums over not being able to fit me in person, and that I should be very careful of upsetting him. For of course, Meg wants everything perfect for her wedding." Christine bit her lip then, thinking of her own hasty wedding, with strangers as witnesses and a priest who was also a stranger to them performing the sacred rites. It was certainly not the wedding she had dreamed of as a little girl.

Raoul frowned, then said, "But you know what a critical time it is here at Chagny—"

It was true. Early spring could be tricky; an untimely frost would send the locals out with smudge pots around the clock, and Raoul could not leave all the work to Monsieur Fournier to manage—he would ride alongside the overseer to make sure no tender vines were lost. Sometimes she thought he loved Chagny all the more because he had never expected it to be his.

And really, that solicitude suited her intentions in this moment, even as they began to form. Meg's impending nuptials were the ideal excuse for her to return to Paris now, without Raoul. Of course, they had both planned to go to the wedding in two weeks; orders had already been sent ahead for the Chagny town house in the Faubourg Saint Germain to be prepared for their arrival. But now Christine felt that she must return to Paris, and alone. She knew her mind would never let her rest until she knew the truth behind these murders near the Opera. Could it be that Erik was still alive? And if he were, what then? Somehow, she couldn't believe he was the perpetrator of these new, gruesome crimes. What earthly purpose could they serve? Why, if he had lain hidden and quiet for the past two years, would he suddenly advertise his presence in such a sensational way?

Not for a second did she believe him incapable of such crimes—she was not quite that naïve. He had killed, and more than once, but not randomly, not without purpose. What reason could he possibly have to commit murder almost on the steps of the Opera itself? Certainly, life had gone on there since the scandal surrounding her own disappearance and the death of Philippe, the Comte de Chagny; although the Paris Opera had shuttered itself for several months afterward, eventually, new productions were mounted with new divas. La Carlotta could not be persuaded to set foot there ever again, and had in fact returned to her native Spain. But the show went on as it always had, with no further whisper of the Opera Ghost, although Meg had written, with somewhat unbecoming glee, that Box Five, his former favorite, had to be let at a substantially reduced rate due to worries that it was still haunted by his presence.

For the past two years, Christine had allowed herself to think Erik dead. It was easier that way. It was easier still to fall into the rhythms of life at Chagny, to do her best to be a proper mistress of the vast estate, even though she had never thought she would be in such a position and quite honestly didn't know what she was doing. Indeed, she sometimes found herself weary of the sameness of her days, which certainly lacked the excitement of the life she had led in Paris while performing at the Opera.

For the most part, the staff had been kind to her; Raoul had always been their favorite, and it was so obvious he loved Christine to distraction that most of them loved her, too. Society had been a different matter, but Raoul refused to allow any obvious snubs to his wife. Even in these latter days of the Third Republic, the antiquity of the family name carried considerable weight, so Christine had found the way easier for her than possibly it had any right to be. And in the round of life at the estate, she had found it safer to let the past lie and to look forward only to the future.

But now that past had intruded on the present, and she no longer found it quite so easy to ignore. Whatever power Erik had exerted over her was not entirely gone, it seemed—even in his absence, he was apparently able to compel her to lie to her husband, to make dissembling plans to return to Paris far earlier than was strictly necessary. Even the barest hint that Erik might still be among the living was apparently enough to unsettle her.

She knew she would never rest easy until she knew the truth.

Christine saw that Raoul was waiting for her to speak, so she said quickly, "I know you can't leave now, dearest, but I should be quite safe, you know. I'll take Jeannette with me, of course, and the Gastons are already awaiting our arrival. I'll just wire ahead and let them know to expect me early. I suppose they might fuss a bit, but they can always get my apartments ready first and then worry about the rest of the house later."

"And you would not mind going to Paris alone?" he asked, nothing but concern showing in his clear blue eyes.

Of course, he was thinking only of her, and of how she had once sobbed passionately to him that she never wanted to return to Paris as long as she lived. At the time, he had been only too happy to accommodate her wishes. But that was before life intervened and he had to take on the responsibilities of being the Comte de Chagny, and long before Meg had found her station advanced almost as much as Christine's, and begged the couple to come back to Paris for her wedding.

When she first heard of the engagement, Christine had been overjoyed for her friend, even though she knew very little of this Honoré de Castelo-Barbezac. But even then she had dreaded the thought of going to Paris once more, knowing she would be forever haunted by the events of two years past, and the echoing beauty of a voice that belonged to a man she thought long dead. She had wondered how she could refuse her friend's request to serve as her matron of honor, even as she knew she would never have the courage to disappoint Meg in such a way. Since Raoul had promised to go with her to the wedding, Christine thought she could face Paris.

She found it ironic that she now schemed to return there without him.

"Perhaps it will be a little difficult," she allowed, knowing Raoul would think it odd that she showed no reluctance to return alone. "But of course, I will be spending most of my time with Meg, and I'm sure she will take care to see that I am never idle. She mentioned perhaps I should order my summer gowns while I'm there and can avail myself of the services of Monsieur Worth for those pieces as well."

Raoul threw up his hands in mock despair. "Well, then, I know I must stay here and make sure the vines get off to a good start this year, or I shall never be able to pay Monsieur Worth's bill!"

Despite herself, Christine smiled. "Oh, I promise I shan't be more than a *little* extravagant. Even among the great families of the Loire, it's not necessary to have four changes of dress each day, as I've heard is *de rigeur* in Paris lately."

"I suppose I must give thanks for that, then," he replied with an answering grin. "I don't think it could do any harm — as you say, you'll be with Mademoiselle Giry, and it couldn't hurt for you to be seen in Paris society with her. We've buried ourselves here the past few years, I think, and I suppose we were both foolish if we thought we could remain isolated here forever."

How sweet he was, really, how considerate of her wishes. No arguments, no admonishments as to how to behave in society, and no real restrictions, either. Her husband had a sunny soul, bright and open and uncomplicated, despite the travails he had endured to win her. She had never been able to explain that her contact with

Erik had changed her somehow, had brought something dark and complicated to a spirit she had once thought as open as Raoul's own. It was that very stain which drove her to return to Paris now, to follow her own desires without revealing the truth to her husband.

Still, she had to thank the Lord that Raoul had retained that essence of himself. It was one of the things she loved about him, even though she sometimes wondered whether she could ever return his love as completely. It seemed there was always some piece of her soul she had given to Erik, some part of her that Raoul could never understand or own. But she would be lying to herself if she didn't admit how gladdened she was by his easy acquiescence.

Once in Paris, perhaps she could put her own uneasy soul finally to rest. She was eager to see Meg again, of course, but even more so, she wanted to know the truth about Erik, and whether he'd had a hand in these murders. And if he had—if he were alive —

To those questions, she had no answers. For the moment, she could only raise a smiling, false face to her husband, and hope that once again, God or fate would sort things out.

CHAPTER 2

Down Among the Dead

*H*e had lain in darkness for an eternity. Hunted, heartsick, he'd had no choice but to go to ground like the wounded animal he was. His home beneath the Paris Opera was no more; ransacked, ruined, with nothing remaining of the hidden sanctuary he had labored over for so many years. Only a few days after Christine left him, he had slipped into the sub-basements through a way only he knew, one that not even his old friend the Persian, who had plumbed most of the Palais Garnier's secrets, had been able to ferret out. But once there, Erik saw that the angry mob who'd tried to chase him down had been most thorough—the furniture had been smashed to splinters, the pipe organ partly disassembled, his books and notes and music a heap of sodden, still-smoldering rags of paper. The acrid scent of smoke lingered there in the darkness, with no way for the foul air to escape.

All along, he had known utter wreckage was probably what he would find, but seeing the destruction for himself instead of merely imagining it was far more painful than he would have thought possible. Every piece of furniture or scrap of his beloved *Don Juan Triumphant* score seemed to scream at him that Christine was gone, the dream dead forever. He wished he could have died then. But the heart that was broken showed no signs of failing him, and even though he wanted no more than to lie down and die, he had prepared himself for this moment.

He had told the Persian—the *daroga*—that he was dying, but as much as Erik had wished for that merciful end, he knew it was not at all imminent. Christine had given the gold wedding ring back to him before she left the house beyond the lake forever, and he carried it with him when he returned there. Let her think he was dead. Let the whole world think the same.

The body was simply that of some unfortunate who had expired in a back alley near the slums of Les Halles; Erik had found the dead man and brought him to the bowels of the Opera House. It was of no real import that he and the mugging victim were only very approximately the same size, for once the flesh had rotted away from the corpse, there would be no one to distinguish a difference of a few inches here and there. No, he had simply dumped the body on the edge of the lake, and covered its face with one of his spare masks. With any luck, no one would return to the shores of Lake Averne for weeks or even months, and by that point, the body would be unrecognizable. The gold ring he had hoped would adorn Christine's graceful hand, he shoved onto the pinky finger of the man's left hand; it would fit no other.

And then he had left, knowing he would never return. For him, an even darker sanctuary awaited.

Beneath the orderly streets of Haussman's Parisian reconstruction efforts lay a vast network of abandoned quarries and catacombs, and within those forgotten spaces were also contained the ossuaries of Paris, a veritable kingdom of the dead. Indeed, visitors to the bone yards—and they did attract their share of tourists—were first greeted by an imposing sign over the doorway which proclaimed: *Arrête!*

C'est ici l'empire de la mort! (Stop! Here is the empire of the dead!)

Beyond that sign lay the ossuaries, first conceived in the late eighteenth century when land became scarce and the decision was made to empty the cemeteries of Paris into sections of the abandoned limestone quarries beneath the city. They were strongholds of bone—skulls, femurs, and tibias stacked in a variety of patterns almost to the height of a man's head. Carefully marked passages outlined the areas in which visitors were welcome, but beyond those tunnels lay miles of unexplored paths that reached far back into the catacombs. It was there Erik found his own *oubliette*, a backwater in the kingdom of the dead where no one could ever find him.

Down in the darkness, he created a makeshift home of items salvaged from the alleys and trash heaps of Paris: bits of furniture deemed too scratched or simply out of fashion for further use, bedding patch-worked together out of scraps gleaned from the rag heaps behind the dressmakers' shops on the Rue de la Paix, precious books and stacks of paper stolen from the carts of vendors along the Boulevard Saint Germain. There in the artificial night of the cata-combs, he labored over a careful reconstruction of *Don Juan Triumphant*, as he had very little else to occupy his time. Of course, there was no question of him rebuilding a pipe organ in the narrow limestone-bordered cell he now called home, but early in his sojourn there, he had stolen a violin from a street musician as the man napped in a back alley. Soon afterward, rumors began to spread of the specter of a dead violinist that haunted the nether regions beyond the ossuaries of Denfert-Rochereau. The tourists and spelunkers took care to avoid that area, as did the prostitutes who had taken to plying their trade underground, far from the watchful eyes of the local *gendarmes*.

In the beginning, of course, there had been hate. Oh, how he had hated Christine for turning from him and going to that damnable boy— never mind that Erik had in fact instructed her to do so. He had thought it was enough that she had let him kiss her, that she had chosen to turn the scorpion figurine instead of the grasshopper, signifying her supposed rejection of Raoul—and thus saving the Opera from destruction, as turning the grasshopper would have ignited the barrels of dynamite Erik had stored in the sub-basements.

How sweet those precious moments had been, when he'd thought she might stay there with him forever in the house beyond the lake, when she had lifted her pure white forehead for him to kiss. But then he knew that even though he might die of love for her, he could not force her to live her life down there, alone in the darkness with only a monster for company. And so she had gone, and the peace Erik experienced after being gifted with her kiss had only lasted a few days, just long enough for him to go to the Persian and tell him that Christine was free and that he, Erik, was dying.

A good story, and one the daroga sincerely seemed to believe. Would that it had been true! But once Erik had come here to the ossuaries, driven to live among the dead, the bitterness and hate had risen in him once again. How dare she fall in love with such a trifling young man, after all, one who had very little to recommend him beyond looks and a title! Shallow, foolish girl! Could she not see beyond such surface considerations to understand the heights to which Erik could have brought her, the passions he could have taught her...the love he could have shown her?

Mercifully, that stage of his despair did not last very long. Much as he might have wanted to, he found he could not truly hate her...not the woman who had laid her gentle lips upon his hideous forehead, who had held him as their tears mingled on his unmasked face. There was regret, of course, but he could not hate the only woman who had ever shown him the slightest affection.

Raoul was much easier to hate, Raoul who had interfered, who had shown Christine the promise of a mortal love. It was easy to hate his guileless blue eyes, his smooth and untroubled features, his easy, charming ways—he had the manner of a man who had never been crossed in his entire life, who had always had the best of everything and the regard of his peers. Until, of course, he come up against the Phantom of the Opera! Oh, then it had been a very different sort of circumstance, had it not? The recollection of Raoul's panicked reaction to Christine's relationship with her "Angel" and the agonies he had suffered to be with her still brought a smile to Erik's misshapen lips. At least the boy had had to walk through hell to claim his bride!

But claim her he had, and they had fled Paris, taking the train to Copenhagen from the Gare du Nord. Erik doubted they knew that they had a watchful angel to the very end, one who had hidden in the shadows to observe their departure, even as Raoul lifted a hand to help Christine into the car, the graceful skirts of her blue brocade gown sweeping the steps. Erik had always loved her in that dress; it brought out the porcelain purity of her skin and the clear forget-me-not blue of her eyes.

Then they were gone, and Erik was left with nothing but the memory of her sweet voice, the scent of roses that always accompanied her, the butterfly whisper of her fingers upon his. He would have given his life for only a few more moments in her presence, but that, of course, was not to be.

There had been no rumor of them for several months, until one day in a discarded newspaper, Erik found a small article that spoke of their return to France once the Comte de Chagny's death had been ruled as accidental. They had come home, but not to Paris, and now Christine was la Comtesse de Chagny.

Erik had considered leaving Paris and going to Tours, which was only twenty miles from the Chagny estate, but he soon dismissed the idea. It was easy enough to hide himself in Paris, where he had found a refuge and where the teeming millions of the city's population shielded him from prying eyes. Tours offered a far different situation; although it was a regional capital and a small, bustling city in its own right, the place certainly did not provide the same advantages as Paris. Besides, if he had possessed the strength to let Christine go, then he had to find within himself the resolve to allow her to live her life. There was no point in torturing himself on the meager chance he might catch a glimpse of her when she came to town.

So he had remained in his hidden lair in the catacombs, and even found a few occupations to interest him once again, since it soon became apparent that his heart was not going to do him the service of failing any time soon. There was the ongoing work with *Don Juan Triumphant*, of course. Once it had been composed, it was recorded in his memory for all time, but the task of transcribing it once again was time-consuming, especially since he had to steal every piece of paper upon which it was written. And after a few months, he even found the will to return to the Opera.

Box Five was let, of course, but his former haunt was not the only place where Erik could hide himself and observe the goings-on. Thank God that La Carlotta had taken herself back to her native Spain; the new diva was a young woman named Cécile Lamont, and Erik was surprised to find that she actually could sing. Not like Christine, of course, he reflected sadly; there would never be another Christine—but the new girl had a very pretty voice, with some of the purity he had admired in Christine's. It was diverting enough to watch Mademoiselle Lamont play Susanna in *Figaro*, even to the point where he began to wonder what he could do to improve her voice if she were under his tutelage. Then he realized what he was thinking and, shaken, had crept away. Impossible that he could even begin to consider replacing Christine. It was only the solitude, he told himself, the weary hours in the chill, damp darkness where the only sound beyond his own heartbeat was the steady drip of moisture from the limestone roof of the catacombs. Perhaps the isolation was slowly driving him mad.

Many months passed before he returned to the Opera after that, and although Mademoiselle Lamont still reigned as diva, he was able to assess her voice more dispassionately. True, she had a certain clarity of tone that La Carlotta had definitely lacked, but her diction was really quite poor, and her midrange only adequate. The new management seemed to be doing a fair enough job under the direction of Monsieur Gailhard, but as always, the Opera's primary importance was to see and be seen, with any artistic pretensions clearly subordinated to spectacle.

After that visit, he stopped in very occasionally, more because it was the only place he could feel halfway safe beyond the catacombs than because he truly cared about the performances. Several times, he staged raids on the costume and makeup departments, taking certain items he needed. Christine had not believed him when he'd told her he would soon have a mask that would make him look like everyone else, but after many failed attempts, he had now come close. In blazing sunlight, of course, he doubted he would fool anyone with keen eyes, but in the soft glow of the street lamps or the uneven flicker of a candle flame, he seemed to be just another ordinary Parisian in better-than-average clothing, albeit one who instinctively chose to walk in the shadows.

The disguise allowed Erik to finally recapture some of the life he thought he had lost forever; never one to scruple at a quick theft when it served his needs, he gradually began to rebuild his funds through some deft sleight-of-hand. The steps of the Opera House were particularly good hunting grounds, for in the jostle of the crowds, it was the simplest thing in the world to relieve some overdressed *bourgeois* of his wallet. With the money thus acquired, he was able to order new suits, procure paper and ink and candles, and purchase heavy new blankets, as the cold of his underground home had begun to affect even his bones. For the first time in many months, he began to feel like a man once more, and not a ghost.

Chance pieces of his former life crossed his path from time to time; it was only a month or so earlier that he had read of Mademoiselle Giry's engagement to the Baron de Castelo-Barbezac, and Erik smiled despite himself. Perhaps his promises to the worthy Madame Giry had been somewhat overreaching, but he felt certain that the Girys of both generations were perfectly happy with a baron and did not regret too much the Opera Ghost's claims that one day Meg would be the new Empress. If nothing else, Meg Giry had been a good and true friend to Christine, and he wished her the best of this world.

Inevitably, he thought of Christine and wondered if she would come to town for the wedding. Silly of him, he knew—what would he do, after all, even if she did come? Loiter in the fashionable streets of the Faubourg Saint Germain, hoping for a glimpse of his erstwhile obsession? Someone would most certainly call the police, convincing mask or no. Better to stay in the shadows and think of his masterwork, now so close to completion...once more. Christine had her life, after all. It was foolish to think he could ever again be a part of it.

It was very late; even the cafés that spilled their light and noise onto the sidewalks were shuttered and dark. A brisk breeze blew off the Seine, bringing with it a smell of damp and something else, something sharp and organic— the smell of returning spring. The trees were still bare, but their naked outlines showed the slightest softening, the first buds revealing the barest hint of green on their dark branches.

That same breeze rustled in the abandoned pages of the day's newspapers, one of which blew up from the gutter and across the tip of Erik's shoe. He looked down at it, then shook his head. No time to waste on scanning the words it contained; he had spent hours walking the city streets, listening to the voices around him, and now he only wanted to return to his narrow bed.

Even ghosts grow weary, he thought, and hastened toward the hidden entrance to the catacombs on the Rue de Valois. No eyes noted his shadowy form becoming one with the darkness on the narrow street, and he disappeared once more from the world.

CHAPTER 3

Friend and Foe

*C*hristine was uncertain exactly what she had expected from Meg's fiancé, but she did know that Monsieur le Baron Honoré de Castelo-Barbezac was not it. The man who greeted her in the main salon of his elegant town house was dressed impeccably, of course, from his white silk brocade waistcoat to his expertly tailored black evening coat and narrow pants, but his hair was just a shade too long than considered appropriate, and the bow tie at his throat almost bordered on floppy. She had been away from Paris for a few years, but Christine could still recognize the telltale signs of the *flâneur*, the idle man-about-town who existed nowhere but on the streets of the City of Light: arbiter of fashion, connoisseur of art and music, admirer of actresses, opera singers...and, of course, ballet dancers.

Still, the blue-gray eyes that met hers when she entered the room were very kind, and the smile that accompanied the obligatory hand-kissing quite dazzling. If nothing else, Honoré de Castelo-Barbezac had very good teeth.

"Ah, the celebrated Christine," he said. "Of whom I have heard so very much — indeed, there were times I thought Meg would talk of nothing else."

"Oh, hush," Meg said, having risen from a seat near the fireplace to come greet her friend. The mischievous ballet dancer with the bow in her hair was nowhere to be seen; instead, Meg was now the epitome of Paris fashion, from her watered-silk rose-hued dinner gown to the sleek chignon of heavy dark hair she wore low on her neck. "Really, Christine, there are times when I can't believe a word he says." But the look Meg gave her fiancé was loving and indulgent, and she smiled even as she spoke. Then she took Christine's hands with some of the impulsiveness Christine remembered of old as she added, "I am so glad you decided to come. I was quite afraid you wouldn't."

"At first, I wasn't certain," Christine replied, although of course, she didn't dare divulge to Meg her true reason for coming to Paris, especially with Meg's fiancé standing there and listening to their exchange. "But then Raoul and I discussed the matter, and we both felt that enough time had passed and that we were ready to return to Paris."

"I know I should die if I had to spend more than a week away," the baron put in, but again he smiled, the corners of his eyes crinkling with amusement.

"Honoré," Meg said, a warning note in her voice.

"Merely expressing an opinion, *ma petite,*" he replied. "But I do think the proper thing now is to introduce Madame la Comtesse to your guests."

For a second, Meg looked guilty, and then she nodded. Apparently, she wasn't quite as familiar with the manners of high society as she would have liked to be. But then she recovered herself and hooked her arm through Christine's, murmuring, "We can face the dragons together, my dear. They *will* try to cut us down, I suppose, but we'll show them that we opera girls have more backbone than that."

And indeed, as Christine was led around the salon and introduced to the dozen people who occupied it, she couldn't help but notice the undercurrent of hostility that ran below the politely neutral acknowledgments she received. She might have married the Comte de Chagny, but she had been born only the daughter of an itinerant Swedish fiddle player, and they would never let her forget that fact, even if those who occupied the upper echelons of Parisian society were too well-bred to say anything to her face.

It also didn't help matters that she felt quite countrified and not at all in step with fashion. The bustle had reasserted itself in full force this season, it seemed, and her narrow skirts looked quite plain in contrast to the exuberant drapings and swags she saw around her. The dinner gown she wore had never been all that becoming; Raoul's oldest sister had passed away from rheumatic fever not quite a year earlier, and Christine had been relegated to the pale grays and lavenders of half-mourning for the past six months. Still, it was her newest gown, and the only one she had thought even remotely suitable to the occasion, even though she knew the lavender moiré made her look somewhat pale and tired. The new style of hairdressing was not at all suited to her heavy curls, and her lady's maid had abandoned any attempt at the fashionable low chignon after her first attempt. So Christine still wore her chestnut curls in a cascade down her back, even though the front sections had been pulled away from her face and secured in place with heavy silver combs that had once belonged to Raoul's mother.

Somehow, she was able to endure the women's cool glances and murmur the necessary polite words after each introduction, although she knew she would never be able to remember all the names of Meg and Honoré's guests. She did find it somewhat amusing that she outranked all of them, except for one doughty old duchess who looked as if she might have survived the original Revolution. But that *grande dame* had been the kindest, even going so far as to pat Christine's hand and say, "I was privileged to see you sing *Faust*, my dear. Although I suppose it was all for the best, your comte did deprive the Paris Opera of its greatest star."

Blushing, Christine replied, "That's very kind of you," even as the duchess waved a be-ringed hand.

"Kindness has nothing to do with it, child. You were such a blessed change after La Carlotta that I would be remiss if I didn't praise you." Then the duchess's faded eyebrows pulled together, and the look she gave Christine was very shrewd. "Of course, I would have enjoyed the opera even more if I had been able to see you actually finish it."

The Aubusson-covered floor beneath Christine's feet seemed to tilt perilously, even as she took a breath to attempt to recover herself. Of course, the duchess was referring to Christine's precipitous disappearance from the stage and the commotion that had ensued. It had been the talk of Paris for weeks. At least, that particular account was what Meg had described to her, but Meg had also been quick to add that no one knew the real truth of the matter, for the managers weren't talking and the principals involved—namely, Christine and Raoul—had disappeared from the scene.

Certainly, neither she nor Raoul had ever made any attempt to explain what had actually happened, save to say that they had made plans to elope, given the disapproval of Philippe de Chagny regarding their match. It was a tragedy that Philippe had for some reason thought they'd gone to ground under the opera house and then had drowned there in the dark waters of the lake, but that was all it had been: a tragic accident. Any mention of an opera ghost had been dismissed as the hysterical imaginings of the young dancers—affectionately referred to as "ballet rats"—and the stage hands.

At least, that was what Meg had reported.

"A foolish prank," Christine managed at last, hoping that she hadn't betrayed herself with any sudden tremors. "Raoul and I have regretted it ever since."

"Ah," said the duchess, whose name Christine had forgotten. "I thought that might have been it. Unfortunate, really. So much fuss over a younger son's choice of bride! Then again," she added as her pale gray eyes took on a sudden glint, "one never knows when a younger son will inherit, does one?" And she looked past Christine to the spot where Meg stood with her fiancé a few feet away.

"Oh, is that the case with Monsieur le Baron as well?" Christine asked, eager to divert their conversation from the events of two years ago. "Meg never mentioned it to me."

"Yes, although most of us who know the family well knew that Honoré would one day be the baron. His older brother was quite sickly." Her tone seemed to indicate that the elder Barbezac's health was entirely his own fault. "But that didn't keep Honoré from running around with the worst sorts—street musicians, café singers, artists, ballet dancers—" The duchess appeared to catch herself before continuing any further with that line of thought, at the risk of insulting the young comtesse to whom she spoke. "You should see some of the daubs he's hung around the house. Not worth the canvas they're painted on, my dear."

"He seems quite an interesting person," Christine replied, thinking that Honoré sounded like a perfect match for Meg. Obviously, he was not overly impressed with his title, which meant he most likely cared little about his fiancée's humble origins. "I'm sure Meg thinks the world of him."

"As to that," the duchess said, "why shouldn't she? He's given her wealth, security, and a title. Although," she added, in an obvious attempt at politeness, "they do seem to be quite besotted with one another. Nothing like in my day—I only met my husband a week before the wedding. None of this modern prating of love *there*, I assure you."

"You didn't...love him?" faltered Christine, who was beginning to feel a little overwhelmed by the duchess. Certainly, she had never heard such frank talk from anyone else of that generation.

The duchess raised her lorgnette and stared at Christine for so long that Christine could feel the blood rush to her cheeks once again. "You *are* quite the *naïf*, aren't you, child?" Then, without waiting for an answer—not that Christine could have managed one—she went on, "We tolerated one another, and that's more than most married couples have, I suppose. But now it's all meant to be about love, which is quite silly, you know."

In that moment, Christine heard the Phantom's words once more in her head, his beautiful voice ragged from weeping. *Christine, I am dying of love of you*, he had said, while she had thought her own heart would break upon hearing those words. She wondered, absurdly, what the redoubtable duchess before her would have to say to such a pronouncement. Probably, the old woman would have smacked him on the jaw with her fan and told him not to be a fool, that a man could die of a heart attack or dysentery, but certainly not of love. Christine had to stifle a sudden impulse to giggle before she replied, "Well, I'm glad I married for love."

Another one of those shrewd, measuring glances. "And I believe you did, child, no matter what other people might say. But now it appears they're calling us in for dinner."

With a start, Christine turned to see the other guests rising from their respective chairs to follow Meg and Honoré into the dining salon. "Oh, dear," she said, "I seem to have kept you quite to myself, your grace."

"Don't you believe it," said the duchess. "If anything, I've been the one keeping you from everyone else. But now, my dear, if you would oblige me...." And she held out her arm to Christine. "I do have a difficult time moving about these days."

At once, Christine offered an arm to help the duchess up from her chair, for the old woman did seem to be quite stiff in the joints. She waited as her companion arranged her black silken skirts, then said, "I've very much enjoyed our talk."

"And I, my child." The duchess smiled at her then, the faintest trace of a dimple appearing in her lined cheek. For the first time, Christine saw that she must have been quite a beauty when she was young. "You may accompany me into the dining hall. I'm sure that Mademoiselle Giry has you seated next to her, but I shall be just across the table from you, next to Honoré."

"Do you know Honoré's family well?" Christine asked as they moved slowly toward the dining salon. She took care to keep her steps small to match those of the arthritic woman.

"I should think so," the duchess replied. "He *is* my grandson, after all."

And having delivered that remark, she continued into the adjoining room, leaving Christine to stare after her in bemusement for a few seconds before she remembered herself and hastened to stay next to the old woman. The duchess gave Christine another smile, then whispered to her, just before they entered the dining salon,

"And don't let the Baroness de Rochefort give you too many airs, my dear. She may be a baroness now, but her father was nothing but a cloth merchant from Lyon."

Christine smiled as well and nodded, then, chin held high, made her way toward the head of the table. Too many of the eyes watching her were still hostile, but she felt curiously light of heart. Whatever else, she thought that she had made an ally this evening…and she sensed that she would need such a friend in the days and weeks ahead.

He waited in the darkness of an alley just off the Rue Scribe, watching the crowds around the opera house gradually thin as the evening wore on. Far away, a bell struck one o'clock, that one mournful note seeming to reverberate on and on in his head, stirring up the agitation he couldn't seem to control, and to which he had long ago surrendered.

This was not the first night he had waited; no, this alley had been his home for uncounted evenings now as he stalked his prey, waiting for the perfect moment to strike. Too often, those he sought strolled this street in company, or were surrounded by enough strangers that he didn't dare make his move. Too many nights he was forced to return to his meager flat and sleep through the day, his only desire to hasten the useless sunlit hours until he could once more take to the streets.

Oh, but the kill was almost worth the waiting, worth the interminable hours, worth the ache in his muscles and the dull gray fog that seemed to cloud his brain most of the time. The only other thing that made his life worthwhile was the heavenly pipe and the oily black bars he smoked in it; under the drug's influence, he suddenly felt clear of mind, certain of his purpose. It was only until he had found and punished all of those who had contributed to his downfall that he could rest and finally put the hashish aside.

Ah, but now he thought his prey might finally be at hand. He had seen the man walk these streets many times over the past few days, going from the Opera to hail a cab on the Boulevard des Capuchines, but the timing had never been right. Tonight, however....

There he was, moving slowly down the Rue Scribe. The street was deserted, bleak and quiet under a waning half-moon, and the sound of the man's infernal whistling could be heard clearly...

some silly pastiche by Offenbach. Otherwise, the only sound the killer could detect was the beating of his own heart.

In the darkness of the alley he waited, letting the drug thrill along his nerve endings, hearing the thin slap of the man's shoes on the damp pavings. Closer, closer —

The garrote dropped over the man's throat as his killer pulled it tight, feeling the familiar bite of the wire in his hands, the pressure of his victim's body against the weapon. But the man was pudgy and weak, no match for the one who had lain in wait for him. His thrashings grew more and more feeble, until he finally slid from beneath the wire to fall in a limp heap on the paving stones. The mark of the wire was a thin, livid line against his throat.

His killer stood there for a moment, staring down at his handiwork. As with his other victims, the man's eyes were bulging and bloodshot, his mouth open in a ridiculous *O* of fright. This one had apparently been so frightened that he pissed himself; the smell of urine rose sharp in the damp night air.

Suddenly disgusted, the killer wound his garrote carefully and tucked it back into the pocket of his overcoat. It would never do for the Sûreté to discover that the murder weapon was a simple garrote; he wanted them to think these men had been killed by something far more unusual, distinctive. He wanted the blame to be laid at the feet of the person who had been the primary source of all his misfortune. If the man hadn't already been dead, he would have killed him as well, but defaming his memory was his next-best revenge. No, all he could do now was continue to send those who had also participated in his ruin to their richly deserved reward.

From around a corner, he could hear the sound of approaching voices, and he turned and darted once more into the shadows, moving quickly and silently through the darkness. Now, perhaps, he could enjoy a few hours of sleep undisturbed by nightmares. Then he would awake, and the waiting would begin again. He knew that several days would have to pass before he deemed it safe enough to commence the stalking of his next victim.

From behind him came a woman's scream, followed by someone shouting for a gendarme. Once, in the beginning, he had stayed to watch as the crowd gathered and the police came in to investigate, but he had soon abandoned that activity as overly dangerous. As much as it would please him to see the consternation that he'd caused, he knew his only hope for continued freedom lay in leaving the area as quickly as possible. He would have to get the rest of the story secondhand, through the newspaper articles he found endlessly amusing. Reading about the bumbling attempts of the Sûreté to discover the identity of the Rue Scribe killer gave him almost as much pleasure as the act of killing itself. Even more diverting was the new series of articles that had begun to connect these new murders to the erstwhile Opera Ghost.

His scheme was working perfectly.

And as long as his luck and the hashish held out, he knew he could carry his plan through to the very end. Oh, there was the minor complication of his chief victim not currently residing in Paris, but he had a feeling fate would sort out that particular problem for him. Now, with three dead men to his credit, he felt all but invincible.

Beware, Paris, he thought, *for now you have a new Angel of Death!*

CHAPTER 4

Faces in the Shadows

*A*ntoine Saint Denis stood in the harsh morning sunlight and scowled down at the unmarked gray-beige paving stones beneath his feet. There was nothing there to show that only a few hours earlier, a man had died violently on this very spot.

At that early hour, the fashionable street was mostly deserted; a few shop girls swept half-heartedly at the stoops of their stores, and occasionally a heavy cart laden with food stuffs for the restaurants and cafés of the Boulevard des Capuchines rumbled by, but otherwise, Saint

Denis and his companion, Monsieur Aubry of the Sûreté, were left very much on their own.

"Just like the others," Aubry said at length, apparently discomfited by Saint Denis' continuing silence. "Throttled by a garrote—or worse. He never stood a chance."

Without answering, Saint Denis drew a chased silver case from the breast pocket of his morning coat, withdrew a cigarette, and then offered the case to Monsieur Aubry. He knew the other man would refuse, just as he had on each separate occasion before, but Saint Denis still felt it was the polite thing to do.

"No, thank you—I don't indulge," replied Aubry, as he always did.

Ritual satisfied, Saint Denis returned the cigarette case to his pocket, struck a match, and lit his cigarette. The rush of nicotine blended with the caffeine from the several cups of coffee he had drunk before leaving his house, giving him a general sense of well-being...despite the circumstances which required his presence on the Rue Scribe.

Or perhaps because of those very circumstances. Saint Denis paid Aubry handsomely but discreetly for the honor of being the first member of the press on the scene of any sensational crime, including the murders he had begun to ascribe to the vanished Phantom of the

Opera. Not that he truly believed the Phantom was involved, of course, but the mere mention of that worthy ghost was enough to increase his paper's circulation by a good twenty percent.

"And who was the poor unfortunate this time?" Saint Denis retrieved a small notebook and fountain pen from another coat pocket; the paraphernalia he was forced to carry with him did nothing for the lines of his expertly cut suits, but he did not want to be burdened with a satchel as he moved about the city. Most of his colleagues thought he was mad, wandering the streets alone instead of waiting properly in his office for informants to come to him, but Saint Denis had made his career out of not caring what others thought, and he certainly wasn't about to change now.

Monsieur Aubry pulled out a notebook almost identical to the one Saint Denis carried and consulted it with the grave air he obviously thought suitable to the occasion. Saint Denis barely had time to suppress a smile before the other man spoke.

"Monsieur Maurice Bertrand, aged fifty-seven." Aubry paused and lifted a sandy eyebrow at Saint Denis, as if waiting to make sure the reporter wrote everything down word for word. "Quite prosperous. He has— or I should say *had*—a house in Passy and a business that supplied iron to the railways. He was married and had two daughters in their early twenties. I believe they're both married and have established their own households."

"Any reason why Monsieur Bertrand was attending the opera alone last night?" Of course, there was the distinct possibility that the man in question had not actually gone to the opera alone, but had parted company from whatever member of the *demimonde* with whom he had spent the evening before heading to the Boulevard des Capuchines, where he would have been more likely to find a cab at that hour.

"I have heard that Madame Bertrand does not particularly care for the opera," Aubry replied, even as his plain, honest features expressed disapproval over what he guessed Saint Denis must be thinking.

"Of course," Saint Denis replied, taking care to keep his tone neutral. It was difficult at times to prevent himself from baiting Monsieur Aubry —the man was so deadly serious, so earnest about his position with the Sûreté—but Saint Denis knew doing so would serve no purpose. He should rather count himself lucky the man was awed enough by his background and his position with the Paris *Presse* that he was willing to divulge what should have been police secrets to a reporter. Of course, the two thousand francs a month Saint Denis paid for that privilege didn't hurt, either. Taking a breath, he went on with the expected questions. "Any financial difficulties? Any enemies?"

"No, monsieur," Aubry said. "Monsieur Bertrand was quite a conservative man, from what we have been able to discover so far. The opera seems to have been his one indulgence."

As it had been with the other two victims. A love of the opera was not the only common thread that tied them together, however; all of the dead men had been in their late fifties to early sixties, prosperous, settled. None of them seemed to have any hidden vices or secret enemies that would have caused them to be the target of a murderous madman. Perhaps it was all completely random—perhaps a true monster stalked the Rue Scribe, killing whenever the mood took him, with no particular thought as to the identity of his victims.

Somehow, though, Saint Denis refused to believe that was the case. There must be some connection among all these otherwise unremarkable men, some element that had drawn the murderer to them. Just because neither he nor the Sûreté had yet been able to discover that commonality did not mean it didn't exist. He had no real faith in the ability of the official investigators to discover the identity of the true culprit;

he had seen them bungle enough cases to know that in many instances, it was sheer blind luck which led the Sûreté to capture an actual perpetrator. That they succeeded enough times to keep the public satisfied was more a function of the law of averages than of the individual ability of anyone on the force.

Aubry was a good man, but he was limited by his education and background. The one thing Saint Denis felt Aubry had in his favor was a certain likability that made people want to confide in him—a useful trait in a policeman. But his most recent promotion to full inspector was due in no small part to Saint Denis' assistance on his last several cases, and Saint Denis knew that if there were to be any breakthroughs in this one, it would fall to him to discover them.

"Do you have Madame Bertrand's address?" he asked at length. "Perhaps I should call—after an appropriate interval, of course." As a newspaper reporter, he did not have the exclusive *entrée* of a policeman, who could call at all hours regardless of the propriety involved, but this could wait a few days. The killer—so far, at any rate—seemed to allow at least three or four days to elapse before he struck again.

"But of course," Aubry said, and consulted his notepad. "In Passy, as I said, Rue de la Printemps. Number fifteen." In an undertone, he added, "The funeral is scheduled for this Thursday."

"Then perhaps I shall go this Friday and offer my condolences to Madame Bertrand." Saint Denis made a notation on his pad, more to appease Aubry than because he really needed to do so. The address was already firmly fixed in his mind. Perhaps in the meantime, he should try to go back and interview some of the relatives of the other victims. There had to be some element he had missed, some vital connection that bound them all together.

"Monsieur Saint Denis?" Aubry's tone was hesitant, worried.

"Hmm?" Already Saint Denis was thinking ahead…to the questions he would ask, the steps he would retrace.

"Do you think he will ever stop?"

The question jolted Saint Denis back to the sunlit street, the bare cobbles that did nothing to reveal the violence enacted here the night before. Such an ordinary view, and yet—

After a long pause, he shook his head. "No, Aubry. I don't think he ever will."

Unless we catch him first, he added mentally, feeling for the first time the burden of proof he had laid upon himself. For if he, Antoine Saint Denis, could not discover the identity of this murderer, who would?

Meg's carriage was almost half an hour late arriving at the Chagny town house, but Christine put her annoyance aside as soon as she saw her friend's rosy, glowing face—one could not be angry with such obvious happiness.

"Oh, don't be cross, Christine," Meg said almost immediately, after Christine had settled herself into the brougham, dispersing the skirts of her cashmere walking gown gracefully about her. "Honoré was having a new picture mounted in the gallery, and of course he *must* have my advice as to the lighting."

"You shouldn't be making your apologies to me," Christine replied with a laugh. "But won't Monsieur Worth be dreadfully angry if we come this late to a fitting?"

"As to that," Meg said airily, "he always makes everyone wait at least an hour, so we'll still be early. Besides, he's grown a little more accommodating with his clients now that Madame Vionnet's gowns have become all the rage."

Christine allowed herself a smile. How different in appearance was the fashionable young woman who now sat across from her, and yet still so quintessentially Meg. But one thing bothered her, something she had wanted to ask her friend the evening before and yet had never found the opportunity to do so. "But where is Madame Giry, Meg? I confess, I was surprised to note her absence at your soirée last night."

For a few seconds, Meg looked distinctly uncomfortable. She turned her head to gaze at the streets passing by outside, her pearl and enamel earrings catching the light of the early afternoon sun. "Maman has not been quite well," she said after a moment. Then she lifted somber dark eyes to meet Christine's, and added with a catch in her voice, "And oh, Christine…that's not all."

"What is it, Meg?" Somehow, Christine knew that as much as Honoré might be besotted with Meg, their path had not been completely smooth.

Haltingly at first, and then with the words flowing quickly as she realized she at last had a sympathetic ear, Meg recounted her troubles to Christine. Honoré's family had been anything but welcoming — except for his maternal grand-mother, the dowager Duchess de Montfort, without whom Meg felt sure she would never have been able to endure their treatment, no matter how much she loved Honoré. His mother had been cold, his sisters absolutely unsupport-able — there, Meg broke off, eyes flashing with some of the spirit Christine remembered from their days at the Palais Garnier. "Do you know, Adèle actually offered me fifty thousand francs to break off the engagement! As if the money mattered!"

"To her, I'm sure it does," Christine replied, somewhat astonished at the bitterness in her own tone. Certainly, her path with Raoul had only been a little more smooth; there had been no disapproving parents to deal with, but the elder of Raoul's two sisters, Louise, who had practically raised him, obviously felt it was her duty to take over where Comte Philippe had left off and express her disapproval of such a *mésalliance*. When presented with the *fait accompli* of their marriage, she had retreated into an icy hurt that no amount of friendly overtures on Christine's part could melt. Her death six months earlier of rheumatic fever left Christine saddened by the distance between brother and sister during the last years of Louise's life, but she had also experienced a certain guilty relief, a completely unworthy emotion she had never confessed to anyone, let alone Raoul, who had been devastated by the loss. Better that he should never know how much Christine had disliked his sister. Raoul's other sister, Eleanor, lived in Cherbourg and had mostly stayed out of their affairs, a circumstance for which Christine found herself eternally grateful.

"I'm sure you're right," Meg replied. "And when Honoré found out—well, I never really knew he had a temper until then. Of course, I wasn't present when he spoke with Adèle, but apparently, they had a terrible row, and Honoré was so provoked that he told her to mind herself, as she was still unmarried and he now had control over her portion of the inheritance, since their father passed away a little more than a year ago. I think that threat was finally what made her abandon her attempts to get rid of me, but she can still barely stand for me to be in the same room with her."

Impulsively, Christine reached out and gave Meg's kidskin-covered hand a squeeze with her own gloved one. Her friend managed a watery smile, and then patted Christine's hand in return before continuing. "But then when Maman got wind of everything, she got it in her head that she was the one causing all my trouble, that she was far too common to associate with the likes of Honoré's family. And so she's stayed away this whole time—won't come to the receptions, or my fittings, or even to meet Honoré and me in a café for luncheon." Tears shone bright and unshed in Meg's eyes. "The most horrible part is that she really is unwell, as if she's willing herself into a decline so she won't be a burden to me any longer!"

"Meg, I'm so sorry," Christine murmured, knowing even as she said them that the words were woefully inadequate. Must it always be like this? Could one never have joy unsullied by pain?

Again, that sad little smile. "Oh, perhaps I've made it sound worse than it really is. Honoré would do anything for me, and Madame la Duchesse is very kind as well. She says she's seen far too many members of the nobility rise and fall to concern herself overmuch with a person's birth, and that a person's character is what determines their worth. She's become quite my protector."

"I did like her very much," Christine said, hoping that Meg would recognize the sincerity of her words. Certainly, she had had no such champion in Raoul's family...save Raoul himself, of course.

In the next moment, their carriage stopped in front of an imposing storefront on the Rue de la Paix, the home of Monsieur Worth's *atelier*. As Christine outranked Meg now and would do so even after her friend's marriage, she was the one first helped from the brougham by the footman and so waited in the warm sun as Meg was also assisted from the carriage. Although the air was cool, Christine began to feel uncomfortable in her gray cashmere traveling suit. It was a good thing, she thought, that she was at Monsieur Worth's to order new spring and summer clothing in addition to the frock she would wear at Meg's wedding. The gowns she had brought with her to Paris would only be suitable for a few more weeks, if even that long.

Meg's earlier words about arriving early proved to be prophetic, for in fact, they did have to wait almost half an hour to see the esteemed Monsieur Worth. He was a smallish man with a neat pointed beard and a manner at once flattering and confiding. His assistant, an angular young woman in her late twenties clothed in the latest fashion, took Christine's measurements as Monsieur Worth exclaimed over her.

"Ah — *quel poitrine!*" he said, noting the tininess of her waist. "And the coloring — so striking, yet so delicate! It will be a pleasure to dress you, Madame la Comtesse de Chagny. Blues, of course, yet a certain green would do nicely — and rose as well, to match your cheeks and lips. And the sketches for the bridal party — "

He laid a few watercolors before Christine, who caught Meg's mischievous grin. The gowns for Meg's attendants were beautiful, of course — aquamarine watered satin and white silk gauze, with pale pink roses draping the bustle. They were colors that would flatter Christine and leave Honoré's two sisters, both of whom were dark, looking positively sallow.

Obviously, Meg had already learned the more subtle forms of revenge.

"They're beautiful," was all Christine could manage before she handed the watercolors back to Monsieur Worth. She had to look away from Meg, or she knew she would burst out laughing at any moment.

From there, they went on to the laborious task of ordering Christine's new spring wardrobe: ball gowns and evening gowns, dinner gowns and visiting toilettes, morning and after-noon dresses, finishing off with a new blue serge riding habit. The estimated bill made Christine blanch, but Meg assured her that all of the items were absolutely necessary, and that the twenty percent surcharge on top of it all to ensure that at least one of each type of dress was ready by the end of the week was a required expense.

"After all, Christine," she said, as Christine handed the last of the swatch books back to Monsieur Worth's assistant, "you're not in the country anymore."

No, I'm not, Christine thought wearily. Toward the end of that consultation, she had thought if she had to distinguish between a *mousseline de soie* and a *lisse* or a damask and a brocade one more time, she would surely scream.

When she was a simple singer with the Paris Opera, she had certainly never given so much thought to her wardrobe—not that she could have afforded to indulge even if she had cared back then. She enjoyed pretty dresses, of course, but her interest had stopped there. At the time, she had had far more important things to worry about.

As she did now, she thought, as she and Meg emerged from Monsieur Worth's *atelier* into the quick-falling dusk of early spring. The day had been clear and sunny, but even as the gas lamps were lit and a different sort of energy took hold of the streets, she could feel the damp rising from the river. It was now, at this tenebrous hour, that her thoughts invariably went to the man who had made the darkness his home. Was he out there somewhere even now, hidden someplace in this vast city, alone with a pain she could not even begin to imagine? Had he raised his hand to kill again, and for what purpose?

"You're far away, Christine," Meg remarked, and Christine jumped slightly.

"I suppose I always have been," Christine responded, almost without thinking. *Head in the clouds*, was what people used to say behind her back. Perhaps they had thought her so dreamy that she couldn't hear what they were saying. But she had, of course. It would have been impossible not to hear those derisive comments. She had never bothered to explain herself, for how could she? How could anyone who had not been raised in a world of fairy tales and dreams possibly understand?

Raoul had understood...or at least he had tried to, even though she'd seen the incomprehension on his features more than once as she tried to explain to him how music was the only thing that ever brought her close to those otherworldly experiences. Even though he had spent those magical days with her when they were children, listening to her father spin his tales of the North, of kings and fairy folk...and, of course, of angels...he could not quite grasp what she was trying to explain to him. Perhaps it was because he had never experienced the true power of her father's words, of the days when she had felt as if the veil between this world and the next was as thin and shimmering as a butterfly's wing, a veil that could be torn easily aside if one only knew the right words.

Was it any wonder, then, that she had fallen prey to Erik and his clever borrowing of the title, "Angel of Music"? There were times she thought she could hate him for that, for such a calculated manipulation of her mind and soul. But it was not in her to hate, and any bitterness she might have felt regarding his actions was quickly subsumed by an overwhelming sense of pity. *Poor Erik*, she had thought then, and still did. If only she had been strong enough to accept his love….

Her reverie was interrupted by the arrival of the carriage, and Meg pressing her to return to Honoré's town house for dinner. "It will only be the three of us, I assure you," she said. "I told him too many formal dinners in a row would tire me, this close to the wedding."

Since Christine had planned nothing but a quiet dinner alone in her own suite at the Chagny home, the thought of spending time with Meg and Honoré away from the pressures of society was immediately appealing. The rapidly rising dark now seemed oppressive, as if there were unseen eyes watching from the shadows, and she wanted nothing more than light and company. "That sounds wonderful," she replied.

"Honoré will be so pleased," Meg said. "He felt he hardly had the chance to speak with you last night. He said he'd like to have a conversation with you 'far from the madding crowd'—or something like that. He's always quoting something I've never heard of."

Christine nodded, then turned to offer her hand to the footman who approached to assist her into the carriage. As she did so, she looked past his shoulder to see another man approaching down the street. Her breath caught in her throat—that dark hat pulled low, the lean, elegant figure—surely it couldn't be —

Then he raised his head, and she caught a sudden glimpse of a pale, handsome face obscured by a pair of dark glasses, and she looked away. Of course, it couldn't be he—Erik would never have walked openly down the Rue de la Paix at an hour barely past dusk. Besides, this man looked relatively normal, save for the dark glasses, which were a little odd, given the time of day...but perhaps the stranger had a sensitivity to light. She'd heard some people did suffer from that particular affliction.

Looking away quickly, not to be caught staring, Christine allowed the footman to hand her up into the brougham and then willed her heart to stop its irrational beating in her chest. *You'll see him in every shadow if you don't stop this*, she scolded herself. *You don't even know if he's still alive!*

She was spared from further brooding by Meg's arrival inside the carriage, along with the inconsequential chatter her friend kept up all the way back to the Faubourg Saint Germain. It was as if Meg wanted to make sure they were both in good spirits by the time they returned home; her revelations of earlier that afternoon might never have been spoken aloud.

Still, Christine couldn't keep her thoughts from returning to the strange man she had seen only moments before. True, there were thousands of men in Paris who wore black hats, and possibly even hundreds who went out after sunset in dark glasses, but how many were that tall, that slender? How many moved with the incomprehensible grace she remembered all too well?

It wasn't him, she thought. *It* wasn't.

But she knew she could never convince herself of that.

CHAPTER 5

Hidden Fears, Hidden Desires

So, she was here in Paris after all. For that one second as her eyes met his, it seemed as if his heart had stopped. Then she looked quickly away and disappeared into a carriage with an unfamiliar crest on the door. Probably Castelo-Barbezac's, since Erik recognized Meg in the next instant, all grown up in an afternoon gown of cascading mulberry silk faille, as the footman handed her up into the carriage as well.

But Christine—she seemed not to have changed a bit, her glorious hair still in its riot of curls down her back, face as delicately lovely as

ever, her figure still slender, lithe in a not entirely
fashionable pale gray walking dress. It was
trimmed in black, indicating half-mourning, but
for whom? Certainly not that blasted comte,
more's the pity—if Raoul were no more, she
would have been in black from head to toe. No,
probably Christine wore the somber gown to
honor a member of Raoul's family who had
passed.

Erik did not attempt to follow the carriage,
much as he wanted to stay close to Christine. He
did not know exactly where the baron's town
house was located, but discovering the address
would be easy enough. Instead, he pulled his
dark fedora a little lower over his face and hailed
a cab, instructing the driver to take him to the
Comte de Chagny's home in the Faubourg Saint
Germain. Better to go there now, while he was
reasonably certain Christine was otherwise
engaged. There were certain facts he wished to
learn about the Comtesse de Chagny's stay here
in Paris, and it would be easier to accomplish
that end while she was occupied elsewhere.

The fashionable streets slid past as he leaned
against the somewhat worn horsehair cushions,
willing himself to remain calm. So much for the
fragile resignation he had attempted to maintain
over the past few months! Now that he had seen
Christine again, Erik wondered how he could

have ever imagined living without her. Surely, no other woman had eyes more blue or more pure, nor a mouth so delicately molded yet ripe for kissing. Closing his eyes, he remembered the touch of her lips against his forehead, the cleansing drops of her tears against his ravaged face.

And she had looked at him! For one shattering moment, their eyes had met, and surely she must have known. Even with his face disguised by the new mask he wore, her soul must have recognized his.

And what of it? a bitter voice in his mind inquired. *No matter what you feel for her—and no matter what she might feel for you—she belongs to someone else. You can never have her.*

Oh, but surely it might be enough to see her, to take nourishment from catching a glimpse here and there of her lovely face—perhaps, if he were very lucky, to hear her sing once again. Surely, she hadn't given it up entirely. She must still sing in company, or perhaps even when she was alone, when she thought she was unwatched and unnoted.

The cab drew to a stop outside the Chagny home, an imposing early eighteenth-century monument of classical proportions, meticulously maintained, the bare, elegant trees out front just beginning to show the faintest hint of green. Erik handed the driver several francs and stepped out, some part of him still astonished at the ease with which he was now able to move among men, thanks to his new mask. The driver stammered his thanks for the generous tip, but Erik dismissed him with a casual wave of the hand. He had more important matters to attend to now.

The house sat on an expansive corner lot on the northeast corner of the Rue Jacob and the Rue Bonaparte, but more importantly, the gardens to the rear of the house opened onto a narrow alleyway, just the sort of place for the scullery staff to empty the refuse bins or splash the leftover bath water. It was now going on six o'clock, and he felt fairly certain it wouldn't be long before someone came out to dump the refuse for the evening, as that seemed to be standard practice in the great houses he had observed.

As usual, his calculations were correct; he had waited in the shadows no more than fifteen or twenty minutes before a dark, fragile-looking *gamine* came out with a pair of buckets that appeared far too heavy for her. After she stepped through the back gate, she set them both down with a sigh, rubbing one of her shoulder blades in an absent-minded fashion.

Erik spoke from the shadows, taking care that his voice was as perfectly pitched, as persuasively modulated, as only he could make it. "Mademoiselle…."

Even so, she jumped a bit as she watched him step away from the wall that separated the town home's gardens from the alleyway. "Holy Mother, you did give me a scare! What are you doing back here, monsieur?"

He held himself still, so as not to alarm her any more than he already had. Voice pleasant, he said, "I know this seems a bit irregular, mademoiselle, but I happen to be an old family friend of the Chagnys, and I thought if perhaps I could ask you a few questions?"

She narrowed suspicious dark eyes at him. Erik thought she might have been pretty if she hadn't looked so tired. Not mistreated, of course; her dress was neat and clean, and so was the sleek black hair under her proper white cap. Her slenderness seemed natural, not caused by any deprivation. No, she was probably lucky in her situation here, but even so, a life in service was a hard lot no matter how generous your masters might be.

Behind the suspicion in her eyes was a gleam of native intelligence. "If you are a friend of the family, m'sieur, then why have you come to the back instead of calling at the front door?"

Cheeky little thing, he thought, but there was more amusement than anger to that reflection. "Because, ma'mselle, I am planning a surprise for the comte and comtesse, and if I went to the front door, I would spoil the surprise." From his pocket, he pulled out a shining gold louis. It was more than she could earn in a month.

"Mmm." She looked from the coin up to his face, but Erik felt certain she couldn't see him clearly. The glow from the street lamps and the few lights inside the house did very little to illuminate the darkness. "What kind of a surprise?"

"If I told you what sort of surprise," he countered, "then it wouldn't be a surprise any longer, would it?"

Nodding with some reluctance, she replied, "I suppose so, m'sieur. Only, I don't want to be a party to any trouble for the comtesse."

"No trouble, I assure you." With those words, he pressed the coin into the girl's thin, work-reddened hand, and she took it without protest, the louis disappearing into a pocket in her skirt.

"Only that she's a right sweet lady, is the comtesse, and I wouldn't want to cause her any harm."

"Of course you wouldn't," Erik said, his voice soothing. "If I may ask, has the comtesse come to Paris alone?"

Another narrow look from underneath her heavy black lashes, but the girl answered the question readily enough. "Just her and her lady's maid, Jeannette. She's come up to town for Mademoiselle Giry's wedding to that baron."

"And does the comte plan to come here at some point?" It would be too much to hope that Christine's sojourn in Paris would continue indefinitely without Raoul's presence.

"Yes—I heard the housekeeper say he was expected in about a week. Stayed down at Chagny to oversee the spring planting and keep watch over the vines, is what I heard. But he'll be up for the wedding. I suppose they were all quite thick, when the comtesse was at the Opera?"

"Yes, you might say that," Erik replied absently, already thinking ahead. Only a week, then, until the thorn in his side returned to town. Better than nothing, he supposed.

Much could happen in seven days.

"The comtesse is out this evening," the girl continued, apparently wanting to make sure she earned the louis in her pocket. "She sent word back that she was to dine with Mademoiselle Giry and her fiancé."

"Yes, I knew that," Erik said.

For some reason, his words seemed to reassure the girl—after all, who but a close friend would have known of the Comtesse de Chagny's last-minute decision to dine at the home of Honoré de Castelo-Barbezac instead of quietly in her own house, as had been originally planned?

"You've been very helpful…." And then he paused. He realized he hadn't even inquired as to her name.

"Lise," she supplied.

"Yes, Lise," he said, and then drew another louis from his own waistcoat pocket. "There'll be more of these for you, if you keep your ear to the ground and keep me informed. Look for me here at the same time each evening — I can't say when I will be back next, but I shall return."

"Of course, m'sieur." She bowed her head, but not so quickly that he couldn't see the gleam in her eyes at the thought of such unexpected riches.

Not for the first time, he marveled at the ease with which people could be bought. Well, he could forgive such a failing in Lise; he was not asking anything so dreadful of her after all, and she was young enough that she might still be dreaming of catching the fancy of a tradesman or skilled laborer and settling down on her own. The sort of money Erik was offering could go a long way in helping a girl like her establish her own household one day.

"*Bonsoir, mademoiselle*," he said formally, then moved with the ease of long practice back into the shadows, heading not out toward the Rue Bonaparte, but east toward the Rue Furstenberg, then south past the Palais Abbatial, where Charles of Bourbon had once held court. Then he made his way back onto the Boulevard Saint Germain. From there, it was short work to hail another cab and return to the glittering streets around the Opera, and the secret entrances to his underground home.

He had much to ponder. The news that Christine would be accompanied by only her household staff for the coming week was welcome, of course, but how best to use the current situation to his advantage? Did he dare approach her? Would she be shocked if he confronted her…horrified…relieved? How had the news of his death truly affected her, and how would she react once she realized that the most painful chapter in her life had never been closed after all?

Too many questions, and none for which he had any answers. That one brief glimpse of Christine had not been enough for him to determine her current emotional state, nor to learn whether she had recognized him in return. All he could do was return to his miserable home and hope the next day would provide more inspiration.

It was almost midnight when Christine returned to the house in the Faubourg Saint Germain. A yawning footman let her in the door, and Jeannette showed all the signs of having fallen asleep by the fire in Christine's sitting room; her normally precise chignon had been pushed to one side, and a few stray blonde hairs fell around her face. Still, she seemed alert enough as she hastened to help Christine out of her gray cashmere walking gown while gently chastising her mistress for not having the sense to come home first to change into something more suitable.

"Why?" was Christine's response. "It was only the three of us, after all, and I'm sure Monsieur le Baron was not overly concerned about my gown."

"You may say that, madame," Jeannette replied, "but you haven't been out in Paris society for some time, and one never knows what sort of impression one might be giving."

Perhaps Jeannette was right, but at the moment, Christine was too tired to admit it. How good it felt to have the iron grip of her stays finally released, to be able to breathe deeply once again! She stepped behind the dressing screen to remove her chemise and draw on the nightgown of fine linen Jeannette had laid out for her; the soft fabric was comforting against her skin, light and yet warm. She said from behind the screen, "At least you should be happy to know that I've ordered my gowns from Monsieur Worth, and that the first of them should be here in the next two days."

"Ah, well, that's something," came Jeannette's relieved remark, and Christine had to smile to herself. As the lady's maid to a comtesse, Jeannette felt it an affront to her personal honor that Christine had been forced to step out onto the streets of Paris in anything but the latest style.

As she moved from behind the screen, Christine drew her warm quilted brocade dressing gown around her. For a second, she recalled the filmy silk and lace robe she had once worn backstage at the opera, and then shook her head. Why did she feel the need to keep dredging up those memories? Why could they not leave her alone?

"I've brought up a pitcher of water for you, madame, and I finally found that newspaper you were asking for this morning. One of the footman mislaid it, apparently." Jeannette allowed herself a sniff. Her opinion of the current household staff was fairly obvious. "Let themselves go slack, they have, madame, more than two years with never the comte in residence. I suppose they've forgotten what it is like to wait on someone."

Christine found it in herself to be a little more forgiving. It had been some time since any of the Chagnys had occupied the home, after all, although Raoul's sister Louise had spent a month there about a year ago. She supposed that some habits were easy enough to forget. But Jeannette, daughter of Madame Rouget, housekeeper on the Chagny estate, did not see things quite the same way. She had been raised to believe that matters in a great house should run exactly thus-and-so, and any deviation from that pattern was enough to arouse her ire.

Hoping to head off any further diatribes on the subject of the current household's inadequacies, Christine said hastily, "But it's very good that you found the paper for me, Jeannette. Thank you."

Jeannette nodded, although it was obvious she was holding back additional comment only because Christine had made it clear that she did not want any more discussion of the matter. "Would there be anything else, madame?"

"No, Jeannette. That will be all."

After that dismissal, Jeannette gave a brief

curtsy and left the room, leaving Christine to utter a small prayer of thanks, accompanied by a rueful shake of the head. Sometimes it was difficult for everyone — Christine included — to live up to Jeannette's expectations.

She went to the side table and poured herself a glass of water, glad of it after a night of too much food and wine at Honoré's home. The "small, private dinner" had consisted of four courses, each with their own wine selection. No wonder her stays had felt so tight! But at least the dinner and the lively conversation which had accompanied it had done their task in banishing any thoughts of the stranger on the Rue de la Paix from her mind.

It was only now, in the softly lit confines of her own elegant bedchamber, that those thoughts began to return. She told herself the man couldn't have been him — he didn't even *look* like him — and what on God's earth would the erstwhile Phantom of the Opera have been doing on that fashionable street, after all? Buying his latest obsession a new hat?

Something was nagging at the back of her mind, though, something he had once said to her. What had it been, in those terrible hours when she had been held captive in the pretty little Louis Philippe room in Erik's house beyond the lake? He had ranted about all sorts of things as she had tried desperately to hold on to her sanity, even as she had been engulfed in terror at the thought of Raoul and his Persian guide trapped in the Opera Ghost's torture chamber.

I can't go on living like this, he had said. What else? Something about a requiem mass, or a marriage mass. She had tried so hard over the past several years to push those moments of horror behind her, to forever forget the torment and anguish Erik had both suffered and caused.

Still, now she was here of her own free will. She had come to Paris on her own, motivated by what? A woman's curiosity, as she had once said mock-playfully to Erik? No, of course it was much more than that. Even with all that he had done to her and Raoul, she had wept upon hearing Erik was dead. Even then, some small part of her had wished fervently that it was not true. If she had the chance now to discover if he really were alive, then she must be strong enough to live with the truth, whatever it might be. She must force herself to remember, to relive those moments if she must, if that knowledge might bring her closer to the mystery of Erik's fate.

She took a sip of water, then another. All was peace and elegance here, in this lovely blue-hung room furnished in stately Louis Quinze pieces that had somehow survived the Terror. There was nothing here that could hurt her.

Now I want to live like the rest of the world, Erik had told her as he knelt at her feet, the horror of his face even more ravaged by tears. *I want to have a wife like everyone else…I have devised a mask that allows me to have a normal face….*

"Oh, my God," she whispered then as realization struck her. "A mask! Yet another mask!"

With a nervous gesture, she set the glass abruptly down on the side table, then strode to the bedroom window and twitched the heavy damask curtain aside. The small, manicured garden below was still, and beyond the low wall topped by decorative ironwork that circled the property, the street was quiet under a waning gibbous moon. Nothing there, of course, but still she could not shake the feeling of being watched.

That's what he does, of course, she thought. *Drifts in the shadow, hides in the darkness. One never knows exactly where he is, or what he hears….*

Feeling suddenly exposed, she pulled the curtains shut again, then stood in the center of the room, irresolute. Now it made sense to her. There had been something slightly odd about the lean face of which she had caught only a glimpse, something too pale, indistinct somehow. She could see how it might pass in the half-light of dusk or the uncertain glow of the street lamps. Up close would probably be another matter.

Still, he feels comfortable enough to walk the streets with men, she thought. *If it was he, of course.*

Christine's thoughts did nothing to reassure her. She had always thought that lighted places full of people were the sort of situations Erik instinctively avoided, but now it seemed quite possible that he mingled with the populace on a regular basis. It meant there was nowhere she could hide from him, nowhere she might go to be safe.

Don't be silly, she scolded herself. *You came here to seek him out! Now you're worrying about hiding from him?*

She told herself she should be glad; perhaps now he might be easier to find. Perhaps it would only be a matter of putting herself in his path once again....

Her gaze fell on the Paris *Presse* Jeannette had laid on the table next to the water pitcher, and she went to pick it up, unfolding it as she did so.

The headline screamed up at her, as she had half-hoped and feared it would: *Rue Scribe Killer Strikes Again!*

Willing her heart to stop its foolish pounding,

Christine scanned the article. Except for the name of the victim, it was almost a repeat of the piece she had first read in the breakfast room at Chagny. Once again, some poor man had met his end in the deserted spaces of the Rue Scribe, his life cut short by a brutal strangulation. The only sign of the murder weapon had been the livid mark left on the victim's throat. And still the Sûreté were mute as to motive or indeed any connection among the victims, save that they were all prosperous men in their late fifties or early sixties. Robbery did not seem to have been the reason for the killings, as the unfortunate men were all found with their personal valuables intact.

Christine laid the paper aside with a shaking hand. In her heart, she knew she had hoped there would not be another article like this, that the first two murders had merely been some sort of aberration. But here the killer had struck again, only five days after the previous murder. The reporter intimated that the Sûreté feared the killer would never stop—unless he was caught, of course.

Deliberately, Christine made herself pick up the paper once more, searching for the byline of the reporter who had written the article. There it was, in smudged italics under the blazing headline. *A. Saint Denis.*

Her only previous experience with reporters had been the critics who occasionally had loitered backstage at the Opera, and she was not disposed to think well of most of them. Their main objective seemed to have been getting on friendly—or worse—terms with the members of the *corps de ballet*, and not actually writing about the Opera or the performances held there. Still, she thought that perhaps she should pay this "A. Saint Denis" a visit. He seemed to have the exclusive rights to report on this story, and perhaps he would be willing to share some of his insights. She knew she could never go to the police. Erik was still a wanted man, even if he proved to be innocent of these current crimes, and she would never forgive herself if she inadvertently led the authorities to discover his whereabouts.

No, better to go about her own investigations in an oblique way, one she hoped would not draw untoward attention toward herself. She did not know Monsieur Saint Denis, and she had no idea whether she could trust him or not. But she knew she must start somewhere, and this seemed the most logical step to her.

Only time would tell whether her instincts were correct, or whether she had innocently set in motion events that could only end in another tragedy.

CHAPTER 6

Devil in Heaven

"*L*ady to see you, sir," announced Jean-Louis, one of the copy boys. "A *real* lady," he added, as if to distinguish this current visitor from some of the more dubious women of Antoine Saint Denis' acquaintance.

Despite himself, Saint Denis smiled. Some of his paid informers were definitely members of the Parisian *demimonde*, most of them no better than they should be. It amused him that, even at fourteen, Jean-Louis apparently had no problem recognizing those women for what they were.

"Show her in," he replied, laying aside his pen and shuffling the scattered papers on his desk in a vain attempt to bring some sort of order to chaos. He didn't like to be too organized; he found that tidiness interfered with his thought processes, but he knew the unbridled disorder on his desk could be off-putting to visitors.

Jean-Louis scampered away, leaving Saint Denis to wonder just who this visitor could be. Madame Bertrand, coming to take him to task for his sensational story about her husband's murder? Somehow, he doubted it. That indomitable lady had sent him packing when he had tried to approach her at her lovely old home in Passy, calling him a ghoul and an opportunist. He had been called worse, of course, but her parting shot had still stung.

"You, sir," she had snapped, "are no gentleman!" And then she had slammed her door with such vehemence that the brass knocker clacked several times before going quiet.

During the cab ride back to his offices at the Paris *Presse,* he had reflected it was a good thing his mother hadn't been around to hear Madame Bertrand's scathing comment. She would have been most disappointed to have seen her son come to such a place.

Antoine Saint Denis was the youngest son of a family that had managed to prosper without ever attracting enough attention to earn a title.

Owners of multiple properties and various banking interests since the early seventeenth century, the Saint Denis clan had weathered war, revolution, siege, and famine without suffering any of the financial setbacks that usually accompanied such calamities. With their wealth had come a certain sense of *noblesse oblige*, even though they had never been gifted with even a baronetcy, and Saint Denis knew that if his mother had still been alive, she would have been mortified by his career choice and the depths to which he occasionally had to stoop to get a story.

In his older siblings, his obsession had engendered mainly a sense of rueful amazement. That he should choose to work when he didn't have to, and further, to become a newspaper reporter of all things, was quite beyond their understanding. But since he lived quietly otherwise, not spending his inheritance on drink or women or gambling or any of the other temptations to which a rich young man might fall prey, they kept their opinions to themselves. There was always the hope that one day he would give up his foolishness and settle down. Until then, best to leave him alone.

When the mystery woman entered his office, Saint Denis knew to stand immediately. As Jean-Louis had said, this was a real lady, from the top of her jaunty feathered hat to the soles of the tiny feet—encased in expensive kidskin boots—that peeped out from beneath the multiple flounces of her Delft-blue walking gown. The only thing about her that didn't speak true to current fashion was her hair, which fell in gorgeous chestnut ringlets down her back. That style had been out of favor for several years, yet somehow, he couldn't imagine this woman wearing her hair any other way.

He found himself staring, and not because she was so outstandingly lovely. There was something familiar about the delicate face that looked at him in inquiry, about the glorious dark-lashed eyes that reflected the soft gray-blue of the gown she wore.

"Monsieur Saint Denis?" she inquired, in a voice as delicate and lovely as she was. She extended a slender gray-gloved hand. "I am Madame la Comtesse de Chagny."

Of course. The object of the Phantom of the Opera's passion—the erstwhile Christine Daaé. Her lovely features had been plastered all over the papers during the time of the scandal at the Opera.

He took her hand and bowed slightly. "Madame la Comtesse. I am honored."

"Thank you for seeing me without an appointment...." And then she hesitated, clutching her reticule as she apparently fumbled for what to say next.

"Please, madame, sit," he said, and came around the desk to pull out the one spare seat his office possessed. It was a worn leather monstrosity on rust-pitted casters, but it was the best he could do.

After she had settled her voluminous skirts about her and declined his offer of tea, he returned to his own seat behind the desk and watched her carefully. He knew that her presence in his office was no coincidence, coming so soon after his articles on the murders in the Rue Scribe and their possible connection to that old legend, the Phantom of the Opera. Perhaps the present Madame la Comtesse had not divorced herself as completely from the past as she believed.

"I know it must seem…quite irregular…my coming here," she said at last, obviously made uncomfortable by his continuing silence. "But I felt I must ask you—that is, I thought you might know—"

"Might know what, madame?" he prompted. Better for her to volunteer whatever it was she had to say, rather than have him drag it out of her.

"I have seen your articles, Monsieur Saint Denis," she replied, and then she did look at him directly. Beneath the air of fragility, he caught a glimpse of something quite different—determination?—in her eyes. Perhaps she was not quite the delicate flower he had first thought. "I can make no secret of my past to you. I'm sure you're quite aware of what occurred at the Palais Garnier some two years ago, and my involvement in those events."

"As much as anyone not directly connected with the case would know, I suppose," he admitted. "At the time, I was not assigned to report on the happenings at the Paris Opera, but I have made some inquiries in the intervening years."

"Then I will not attempt to prevaricate, monsieur," she said. "I have read what you have written, and I must say that it has distressed me. I have been led to believe that Er—the Opera Ghost passed away several years ago. Yet you think he has some kind of connection to the horrible events occurring now in the Rue Scribe?"

For an unending moment, Saint Denis found himself drowning in those huge blue eyes. How to explain to her the ongoing need to sell newspapers, the casual way he—and other reporters, for he was not alone in utilizing such methods—played with people's lives in their never-ending pursuit of the story? He had a sudden intuition that this woman had been hurt badly, that her apparent calm was only a fragile façade. Even so, he did not like being questioned on his own territory.

As usual when pressed, Saint Denis resorted to the easygoing charm that had gotten him out of similarly tight spots before. He allowed himself a reassuring smile before saying, "I assure you, madame, that it is a most complex issue. The truth, sometimes, can be most elusive—"

"Don't patronize me, monsieur," she snapped, and for a second, she appeared truly angry. When she went on, however, her tone was somewhat more restrained. "Either you have some sort of information regarding these crimes, or you are merely fabricating stories to sell more newspapers. Which is it?"

His smile faded. The kitten had claws, did she? Voice even, he replied, "You must understand, madame, that certain things have been spoken to me in confidence—things I am not at liberty to say."

"Is that a polite way of telling me to mind my own business, monsieur?"

Tone still neutral, he said, "I would not presume, madame."

Thwarted, she sat quietly for a moment, fiddling with the silver chain of her reticule. "Perhaps if I were to tell you of certain things

that I know? In confidence, of course—by way
of establishing trust between us."

"Perhaps," he said with a show of reluctance,
but inside he was alight with excitement. Who
knew what secrets Christine de Chagny might
have kept about her previous association with
the Phantom of the Opera?

She spoke again, and this time her voice was
so soft that Saint Denis was forced to lean
forward to hear her clearly.

"The method of killing—how he used to—"
And there she stopped, the faint pink of her
cheeks fading. "I assume you knew of that—and
that these people have been killed in the same
fashion."

"Garroted, every one of them," he said
briskly. There was no danger in telling her that
particular detail—it had been in each of his articles, after all.

"No, monsieur," she said, and he watched the
worry in her eyes slowly transform into…what?
Hope? Relief? "On first glance, perhaps you
would think it the same thing. But the Opera
Ghost was much cleverer than that. He had a
singular form of execution, one that he learned in
—in a foreign land. It would leave only a narrow
mark on the throat, with no broken skin."

Whereas Saint Denis had seen for himself
the black flecks of blood on the necks of the

victims where the skin had been broken beneath the thin red line left by the garrote. "And how would you know this, madame? Have you seen him kill?"

She hesitated for so long that he was afraid she would not reply. When she did speak, her voice was barely above a whisper. "No, monsieur, praise God that I have not. But some of the members of the *corps de ballet* saw poor Joseph Buquet's body before he was removed from the Palais Garnier—and gossip spreads quickly backstage at the Opera, as you may not realize. The details were known to all within a few hours."

"And so you think because of this that the Phantom of the Opera could not be involved in these present-day killings? Could he not have altered his method of murder?"

"No," she replied, and her voice sounded firmer, although exactly whom she was trying to convince—Saint Denis or herself—he was not sure. "He is dead, monsieur. He has been dead these two years."

"But was he not a ghost to begin with?" Saint Denis inquired, in a brittle attempt at humor.

Christine de Chagny shivered, and her gloved hands gripped her reticule more tightly. "No, monsieur. He was a man. A most peculiar man, but—" And there she stopped, a small frown creasing her brow, as if she feared she had already said too much.

Although he burned to ask her more questions, somehow Saint Denis knew she would not reveal anything further. "So, what is it you want from me, madame?"

"Stop telling lies," she said at once, meeting his eyes squarely. "Stop slandering a man who cannot defend himself. There is someone killing these people, monsieur, but the murderer cannot be the Opera Ghost."

Saint Denis shrugged. "If he is dead, what does it matter?"

The look she gave him then was so reproachful, he wished he could have taken back the question, delivered in such an off-hand manner. "It is a matter of right and wrong, Monsieur Saint Denis," the comtesse said. "I think you cannot have completely forgotten what that means."

He had thought himself too sophisticated for shame, but her words mortified him. Hoping the flush in his cheeks was not too noticeable, he replied, "I am afraid you must have a very low opinion of me, madame."

"That remains to be seen. Perhaps you can yet redeem yourself." With that mild rebuke, she gathered up her skirts and stood, and he rose quickly as well, caught off guard by her sudden movement. She said clearly, "It was a mistake for me to have come here."

"Madame la Comtesse—"

But she shook her head, dismissing whatever it was he had been about to say. "Good day, monsieur. I pray that you will keep in confidence what I have told you this afternoon." And she turned and left, the heavy faille of her trained skirts rustling against the worn parquet floor.

Saint Denis made no move to stop her. He knew doing so would have been futile. All he could do was stand there, watching the door to his office long after she had gone, and wondering what he could have done differently to gain her trust. He had the troubling thought that he would have to start all over as a different man before she would ever confide in him again.

Christine emerged from the offices of the Paris *Presse* with her head held high, but inwardly, she was writhing. Thank God no one had been witness to her interview with Saint Denis—she had dismissed the reluctant Jeannette for the afternoon, with the airy comment that it was not necessary for ladies to be accompanied on the streets of Paris these days. Such an assertion was mostly true, although ladies of fashion were

rarely seen without their maids in attendance —
for the simple reason that assistance was often
needed for carrying bandboxes and shopping
bags. Still, it was no afternoon of leisurely
browsing through the ateliers of the Rue de la
Paix that had brought Christine out on this
errand, and Jeannette would only have been an
encumbrance.

With an effort, she arranged her features in
more placid lines and stepped to the curb to hail
a cab. Best to go home and take a long, hot bath,
and try to forget why she had gone out in the
first place. The handsome, faintly mocking
features of Antoine Saint Denis rose up in her
mind, the subtle jabs he had made. Had he
thought her completely ridiculous?

Perhaps she was. Perhaps she was a fool to
think she could trust someone who was clearly
more interested in increasing the circulation of
his paper than telling the truth. She thought she
might have finally scored a point at the end of
their dialogue, but with someone as self-
possessed and urbane as Monsieur Saint Denis,
it was hard to say. He was not at all what she
had expected — in a way, he had reminded her of
all the casually polite but subtly disapproving
high-born men in Raoul's circle. Once again, she
thought, she had been dismissed as insignificant.

He *never thought you insignificant*, that clear

little voice in her mind said. *He made you the center of his world. Yet that still wasn't enough for you, was it?*

The thought was unbearable. Luckily, a cab pulled up at that moment, and Christine was able to ignore the insidious inner voice during the laborious process of climbing into the cab and arranging her voluminous skirts about her so they wouldn't be too badly crushed during the ride.

The cabbie asked her destination, and she opened her mouth to give the direction of the Chagny town house. However, what came out instead was, "The cathedral of Notre Dame, monsieur."

He tipped his cap. "Of course, madame."

Christine settled back against the cushions, wondering at herself. Where had *that* come from? Yet even as she uttered the words, she had experienced a rush of desire for the cool stillness of the cathedral, the hushed reverence of a place where people had sent their prayers heavenward for more than five hundred years. Perhaps it wasn't that odd. She needed time to calm her thoughts, to find her center, before she returned home to the multiple little commonplaces of life in the Chagny household.

The cab let her off near the Pont Neuf, as no carriages were allowed on the Ile de la Cité. She walked across the ironically named bridge—it had ceased to be new some time during the twelfth century—surrounded by fellow Parisians in search of spiritual guidance, or perhaps those simply wishing to catch an enviable view of sunset from the gardens surrounding the cathedral. They weren't all Parisians—Christine caught snatches of German and Italian and English, some of that particular language spoken with an odd, flat accent she thought must be American.

The scent of the cathedral caught her as it always did, the smell of damp stone overlaid with the essence of incense that had burned there for hundreds of years. Inside, her first impression was of darkness, starkly contrasted with the glow of sunset filtering through the stained-glass windows on the west side of the building. Then her eyes became accustomed to the dimness, which was only partially relieved by the flicker of hundreds of candles lit at the altars of the various saints.

Vespers was just about to begin. All around her, people filed into the cathedral, taking their seats, but Christine chose a pew toward the back, away from the main group of worshippers. As the familiar rise and fall of the Latin mass began, she bowed her ahead along with all those around her, but she feared her thoughts were not on the liturgy. Instead, her mind raced, retracing her conversation with Saint Denis, worrying she had said too much, fearful she hadn't said enough. Perhaps he really did possess information that would have been helpful—or perhaps he was merely a practiced liar. She had always worried that her instincts with people were not quite as good as they should be. Too often she had trusted when she should not. Her experiences with Erik were proof enough of that.

Still, she had learned one thing of value from Saint Denis. These poor men were being killed by an ordinary garrote, not Erik's Punjab lasso. The irony of feeling relieved that people were merely being garroted and not choked by the lasso was not completely lost on her, and she did smile at herself, shaking her head slightly. Even from the grave, Erik seemed to be exerting a most unholy influence on her.

Too late, she noticed that mass had ended, and the cathedral was emptying of most of its worshippers. Not all, of course—the doors of Notre Dame were always open, allowing those in need of spiritual guidance entry at any hour, but she was left very much alone in her isolated pew. The darkness seemed to close in around her again, and she fumbled with her reticule, seeking the rosary she always carried there.

Somehow, though, she could not concentrate

on the words of the prayer she attempted to whisper. Her fingers slipped over the carved angel-skin coral beads of the rosary—a relic of her mother's—but she lost count of the decades and had to begin all over again. The scent of incense seemed to be growing stronger, making her head swim. Candles flickered at the altar nearest her, tiny flames like molten gold in the dark.

Two of those flames seemed to coalesce from the darkness, growing stronger, moving closer....

She blinked, and suddenly the flames were not flames at all, but eyes, eyes glowing gold in a pale, handsome face. He came out of the darkness as if it had given birth to him, the dark hat pulled low, the cape swirling around him like an animate shadow.

"Dear Christine," the shadow said, and its voice was his, a pure, aching tenor that even now awakened every nerve ending in her body. "Have you missed me?"

CHAPTER 7

Unexpected Arrivals

*H*er head swam. Certainly, he must only be a dream, or perhaps a hallucination brought on by her own exhaustion and the overwhelming scent of incense that swirled through the dark expanses of the cathedral. Christine clutched her rosary and stared at the unfamiliar face before her, even as the apparition went on,

"So silent, Madame la Comtesse? I confess, I had expected a bit more from you, considering how we last parted."

"You can't be real," she said at last, her voice barely above a whisper. "You *can't*."

At that assertion, he merely smiled, teeth white but ever so slightly sharp between the beautifully molded lips. "But I assure you that I am, Christine," he replied, and with those words he laid one cold hand on her arm.

Even through the heavy silk faille, she could feel the chill of his touch. Oh, how she remembered the iciness of his fingers, as if he carried the cold of the tomb with him wherever he went. And the eyes were as she remembered, that oddly gleaming gold, like a cat's eyes. But the face surrounding them—that was as different as could be. Even now, her mind shuttered itself against the horror of Erik's remembered visage, the sunken cheeks, the waxy pallor, the unspeakable void where the nose should have been. She could not reconcile the tattered remnants of those memories with the oddly perfect face before her now. True, it was too pale, and quite without expression, except for those burning eyes, but there in the dimness of the cathedral, he could have passed for quite an attractive man —as long as one had no idea what lay beneath the mask.

"What have you done to yourself, Erik?" she asked finally, making a show of placing her rosary back in her reticule so he would be forced to withdraw his hand.

His mask revealed nothing of what he was

thinking, but he allowed her to pull away from his touch without comment, answering simply, "What I promised to you before, madame. I told you I had developed a mask that would allow me to be as other men, to walk with my wife on Sundays. The wife has been denied me, alas, but at least now I have some measure of freedom I did not possess before."

"And yet, you let me believe you were dead," she said, somewhat surprised by the reproach in her voice. *Would it have made a difference?* she thought. *Could I have gone away with Raoul if I had known beyond a shadow of a doubt that Erik was still alive?*

Her only answer was a wary stillness as the gold eyes watched her carefully. "It was for the best," he replied at last. "You had made your choice quite clear."

Christine looked down at the reticule she clutched in her lap, shutting away the oddly still, pale face that hid Erik's true features. "If you had truly wanted me to believe you were dead, you would have stayed away," she murmured as she continued to stare down at her silken skirts, not wishing him to see any betraying expression in her eyes.

"Ah, my dear—but *you* did not stay away, did you?" he countered. "Two years gone, and back in Paris only now. Why?"

It would have been so much easier if his voice had changed as well, had lost some of the persuasive music that made her will seem not quite her own. The very sound of it stirred something within her, an ache she could not dare to acknowledge. Still, she managed to assume a lighter tone and glanced back up at him, saying, "For Mademoiselle Giry's wedding, of course. Perhaps you did not know that she is engaged to Honoré Castelo de Barbezac?"

"My felicitations," he replied dryly. "And that is all? Your loyalty to your friend is to be applauded, madame. I can only imagine what effort of will it took for you to return to—how do they say it?—the scene of the crime."

Erik's words brought back to Christine the real reason behind her return to Paris. Was it possible, though, that he had no idea a new series of crimes was being perpetrated and blamed on him? She had no idea what his life was now. Perhaps he was able to walk among men, but did he really participate in their world? And if he truly was oblivious to the current circumstances, how could she ever tell him?

How can you not? came a calm voice from somewhere deep inside her. *Did you not just defend him to Antoine Saint Denis? Does Erik not deserve at least that much courtesy?*

"There is...more," she replied, the words

halting. She feared his reaction more than she feared him. Sometimes Erik had been known to perpetrate hideous acts while in a rage that he would never have committed had he been in full possession of his faculties.

It was not possible for the unfamiliar face before her to grow more still, but the expression in the eyes altered, became wary. The sardonic note in his voice never changed, however. "Should I be offering you my congratulations, Madame la Comtesse?"

For a few seconds, she could only stare at him, uncomprehending. Then she slowly realized what he must be insinuating, and she let out a short, nervous laugh. "Oh, no, nothing like that, I assure you."

"The Comte must be very disappointed."

Christine thought of Raoul's patience as month after month went by with no sign of an heir to the Chagny name. He had never reproached her, but she could sense his growing frustration. That frustration no doubt was the source of those furtive glances toward her waist-line, the oblique questions he couldn't quite hold back. The uncomfortable situation was no doubt the source of the tension which had begun to grow between them of late...and how she resented Erik for reminding her of that now!

"The comte is a gentleman," she snapped, her

sudden annoyance breaking the momentary spell of the Opera Ghost's voice.

"From which I am to infer that I, in fact, am not." Again, the unnaturally chiseled lips quirked. "I have been called worse, in my time."

"Indeed," Christine replied, her tone frosty. Inwardly, she was amazed that she was able to stand up to Erik at all, but perhaps the two years that had elapsed since they last parted had taught her more about difficult social situations than she thought. After having to face down the stiff-necked, disapproving nobles of the Loire Valley countless times, a sarcastic Opera Ghost didn't seem quite as difficult to manage.

He was watching her carefully, as if really seeing her for the first time. "It has been two years," he said softly. "It seems they were of more value to you than they were to me."

Were those words some sort of underhanded compliment? He was clever, after all, far cleverer than she, and too often she'd had a difficult time comprehending the meaning of all his utterances. "*Merci, monsieur le fantôme,*" she replied lightly, and was gratified to see the golden eyes narrow. At least she was capable of landing a barb every once in a while.

However, he said only, "And to what other motive should I attribute your presence here in the city?"

This was it, then. Best to say the words and be done with them. She met his gaze squarely and replied, "I can't imagine you haven't heard of this, Erik, but it seems that a series of murders is being carried out near the Opera, on the Rue Scribe. The papers are saying that the murderer is the Phantom of the Opera."

Silence then, a quiet so deadly, she wished she could put her hands up to her ears to shut it out. She found herself straining to hear the ordinary sounds of the cathedral around her, the soft whispers of the worshippers who prayed at the various altars, the muffled echoes of leather-soled shoes on stone that had been worn smooth by centuries of use. Anything to fill the awful gap between the two of them.

"The papers?" he said finally, and although his voice was calm, underneath it lurked that thin thread of menace, so painfully familiar.

Christine thanked God for whatever presence of mind which had led her to omit any mention of Antoine Saint Denis' name. Certainly, she was angry with the reporter, offended by his casual slander of a defenseless dead man—not so dead after all, as it turned out—but the last thing she wanted was for Erik to discover Saint Denis' identity and seek to avenge his ruined name. Perhaps such a thing was inevitable, and yet if Erik eventually learned of the reporter's stories, at least it would not be because she had betrayed him.

"*Which* papers?" he asked, his tone ominous.

"Does it really matter?" Christine waved a hand. "All of them, I suppose. I don't usually pay much attention to papers," she added, with what she hoped was the correct note of airy unconcern.

"But obviously, you paid attention to at least one."

She gazed at him then, as if she was seeing him for the first time. Somehow, she couldn't reconcile the pale, perfect face before her with the sound of *his* voice emanating from the mask's lips. Perhaps this was only a dream after all. Hadn't she sometimes thought, in the darkest recesses of her soul, places she hadn't even known existed before she met Erik, that matters would have turned out so very differently if her Angel had possessed the face of a normal man?

But now was not the time to be losing her wits. Of course, this wasn't a dream, even though the scene around her still had an air of unreality, in the dim cathedral filled with hushed whispers and the smoky, sweet fragrance of incense. But the man who sat in the pew before her was all too real, and she must remind herself of that—and of how dangerous he could be.

"I don't recall," she said stubbornly. "Something Raoul had lying about the house. You must understand my shock when I saw your name in a blazing headline."

"Of course." The words were only faintly mocking.

"I felt I had to come," she went on, not looking at him. "You were dead—you had to be. The announcement in *L'Epoque* had said so. How was I to believe anything else?"

"But some part of you must have been uncertain," he said, "or you would have dismissed the headline as mere sensationalism."

"Yes," she admitted. "How could one ever be sure of anything when you were involved, Erik? You were the king of traps and mirrors, after all —I'm sure, given time, you could have convinced me that the sky was green and up was down."

"You do me too much credit," he said, but from his tone, she could tell he was amused rather than offended.

"At any rate, I thought that I should come to see if I could discover anything for myself. Besides, it is true what I told you about Meg's wedding—she did so very much want me to be here."

There was more to the current situation than that, of course, so much more, but she was afraid to say anything further. Let him fill in the blank spaces as best he could.

"And have you learned anything?"

"Just—just the smallest details. But it was enough to convince me that you could not be the killer. So, I thought you must be dead."

"And did that sadden you, Christine?"

How had she felt, during that moment in Saint Denis' shabby office when she realized Erik could not be the Rue Scribe killer? Relief? Certainly, for she had firsthand experience of the extremities to which her Opera Ghost could go when forced, and she was not naïve enough to believe he was incapable of such crimes. Relief, then, but coupled with regret, as if learning he could not be connected with the current murders had undone her last lingering hope that he might still be alive.

"Yes, Erik," she replied. "Does that surprise you?"

The merest lift of the shoulders under the fine wool of his frock coat. They seemed broader than she remembered; the Opera Ghost she had known had been painfully thin, his body skeletal to match his terrible face. Had he somehow managed to put on some weight over the past few years, or was his coat carefully padded, an illusion to match the mask he wore?

She couldn't know, and she wouldn't allow

herself to ask. Because he didn't seem inclined to speak, she added, "At any rate, although these men have been killed by strangulation, it was by a garrote, and not your lasso, Erik."

Again a long silence, and then he asked simply, "How many?"

"'How many'?" she repeated, not sure what he meant by the question.

"How many have been killed?"

"Three, I believe."

"Three," he said, then shook his head. "And besides blaming it on me, have the police or the papers done anything to catch this man?"

All she could do was give a helpless lift of her shoulders. "I only know what everyone else knows, but of course, they are trying very hard to discover who it is. The killer is cunning, I have heard—he waits until his victims are alone, and then commits the murders quickly and quietly, with no witnesses."

"How convenient."

Not for the victims, she thought, but she said nothing aloud. Somewhere else in this city, three women grieved for husbands who would never come home, fathers who would never see their children again. She had been so wrapped up in her concern that Erik might be involved, she had forgotten about the very human sorrow those murders had left in their wake.

"Christine." He spoke her name so softly, it was almost a whisper; she had to lean forward to hear him clearly. "You won't...tell anyone, will you?"

Poor man, did he really think she would betray his presence here in Paris? What she had done, she had done for herself, to set her mind at rest—or possibly to roil it up again—but she would no sooner reveal his whereabouts than dishonor Raoul.

"You can trust me," she said quietly, and forced herself to reach out and touch him briefly on the hand. The chill of his flesh shook her once again, but she ignored it. The discomfort was worth the expression of relief she saw in his eyes. "Besides," she added, "who would believe me, after all? 'Poor Christine, she really has gone daft this time!' I can hear them now!"

"Thank you," was all he said, but she knew he meant much more than that. She had betrayed his trust once before, betrayed him to Raoul, when she had been half-mad with the conflicting desires in her heart and hadn't known what else to do. The very least she could do was make sure that never happened again.

"And you won't—won't do anything about the newspapers?" she asked. Fear for Saint Denis was still worrying at her. After all, Erik could be so very unpredictable.

"You're protecting someone, that much is obvious." Then he sighed. "But I suppose it is only your natural inclination to keep people you know from harm. Besides, even if I were to rid the world of one troublesome reporter, there would only be ten more to take his place. One is reminded of the little Dutch boy with his finger in the dike."

Christine let out a breath she hadn't realized she had been holding. "So, what should we do?"

"*We*," he said, turning to look at the stained glass windows on the west side of the building, now almost as black as the rest of the interior, "need to make sure you get home safely. It is getting late, and I dare say you will be missed for supper."

The very prosiness of that statement, coming from the erstwhile Opera Ghost, almost made her laugh. She had felt so apart from the world, caught in a little bubble of aloneness with Erik, that she had forgotten life still carried on outside, and that certainly someone would be alarmed if she was much later in returning home.

"I dare say," she agreed, and rose.

He did the same, following her to the rear door of the cathedral, where they emerged into the last fading purple glow of sunset. Most of the tourists who had thronged the gardens of Notre Dame had long since departed, off to their various dinner engagements or other entertainments. It felt odd to have Erik walking beside her in the dusk, odder still to have him hail her a cab as any ordinary man would have done. Somehow, the air between them had grown easy, as if they were old friends becoming reacquainted and not a mad genius and the soul-lost singer he had once courted.

Is this what time does? Christine thought then. *Does it smooth away the edges, so that we can go on in this prosaic fashion, as though he had never wept in my arms and I had never kissed the tears from his cold forehead?*

She was not even sure whether the thought caused relief or regret.

But then he handed her up into the cab, and she knew she wasn't imagining the sudden pressure of his fingers on hers, or the unexpected gleam in those gold eyes before he looked away. No, perhaps not as much had changed as she had thought.

Still, she had to admit to herself that it was as if a pressure lifted itself from her mind when he shut the door to the carriage and she finally felt herself drawn away from him. If nothing else, he was certainly the most overwhelming personality she had ever known.

Rummaging inside her reticule, she found the tiny silver pocket watch Raoul had given her the previous Christmas and flipped it open. Almost six o'clock. Indeed, she was very late, and although she had planned nothing more than a simple supper in her own rooms, she knew she would have to give Jeannette some kind of explanation for her tardiness. Of course, what could be more respectable than attending Vespers at Notre Dame and then staying to light a candle for her father? Odd, what a liar Erik could make of her....

The cab pulled to a stop and she paused, trying to locate a couple of sous for the driver.

"Already taken care of, ma'am," he said, giving her a yellow grin and revealing a gold louis held between two callused fingers.

Trust Erik to be so extravagant. She nodded at the driver and smiled, then turned to walk up the front steps. The footman let her in immediately, of course, but what caught her off-guard was the sight of Jeannette, who hovered anxiously in the foyer.

"Oh, madame," she breathed. "We were so terribly worried. I thought you would be home hours ago, and—"

"I decided to go to the cathedral," Christine said, wondering at her maid's overly dramatic tone. "Perhaps I should have sent word that I would be later than I thought, but really—"

Jeannette cast a frightened look over one

shoulder. "Well, madame, of course it was your discretion, but—"

Her words cut off abruptly, however, as the door to the library was thrown open, and Raoul strode out into the foyer. Christine barely had time to register his presence before he fastened her with a grim look and said, "I suppose you'd like to explain to me the meaning of this?" Then he tossed a folded-up paper onto the gilt table in the center of the room, missing the vase of roses that stood there by mere inches.

She looked down, suddenly finding it very hard to breathe. There, staring up at her, was yesterday's headline: *Phantom of the Opera Strikes Again!* The words seemed to swim before her eyes, and before she could open her mouth to speak, she sagged and fell into blackness.

CHAPTER 8

Sunlight and Shadow

he scent of something harsh and medicinal filled her nose, her throat. Christine sneezed, then opened her watering eyes to see Jeannette hovering anxiously over her, with Raoul standing just behind her maid's black-clad shoulder. Whatever fit of anger had caused him to raise his voice seemed to have passed; his blue eyes were clouded with worry, his finely sculpted features filled with remorse.

"My God, Christine," he said, and although of course his voice did not fill her with the same heady mixture of anticipation and dread that

Erik's did, still, it was a very pleasant voice, a gentle baritone that at the moment shook with concern for her. "Are you all right?"

"It's nothing," she said, and pushed against the soft down-filled cushions beneath her, forcing herself to sit up. Apparently, Raoul had carried her to the settee in the front parlor after her collapse; now that she'd come back to herself, she recognized the striped blue and rose silk upholstery upon which she lay.

"Nothing!" he exclaimed, even as Jeannette stepped back, shaking her head. Like any good servant, she knew when to make herself invisible. "Christine, you fainted dead away!"

"Perhaps I was a bit startled," she murmured, realizing even as they left her mouth how foolish those words sounded. She added in a more normal voice, "It was my own fault, really. I'd had nothing to eat since an early lunch, and I was very late coming back from the cathedral. I should have stopped at a café and had a bite before I went to Vespers."

The explanation sounded plausible enough... she hoped. Really, it was true, when one looked at the situation logically. How long had it been since she'd eaten? Eight hours? Nine? Between her empty stomach and tight stays...and the emotional exhaustion which followed her interview with Erik...it was no wonder she had collapsed. Of course, she knew better than to breathe a single word to Raoul about her meeting with the Opera Ghost.

Her husband still watched her carefully, but at least there was no hint of suspicion in those clear blue eyes, so different from Erik's golden, catlike stare. At length, he nodded and said to Jeannette, "Would you be so kind as to fetch the comtesse a tray? Some broth, I think, and bread and butter. And tea, of course."

Jeannette dipped a quick curtsy and hurried out, but not before she gave Christine a quick, considering glance, as if she thought there might be more going on than met the eye but didn't dare say what. Christine knew her lady's maid missed very little, if anything, and she could only hope that Jeannette would keep her own counsel when it came to any suspicions she might be harboring. For the moment, Christine knew she would have her hands full dealing with her unexpected husband.

She knew that to dance around the issue would only make matters worse, so she took a breath and said, "You surprise me, Raoul. Did you really come all the way to Paris because of some scandalmongering reporter's lies?"

Her directness surprised him, she could tell.

The dark gold brows lowered a bit, and she detected a faint tightening of his jaw. "So, there are no murders?"

"I didn't say *that*, Raoul," she replied. "Unfortunately, some madman does seem to be stalking the Rue Scribe at present. But of course it can't be *him*, darling—he's been dead these two years."

"So we were told," Raoul said.

"It was confirmed beyond a shadow of a doubt," Christine said, in a tone which—she hoped—blended the right mixture of sadness and relief. "Meg sent me a letter saying they had found his skeleton in the cellars of the Opera."

His frown only deepened. "You never told me anything about that."

"I knew how much discussion of—of him upset you, Raoul. We were far away from it all by then. Why bring up the past?" For so long they had run from it, turned their backs on it, tried to forget it—but the past was not so easily discarded.

Like Erik, it was not as dead as it had seemed.

For a long moment, Raoul watched her, and finally the tension seemed to leave his body. He came toward her, then knelt next to the settee. "I'm sorry, Christine—sorry that I doubted you —that I came running to Paris like a madman—"

"It's all right, darling," she said, and took his hand. Such a warm, strong, human hand, so different from….

She could not let herself think of him. Not here, not now. She couldn't allow the slightest betraying expression to cross her face. Later, when she was alone, perhaps she could try to sort all this out. For the moment, though, she must only be Raoul's wife, the woman he thought he trusted. Her soul twisted at the lies she had already told him, and the lies she must continue to tell. Raoul deserved better, but she did not know what else to do. She could not allow herself to betray Erik…not when she'd promised to keep his secrets.

Managing a shaky laugh, she said, "Really, I suppose I should be flattered that I should rouse such a protective instinct after two years of marriage!"

He smiled at that comment, as she had hoped he would. "Two hundred years of marriage couldn't change how I feel about you, Christine."

Those words brought sudden tears to her eyes. How sweet he was, so utterly without guile, so easy in his declarations of love! Why couldn't she simply accept the gift for what it was? How was it that Erik could somehow leave a dark taint on her soul, like a bloodstain that could never be washed completely away? What was it about him that left her brooding and anxious when she should be content with a husband who adored her and a life certainly more comfortable than anything she could ever have imagined? Why couldn't she be satisfied?

She was saved from making a reply to her husband's declaration, however, by the arrival of Jeannette with the dinner tray. Christine allowed herself to be fussed over as Raoul got to his feet, busying himself with plumping the cushions at her back, even as Jeannette spread a napkin to protect the silken folds in her lap and then handed her a soup spoon.

The bouillon smelled wonderful, and Christine's empty stomach twisted at the thought of food after so many hours of deprivation. Still, she said, "There's no need to fuss—"

"Then you shouldn't have fainted, madame," Jeannette said crisply, and Christine could see Raoul smile again.

He added, "It's good to be fussed over every once in a while, Christine. Obviously, you haven't been taking as good care of yourself as you should—although I'm sure that's not through lack of trying on the part of the staff."

That was the Raoul Christine remembered, with the laughter lighting his blue eyes and the charming way he had of putting all those around him at ease. He cared so much about everyone, from the lowliest scullery maid to the members of his immediate family, and hated to see anyone out of sorts or upset.

Christine watched the worry leave Jeannette's eyes as she warmed to Raoul's words. Although sometimes Jeannette could be irritating, with her precise ideas of what constituted acceptable behavior in polite society and what did not, Christine knew that her lady's maid always had her best interests at heart. She was fiercely protective of Christine and had probably spent the time since her collapse berating herself for not keeping a closer watch on her mistress.

"I have to say that Meg has been running me ragged with all these dinner parties and fittings," Christine said at length, with what she hoped was the right note of levity.

"Then I will have to have a word with Mademoiselle Giry when I see her," Raoul replied, but he still smiled.

Obviously, her explanations were enough for him...for now. Christine dared not think what might happen if he discovered her subterfuges, if he ever found out that the Phantom was not quite the ghost he thought. The brief flash of anger she had witnessed in the foyer earlier would be nothing compared to his rage at that particular revelation, she was sure. Her husband was the most easygoing of men...most of the time. The subject of the Opera Ghost was the only one that guaranteed his disapproval, for although he would most likely never admit such a thing, Christine knew he did not like to admit that Erik had occupied a place in her heart before Raoul appeared on the scene. Yes, they had known one another as children, and yet a child's heart was not quite the same thing as the heart of a woman.

For the moment, though, it was enough for Christine to smile up at her husband with lying eyes, exchange light words with Jeannette, and underneath it all wonder, worry...and hope.

At first, he was content with the mere intoxication of her, the memory of the sweet sound of her voice, the faint scent of roses that clung to her hair and clothing—almost overpowered by the incense of the cathedral, but still there. After she disappeared into the cab and left him standing alone at the curb, watching until she had been gone for several minutes, Erik was almost happy as he walked the streets of Paris, for once feeling at one with the men he passed. Had he not just spent a sweet, stolen hour with the woman he loved? Had he not felt the gentle pressure of her gloved fingers against his, the wakening desire in her eyes? Perhaps he was not as unlike those other men as he had once thought. True, she belonged to another, but he was certainly not the first man in Paris to tryst with another man's wife—nor, he thought wryly, would he be the last.

But the afterglow did not last long—not much past the time when he returned to his grim cell in the catacombs of Denfert-Rochereau. He could not help but contrast the damp rock walls and the shabby scavenged furnishings with the grandeur of the Chagny house on the Rue Jacob.

Oh, she would be the very queen of air and darkness down here, he thought bitterly after he had divested himself of his fashionable garments bought with stolen coin and wrapped himself in a crazy quilt of opulent fabrics scavenged from the dustbins of the Rue de la Paix. He could no more imagine Christine in this living hell of bone and rock than he could imagine Raoul de Chagny wielding a Punjab lasso.

We are all what we are, came the galling thought, and he turned over on the lumpy mattress, pulling the quilt closer to himself. Those bitter ruminations were all-too-familiar companions down there in the dark, but that night, they seemed even more painful when contrasted with the beauty he had just seen and breathed in, even dared to touch.

She had faced him and spoken with him, and not flinched. The mask had been a victory, then —she had dealt with him almost as she would a normal man. Perhaps one day she could forget what lay behind it....

He held the memories close, the only warmth in that chill, unforgiving darkness. The pretty dimple at the corner of her mouth, the down-swept dark lashes, even the unexpected flashes of spirit that had caused her to snap at him, a kitten unsheathing its claws for the first time. All those charmed moments gave him the strength to shut his eyes against the night and, for the first time in he didn't know when, hope for the next day's dawning.

Of course, when day came, with it came as well an awakened restlessness. The score for *Don Juan Triumphant* seemed suddenly stale and tired. He dropped his pen after a few abortive attempts and gathered up his clothing in preparation for the day ahead.

The dankness of the catacombs hid one trea-sure that Erik had discovered soon after his arrival there—in a forgotten chamber, a hot spring bubbled up through the limestone, and he, fastidious as ever, had taken advantage of the unending supply of warm water to make sure he was always freshly bathed and his garments kept clean as well. One may live in a bone yard without smelling of it, he had been relieved to find, and that single comfort had done much to make him feel more like a man and less like a corpse.

He wanted to know how matters fared with Christine, what was happening in her world. It was far too early for an assignation with Lise, the scullery maid, but he found himself haunting the streets of the Faubourg Saint Germain, not daring to come too close to the house on the Rue Jacob. He was rewarded with a glimpse of a carriage with the crest of the Chagny household driving away some time past noon, but he could not get close enough to determine who its occupants might be. Finally, he hailed a cab and handed the driver a wad of franc-notes, instructing the man to drive through the city until night fell.

The cabbie must have thought his new fare a madman—and perhaps he was, Erik thought with grim humor—but no enterprising businessman would have turned down such a profitable proposition, insane as it might sound. So, they rattled through the streets, down the wide boulevards of Haussman's master plan for the city's reconstruction, the thoroughfares straight as an old Roman road, out through the Bois de

Boulogne, and back again, until the merciful early dusk of March began to fall and Erik could finally dismiss the cab so that he once again stood by himself on the Rue Bonaparte. He made sure he was quite alone before he glided down the dark alleyway that backed up to the great houses on the Rue Jacob and paused at the gate that led to the Chagny town home.

Lise appeared to have been waiting for him, peering out through the chilly semidarkness of a spring twilight. "Bit late, aren't you, m'sieur?"

Her pertness was almost welcome. At least to her, he wasn't a tired, aging ghost, but someone she could have a good gossip with and make a profit from at the same time.

His only answer was the flash of a golden louis, and she grinned as she took it from him and hid it in her pocket. "*Such* goings-on, m'sieur, as you can't imagine!" she exclaimed. "Only last night, his lordship shows up out of nowhere, and the comtesse faints dead away on the doorstep!"

For a few seconds, Erik could only stare at the scullery girl, not entirely comprehending. Then realization struck...along with a boiling rage. That interfering, pestilential boy! Would he not give Christine a moment's peace?

The mask, of course, hid all true emotion, but something of his anger must have revealed itself despite that impediment, filling the night around them. Even in the darkness, he could see some of the color leave the servant girl's cheeks.

"Course she was fine, sir, really!" Lise said hastily. "Just a bit startled, was all." She paused, then gave him a careful, sideways glance. "No one was expecting the master to come to town so soon. I heard he was angry about something at first, but it seems the comtesse smoothed things over, whatever it was."

Erik barely heard the words. Now, damn him, why *now?* He hadn't realized how much he had looked forward to the next week, a precious seven days during which Christine would be free in town with no Raoul de Chagny to trammel her in…and now this. That damned boy had had her for two years—could he not even give up a single week of her time?

The silence grew, and he finally realized Lise still stood there, watching him, and her expression was so strange that it took him a moment to recognize it for what it was. Pity showed in her sharp, pretty features…along with an odd sort of understanding.

"I'm sorry, m'sieur," she said then, and made an abortive little gesture with one hand, as if she had begun to reach out to touch his sleeve before thinking better of it. She looked up at him through a fringe of thick black lashes. "Do you love her, then?"

The irony of it, he thought, *to be found out by a little servant girl! Is this what having a real face does—makes one vulnerable to discovery? How do people bear it?*

"I don't see how that's any concern of yours," he said coldly, and she stiffened, lifting her chin.

"Perhaps not, m'sieur." This time, her gaze met his directly, and he was suddenly thankful for the dark glasses he wore at all times while out in public. "But it does make a girl suspicious —you wanting news of the household, and getting angry when the comte comes to town. I won't be party to any dishonoring the family, and that's that." She hesitated a moment, then reached in her pocket, removed the louis he had given her, and held it back out to him.

Despite himself, he was touched by the gallantry of her gesture. What was it to Lise, after all, whether her mistress cuckolded the master of the house a hundred times over? But somehow, it did matter to her, and he wondered at that quality in Christine which seemed to inspire protectiveness in all who met her, down to the lowest scullery maid.

"Keep it," he said, and he was unable to keep the weariness out of his tone. "There has been no dishonor, Lise, I assure you of that. I did love the comtesse once, years ago, but she was faithful then and remains so to this day." *And that is the paradox of it all,* he thought. *As much as I want her, I know I would esteem her less if I thought she would ever willingly leave Raoul.*

Lise stared at him, then looked down at the shining gold coin she held. She bit her lip and said, "I *am* sorry, sir," before turning and hurrying back down the path that led to the kitchen door.

He stood there alone in the shadows for a moment, knowing he would probably never see the girl again. Why that thought should give him such a pang, he wasn't sure. There were other ways, probably more reliable, by which he could gather information about Christine. No, it was more than that. It was the look of pity on the girl's face. Pity, and understanding. Quite possibly, she was the only human being who had ever experienced the slightest ounce of sympathy for him and his situation, who had ever considered his feelings for Christine with anything except horror.

Of course, she had no idea who he was beneath the mask — *what* he was beneath the mask, he corrected himself. No one who knew what a monster he was would ever feel pity for him...

...no one except Christine. And the hell of it

was, he didn't want her pity. He wanted her love. And that, he told himself, as he slipped away into the shadows, was the one thing he could never have.

At least while Raoul, Comte de Chagny, lived.

CHAPTER 9

Puzzle Pieces

$\mathcal{A}$ntoine Saint Denis walked the streets of Paris in the clear light of an early spring afternoon, but he paid little heed to the glory of the blooms that were just beginning to burst forth in window boxes and terrace gardens. Likewise, he was oblivious to the slanting silver-gilt light that turned the waters of the Seine into a shimmering trail of fairy dust and seemed to cast a gentle glow on even the most shadowed and careworn faces in the crowds which surrounded him. No, he had much darker matters occupying his mind.

Although he had busied himself with other

concerns—the Rue Scribe killings were not the only crimes he was currently following, though of course they were the most sensational—Saint Denis had been unable to keep the Comtesse de Chagny's words from his mind. *It is a matter of right and wrong, Monsieur Saint Denis. I think you cannot have completely forgotten what that means.*

And of course he hadn't, he tried to reassure himself. Oh, from time to time, the niceties must be overlooked in order to bring a story to the public eye, but wasn't it his duty to do so? Ever since he could remember, he'd had a questing desire to know the truth, to understand the mechanics of why and how things happened. If he'd been born to a different station in life, he supposed he could have been a policeman like Aubry. Aubry was a good man, if a little lacking in imagination, and if Aubry's successes of late were to be attributed more to his consultations with Saint Denis than any native sleuthing talent, so be it. Any self-doubt Aubry might have experienced in relying on a reporter to help solve his cases was no doubt assuaged by the handsome monthly stipend Saint Denis gave him for the privilege of doing so. Of course, Saint Denis benefited as well, since Aubry was generous with the details of his casework as long as Saint Denis was careful not to reveal his sources.

Only now, after hearing the reproachful words of the comtesse over and over in his head, had Saint Denis begun to realize there was a distinction to be made between recognizing the truth and understanding the difference between right and wrong. He'd known all along it was not the Phantom of the Opera who was committing these terrible crimes, and yet he hadn't scrupled to use the dead man's name in the pursuit of selling a few more papers. That practice would have to stop now, of course; he'd given his word to a lady, if an unspoken one, and he could not go back on such a promise, no matter what the consequences might be. Saint Denis envisioned the bitter dispute he was sure to have with his editor over the matter and smiled grimly; there were times when doing the correct thing was, at the very least, difficult if not downright unpleasant.

But along with that realization came the dawning insight that as much as he liked to think his articles boosted circulation, or however much he might enjoy Aubry's deference to him in matters of the criminal mind, what he thirsted for the most was the answer, the solution to the puzzle. As neatly as the riddle might have been solved by having the former Opera Ghost turn out to be the perpetrator, Saint Denis knew now that was not the case.

And so, then, who? Certainly, the killer was cunning, killing in stealth and darkness, and very careful to avoid leaving any clues as to his identity. But as elusive as the murderer might be, Saint Denis was certain there must be a pattern to these killings, even though that pattern might not be easily discernible yet. He had a feeling that each one of these victims had been carefully selected, though to what purpose, he could not imagine.

His intuitions had served him well in the past, however, and he acknowledged this one even as he recognized that he had no concrete proof as of yet to back up the insight. Time would tell. Sooner or later, the killer would do something to betray himself; Saint Denis believed the man must be mad, after all, and no madman could continue indefinitely without making some sort of misstep.

In the matter of the Comtesse de Chagny, his curiosity had been pricked as well. There was a wealth of secrets behind those apparently guileless blue eyes, secrets that went far beyond her surprising knowledge of the Phantom's true method of killing. Saint Denis was familiar with the outlines of the story, of course, but somehow, he had gotten the notion that the Comtesse de Chagny's attack on him had less to do with outraged feelings of right and wrong than with an instinctive desire to protect someone for whom she had once cared—even if she might vehemently deny that fact when pressed. Because of how matters between them currently stood, there was no way he could question her further on the subject...but there had been others involved in the scandal, of course.

He thought of the former opera managers, but decided that trying to interview them would be a dead end. The rumor had circulated that the Opera Ghost had extorted large sums of money from them before he died, and Saint Denis very much doubted they would care to admit such weakness to a reporter. Besides, he was fairly certain neither of them lived in Paris any longer; Monsieur Moncharmin had retired to the countryside near Chartres to write his memoirs, and rumor whispered that Monsieur Richard apparently had suffered some sort of nervous collapse after the scandal at the Opera and was now residing in a sanatorium in Basel.

Meg Giry was a possibility, but even Saint Denis scrupled to approach a young lady so absorbed in her own approaching nuptials. True, she had been a good friend to Christine, and apparently was still, but he did not think he would be granted an audience with her. Also, he had the thought that even if he were able to speak with her, she would certainly relate the details of her conversation with him to Christine, and that wouldn't do at all.

But Mademoiselle Giry's mother was an entirely different matter. Rumors had swirled amongst the petite rats of the *corps de ballet* that the worthy woman knew far more about the Opera Ghost than she cared to let on. As Saint Denis had told Christine, he was not one of the reporters who'd been assigned to the scandal at the Paris Opera—more's the pity—but the case had fascinated him from the beginning, and in the intervening years, he had pursued his own investigations, more to satisfy a personal curiosity than with any idea of reporting his findings. Madame Giry seemed the least likely person to be involved in any sort of intrigue, but several members of the *corps de ballet* had reported that Meg had been in possession of rather more detailed information regarding the Opera Ghost than anyone could reasonably expect, and that this information seemed to have been mostly gathered from her mother.

He knew that Madame Giry now lived in a small but luxurious flat on the Rue de Rivoli, purchased ostensibly by Meg but no doubt funded by the worthy Baron de Castelo-Barbezac. Certainly, the elder Giry's previous lodgings just south of the Gare d'Orleans had left much to be desired, and it wouldn't do for the future mother-in-law of a baron to be seen in such surroundings. So, she had been moved to a more respectable neighborhood, even as she was seen less and less in public with her daughter.

Although Saint Denis had never run in circles as elevated as those in which Mademoiselle Giry now socialized, he knew quite well what was probably going on. The baron was marrying far beneath him — marrying for love, if the society columns were to be believed — and Madame Giry was an unfortunate adjunct to the relationship. Better that she be kept out of circulation as much as possible to avoid any possible embarrassment for her daughter or future son-in-law. Sad, really, that just as the woman's greatest ambitions for her daughter were about to be realized, she should be shuffled out of the way, sent out to pasture like a worthy draught animal which had given good service but was now far past its days of usefulness.

However, it was often the case in such circumstances, when people felt they had been misused or ignored, that they were far more apt to pour out their troubles to a sympathetic ear — even if that ear happened to belong to one of Paris' most notorious reporters. Perhaps the neglected Madame Giry would finally let slip some of her carefully guarded secrets regarding the Opera Ghost — and who could blame her?

Certainly not Antoine Saint Denis, he thought, pausing on the corner of the Rue Saint Augustin and the Avenue de l'Opéra. He reached in his overtaxed coat pocket and pulled out the little notebook he carried with him at all times. A month or so ago, when he had first heard of Madame Giry's new lodgings, he had taken note of that detail and written down her new direction. Yes, there it was. Number twenty-six Rue de Rivoli.

Smiling, he returned the book to his coat pocket and looked around. It was a glorious afternoon, he realized. Only Paris on a spring afternoon could acquire such a fine patina, as if everything had been overlaid with a thin coating of burnished gold.

A pretty young woman approaching him caught his smile and returned it, dimples showing in the soft white flesh near her pink mouth. In response, he tipped his hat, then set off toward the Rue de Rivoli. He was sure that such an outstanding afternoon should not be wasted on a cab when his destination was only nine or ten blocks away.

As he went along, he could not help but continue to smile. His good humor was contagious, and more often than not, he was greeted with an answering smile. Who wouldn't be cheerful on such a spring day in Paris, after all, when the very air was gilded and every breath of the gentle breeze whispered of promises given and hopes fulfilled? Not he. All of his previous doubts seemed to have been but foolish fancies, and he walked confidently along the Avenue de l'Opéra, certain of his task and the reception he would receive at the end of his journey.

He sat in the dimly lit room, clutching the list, rocking back and forth slightly in the hard chair that was the only seating the flat offered besides the narrow bed placed up against one wall. Around the edges of the shabby curtains, a certain glow hinted at the brightness of the day outside, but no beam of light penetrated the general darkness of the room. He hated the daylight and kept the curtains drawn at all times; he only wished they were made of heavier material so they would do a better job of completely blocking out the sun.

The list of names was fairly short and at first glance quite innocuous; they had been neatly typed on a thin sheet of paper, now slightly yellowed around the edges. The paper was smudged with dirty fingerprints and looked as if it had been crumpled into a ball at one point in its existence, but he held it now with excessive care, as though worried that it might shiver into dust with too heedless a touch. There were six names on the list; three of them now had emphatic black lines drawn through them.

"Soon," he murmured, reaching down to the table in front of him and stroking the thin piece of wire that lay there. A thrill went through him at the mental image of that wire being pulled taut against an unsuspecting throat. Sometimes, he thought the garrote itself had taken on a life of its own, whispering to him in the dark, murmuring of its thirst for the blood of his next victim.

So much lay in the hands of fate. He had no control over who would be next; all he could do was watch and wait and hope that one of those chosen six would stray across his path. Three down, but three still to go, and the biggest catch of all continued to be completely out of his grasp.

On the nights he did not go out hunting—the Opera was dark, or he felt in his bones that the gendarmes would be straying too close to his killing grounds—he would lie here in the darkness, dreaming of their deaths. One by one they would go down into oblivion, even as they drowned in their own blood. He could only hope that they experienced even one-tenth the pain and despair he had been forced to suffer over the past uncounted months.

In some tiny portion of his mind, the part that still functioned enough to keep him from looking like a gibbering madman as he went to procure his one daily meal or pick up his monthly stipend from the public house he had given as his direction, he looked at his new existence and despaired. Surely, he had been born for something better than this. Somewhere, as if from a hazy dream, he remembered a world of light and elegance, of beautiful women and flattering underlings. But those flashes seemed to come to him less and less frequently these days as his thoughts floundered and slipped in images of darkness and blood. Perhaps once they were all gone, he could finally find his way back to the light. Perhaps then the demon that raged in his mind could finally be put to rest.

But those moments of lucid despair came more and more sporadically as time wore on. There were days when the names on the list were more familiar to him than his own, days where he could not have answered clearly if asked where he was born but knew to the decimal place the calculated wealth of each of his victims. The accumulation of wealth was not his goal, though, of course not. It would have been easy to steal the wallets, heavy gold pocket watches, finger-rings and fobs of his victims, but robbery had never been his intent. To steal from them would have diluted the purity of his mission, the reason they all had to die. It was a motive as simple as the rising of the sun, and nearly as old.

"*Revenge*," he whispered, and began to laugh.

Erik reflected bitterly that he would never have thought he'd be reduced to the role of voyeur at this stage in his life, but that seemed to be exactly what he had become. The day after Lise, the scullery maid, had dismissed him so unexpectedly, he found his steps drawn, as if by some inexorable force, back to the Faubourg Saint Germain and the Chagny town home there. All he could do was wander the streets aimlessly, hat pulled low over his face—an act suspicious enough in itself on such a fine spring day—hoping for the merest glimpse of Christine.

He caught that glimpse...but she was accompanied by the comte, who handed her up into his carriage before disappearing into its recesses himself. At the sight of his former enemy, Erik could feel his mouth pull into a snarl. Whatever stories Christine had been feeding Raoul, they seemed to be working. The boy—really a man now, Erik reflected sourly; he had grown broader and browner over the intervening two years—smiled sunnily at the driver even as he helped Christine into the carriage. Obviously, Raoul had no idea that Christine had been consorting with her former Angel of Music.

There was no way for Erik to follow the carriage without attracting far too much attention, and so he had had to comfort himself with that brief glimpse of Christine, elegant and glowingly beautiful in a visiting gown of deep rose silk faille. Quite possibly, they were off to visit Meg and her baron. His soul ached at the thought of Christine going about her daily activities, at the thought of all the smiles he had missed, all the little commonplaces he'd never thought he cared about—until Christine. When he first met her, it became terribly important to him that he could live a normal life, that he should be able to escape the black box of a home he had made for himself under the opera house, in that place beyond the underground lake. And now, when he had finally achieved that end—when he could walk among men with only the occasional sideways look—it didn't matter. All of her smiles, her downcast glances, her gentle humor and exquisite patience, were gifts to Raoul, Comte de Chagny, and not to Erik.

Discretion had prevented him from following the carriage, although of course he knew the location of the Baron de Castelo-Barbezac's home as well as he knew Christine's. What would be the point? To see the two happy couples together, secure in their wealth and beauty, their complacent knowledge of their exalted positions in the world? Even he did not wish to bring such torture upon himself. But at least he had seen her—and Christine had not shared her husband's sunny smile. Her face had been serene, almost expressionless, but he knew her well enough to see the tension in the set of her shoulders, the way the leather of her gloves stretched taut across her knuckles as she grasped her parasol. No, the comtesse was not quite as untroubled at heart as she would like others to think.

If there were any way for him to relieve her worry, he would do so unthinkingly, but as he himself was very likely the cause of her current troubled state, there was not much he could do...save leave her alone. Now, though, having seen her once again, he could no more walk away than change the Seine in its course. Some small part of him was even heartened to see her struggle, to know she was not as indifferent to him as she might pretend. If she truly cared nothing for Erik, she would have had no trouble denouncing him to Raoul and ensuring that the authorities were called in to arrest the erstwhile

Opera Ghost. He was, after all, still wanted for the deaths of Joseph Buquet and the former Comte de Chagny—even though the latter's demise had been purely accidental.

Erik was fairly certain no one would believe his protestations of innocence on that account.

He'd had a secondary mission when he set out this morning, however. Christine's revelations in the cathedral the evening before last had led him to do some investigations on his own, and he soon discovered that the man who had been spreading the notion that the Phantom of the Opera was the murderer in the Rue Scribe killings was a reporter named Antoine Saint Denis.

It was most certainly Saint Denis whom Christine had been trying to protect, although Erik was not sure why. Certainly even she, in her innocence, should have realized he could easily discover the name of the reporter without her assistance. Some further reading and a few carefully placed questions had given him all the information he needed—that Saint Denis had worked for the Paris *Presse* for almost seven years now; that he was a gentleman by birth if not by title; and also, Erik recalled with a scowl, that he was handsome, charming, and almost generally liked, except by those who'd had the misfortune to be skewered by one of his exposés.

The waitress at one of the cafés on the Boulevard des Capuchines who had volunteered most of this information had smiled dreamily when recounting the apparently numerous charms of Antoine Saint Denis. "He's often on the streets along here and the Place de l'Opéra. You can't miss him—he's quite tall, with brown hair, and he usually wears a deep blue silk scarf."

At the time, Erik had thought her a little deluded; after all, there were quite a few tall brown-haired men who frequented the fashionable streets around the Opera, even accounting for those who might be wearing blue silk scarves. But now, as he returned to that district, he thought he might have found the man he sought.

Only a few yards ahead of Erik walked a tall brown-haired man in an impeccably cut frock coat—impeccable except for an oddly bulging right pocket. One end of a royal blue scarf waved jauntily in the breeze over his left shoulder as he moved with an easy haste along the crowded sidewalks. Even from behind Saint Denis—if the man truly was the reporter in question—Erik could see the pleasant nods and outright smiles the man received as he walked along. Either he was well-known, or he truly did possess the sort of charm that caused even strangers on the street to respond to him favorably.

Obviously, the man had some destination in mind; he walked with great purpose along the Avenue de l'Opéra before turning down one side street, then another. All of the roads around the opera house were as well known to Erik as the lines on his palm, and he knew at once where the stranger was heading. He found his heart beginning to beat with irrational urgency in his chest, and he shook his head at himself.

What does it matter? he thought. *It has been a long time. Perhaps he, too, is dead.*

Nevertheless, the familiar buildings that met his gaze as he turned onto the Rue de Rivoli seemed to be tinged with a sort of dread, as if each of them housed an unspoken threat. It was all he could do to walk past number four without turning to stare at its shuttered windows. In that genteelly shabby flat, he had once broken down and poured out his heart to the only man he had ever considered a friend.

But those confidences and that friendship were all in the past, and now he had a quarry to pursue. He had no plan in mind as to what to do with Monsieur Saint Denis once he caught up with him; Erik supposed he was motivated as much by curiosity as by anger. What was Saint Denis' destination, after all? He didn't live on this street, that much Erik knew. Perhaps he kept a mistress here, in one of the small but well-maintained homes that grew steadily larger and more elegant as the street numbers ascended and the Rue de Rivoli approached its junction with the Place de la Concorde.

Suddenly, however, he found his way barred by a man who stepped out of a small alleyway that separated two properties. Erik looked up, all words of protestation stifled by the eyes that met his—two eyes of a peculiar jade green, eyes that burned out at him past heavy brows, now more gray than black.

"Where are you going, Erik?" demanded the Persian.

CHAPTER 10

Tea and Sympathy

Of all the ways Erik had thought he might spend this afternoon, sitting in the daroga's parlor and sipping hot tea flavored with lemon was certainly not one of them. He had accepted the Persian's invitation to tea because making a scene on a street corner hadn't seemed terribly prudent, and the other man had been quite insistent.

Now that they were safely indoors, however, it seemed the daroga did not know exactly what to say. He sat in a well-worn armchair and gazed at his guest, his expression one of mixed consternation and puzzlement. At last, he set his tea and saucer down on the marble-topped table next to his chair and said, "How on earth did you manage it, Erik?"

"Manage what?" Erik responded smoothly. Drinking the tea was not as difficult as he feared, so long as he was careful to tip the liquid as directly into his mouth as he could without allowing it to touch the false lips of the mask he wore.

The daroga waved a hand at Erik's face. "That. It is…uncanny."

"In a good way, or a bad way?"

That question—delivered in an ironic tone—only made the Persian frown. He did not seem to have fared well over the past several years; his shining black hair was now mostly gray, and he moved stiffly, as though his joints pained him. But the piercing green eyes were as brilliant as ever, and they narrowed as the man took in his guest's altered appearance.

"Neither," he said. "More, I suppose, that it looks so very normal, and yet I know what lies beneath."

Erik shrugged. Lately, he had been doing his best to eat more, and he knew that his body had begun to fill out, was not as painfully thin as it once had been. Just another part of the subterfuge, another way to make himself appear to be an ordinary man. "What lies beneath is known only to us," he replied. "And it is of no import to those I pass on the street. You cannot know, my friend, what it is like to be utterly unremarkable, to walk amongst humanity and not have any of them give you a second look. It is a rare gift, and one I treasure."

This revelation only made the Persian blink and take another sip of his tea. For a moment, he was silent. Then he said, "You made me think you were dead."

"It seemed safer that way."

"Ah." Another silence, broken only by the ticking of the old brass clock on the mantel. When he spoke, his expression was still troubled. "And what am I to think of this return from the dead? Odd that it should just happen to coincide with the return of the Comte and Comtesse de Chagny."

The mask was a very handy thing in moments such as that, since Erik knew it would not reveal any of his emotions unless he frowned fiercely indeed. He held himself still, then said, "It is no coincidence at all. True, we only crossed paths this day, but I never left Paris. I have been here all along."

"Indeed? Where?"

Perhaps the daroga only wished to satisfy his own curiosity…or perhaps, once a policeman, always a policeman. No, Erik had committed no recent crimes, save for the petty larcenies that kept coins in his pockets and new, respectable clothes on his back, but the murders at the Opera weren't so buried in the past that they had been forgotten. He knew he would never give the man who sat in the chair opposite his a proper answer to that question.

"Here and there," he said vaguely. "For of course, my former home in the cellars of the Opera was no longer available to me. I have made do these past few years."

"And what have you done to occupy yourself?"

Really, a former inspector from so ancient a land as Persia should possess a bit more subtlety. Erik made himself sip from his cup of tea to compose himself before providing an answer. "I have been composing," he said. "It is the best occupation I have found to fill the empty hours."

Those words appeared to evoke an expression of pity in the Persian's cool green eyes. Seeing it, Erik experienced a flare of irritation. He didn't want the man's pity. After all, he had done well enough for himself these past few years.

Only…he truly hadn't. A miserable cubbyhole in the depths of the boneyards was not what anyone could view as a comfortable life.

"And you have done nothing else?"

The question seemed innocuous enough, but Erik knew better. He might not have asked directly, but the Persian no doubt wanted to know whether his erstwhile friend had anything to do with the murders that were currently rocking the city.

"Nothing like what you're thinking," he snapped, letting his annoyance get the better of him. Really, did the daroga believe him so lacking in subtlety that he would make the mistake of committing such sensational crimes? Besides, while Erik knew his hands were less than clean, the men who had died at those hands had done so because they had made the mistake of crossing him. He never killed without cause.

"Indeed?" returned the Persian. However, something in his posture relaxed slightly, belying the ironic tone that had entered his voice.

"Indeed," Erik said. "I have no doubt that you have done your own poking and prying into the situation, and if that is the case, then you must know as well as I do that I had nothing to do with any of it."

Rather than appear offended by the "poking and prying" comment, the other man smiled and sipped some of his tea. "Well, I have not been able to get close enough to know for certain, but it did seem to me that these murders were not quite your style. For one thing, there does not appear to be any discernible motive."

"There isn't," Erik replied, somewhat mollified by the daroga's admission. "And say what you like about me—you know that I never killed without having a very good reason to do so."

"True enough," the Persian allowed, "even though there are some who would say that your 'reasons' were not perhaps as justified as they should be."

Perhaps. Erik would not waste his time arguing the motivations behind the murders he'd been forced to commit; he had been there, and the daroga had not. Rather than continue with that particular argument, he said, "And there is also the small detail that these men have all been garroted, rather than killed with the lasso."

"Ah, is that the truth of it?" Rather than wait for his guest to respond, the Persian continued. "The papers said it was a garrote, but I could not be certain whether that was truly the murder weapon, or whether it was presented as such because the Sûreté could not tell the difference between a garrote and the Punjab lasso. That is some relief, I suppose."

"I suppose," Erik observed dryly. "Or at least, it would be if it were not that the papers are seeking to sensationalize these crimes even further by connecting my name to the murders. I know I am a ghost, but even a ghost dislikes having his name sullied."

The Persian lifted a gray-frosted eyebrow. "Oh, but you are not a ghost, are you, Erik? You have now the appearance of a prosperous man, someone who can move freely about the city. What is it you intend to do with this newfound freedom of yours?"

A good question, and one Erik had not yet answered to his own satisfaction. He had thought the restlessness that had grown in him over the past few days had everything to do with Christine Daaé's presence in the city. As he pondered the daroga's words, however, he found himself wondering if it was something more than having the woman he loved so tantalizingly close and yet forever out of reach. The recent alterations he had made to the mask appeared to have refined it to the point where he truly could pass among men with no one around him lifting an eyebrow. Or rather, he still received a curious glance from time to time, thanks to the dark glasses he wore to conceal his unusual amber-gold eyes, but the glasses were certainly not enough to prevent him from mingling with humanity. The disguise was nearly perfect. What then, did he intend to do with it?

"As to that," he said, his tone as careless as he could make it, "I suppose I hadn't thought so far ahead. Perhaps I will attend the Opera—not in Box Five, of course—or go drink absinthe at the Café Riche."

"That is all?" the Persian asked. "You have returned from the dead, only to occupy yourself with trifling amusements?"

"Ah, but they are not so trifling to *me*, daroga," replied Erik. "For you see, I have never been able to comport myself as an ordinary man. I daresay it will take several years for the novelty to wear off. But in the meantime, there are a grand variety of harmless amusements that this city has to offer."

The Persian tilted his head to one side, regarding his guest. "And some not so harmless," he said. "But I suppose you more than most men know how to be careful."

"I do." Or perhaps not. If Erik were truly the careful sort, he would not have allowed Christine to slip into his heart, would not have let himself dare hope that she could look beyond his outward ugliness and see the yearning that lived in the deepest recesses of his soul. Allowing himself to care had given her the power to hurt him...and oh, how she had hurt him.

But he could not let himself dwell on such matters, not when the daroga sat a few feet away and watched him with careful eyes the hue of celadon. At any rate, Erik knew the mask he had created would allow him to do things he'd never been able to do before, the sorts of accomplishments that would seem terribly commonplace to those who had never suffered a disfigurement, who had never been cursed with a face that doomed them to live outside the world of ordinary mortals.

"And I will be careful," he added, when it seemed the daroga was waiting for him to continue. "I have no desire to attract attention. If that had been my goal, why would I have kept myself hidden away these past two years?"

For a long moment, the Persian said nothing, only sat there with his cup of clumsily painted china in one hand, the pale porcelain incongruous against his dark fingers. What passed through his mind in that moment, Erik couldn't say for certain. He would not allow himself to hold his breath, for doing so would only signal that he feared what his old friend might say.

"I suppose you are right," the daroga said at length. He sipped his tea before adding, "And I also suppose I can only hope that you will continue to be circumspect."

"Having no wish to meet my fate at the hands of Madame Guillotine," Erik responded, "I have no other choice."

This wryly morbid observation evoked a faint smile. "Yes, I suppose that would be something of a deterrent. But what is it that brought you to the Rue de Rivoli today?"

Well, at least there was a question he could answer truthfully. "I was following a man—a reporter," he added, as the Persian began to frown. "His name is Antoine Saint Denis, and he has been writing rather sensational pieces about the murders in the Rue Scribe. Since I was being libeled in those articles, I thought it a good idea to follow Saint Denis and see where it is that he has been getting his information."

"Then I am sorry I interrupted a mission of such importance."

Erik made himself shrug, although inwardly, he still was irritated that the daroga's interference had prevented him from following the reporter to his destination. "No matter," he said. "I know he works for the Paris *Presse,* and so it will not be difficult to pick up the trail at my leisure."

He also knew the address of the handsome house in the Quartier Saint-Georges where Saint Denis made his home, but Erik guessed it would be better not to mention that particular piece of information. It was one thing to stalk a man from his place of business, and quite another to lurk in the streets and alleys that surrounded his home. Better to make the Persian think that he was doing his best to remain on the straight and narrow…and better still for the other man to believe that Erik had nothing more on his mind than determining if there was any way to clear his name.

However, it seemed the daroga wasn't quite ready to abandon his questioning. "And what of Christine Daaé?"

"La Comtesse de Chagny, you mean."

A dismissive gesture with the hand that wasn't holding a teacup and saucer. "She is in Paris. But of course, you already knew that."

As much as he wanted to deny such knowledge, Erik also knew that the Persian would easily spot such a lie. "I believe I saw it in the papers. What of it? She is the comte's wife, and lost to me."

Once again, the Persian was silent for the span of a few seconds. Was he wishing he could see Erik's true face, if only to detect from his expression whether he was telling a falsehood? When he spoke, his tone was quiet and grave. "She was lost to you long before that, I fear."

Fury burned within him, but Erik clenched his jaw and waited for the moment of rage to pass. Too often in the past, he had allowed such anger to fuel acts of violence he later regretted. It certainly would not do to murder the poor Persian in his flat simply because he had uttered an uncomfortable truth.

"As you say," he returned, then swallowed the rest of his tea. The conversation had taken an unwelcome turn, and he had no wish to have the daroga probe at wounds that still remained unhealed. He thought then of Christine being handed up into the carriage, of the graceful sweep of her rosy skirts and the way her chestnut hair had gleamed against the sumptuous fabric. How he wished he could see where she had gone, could see what it was like to be with her in company, rather than in stolen moments where the two of them were hidden away from the world.

The thought which struck him then was so singular, he had to prevent himself from sitting up in shock.

Why *couldn't* he be with her in company? Why could he not go to the home of the Baron de Castelo-Barbezac, and introduce himself as one of the guests? He had done such a thing once before, after all. Oh, not in such exalted company—it had been a gathering of the opera managers and their guests—but still, he had worn one of his earlier masks and no one had questioned his presence. Now, when his mask had been perfected and the daroga himself had said the illusion was uncanny, Erik thought it should be safe enough. To be near her...to hear her sweet voice and the silvery ripple of her laugh…oh, yes, that would be worth any risk.

He set his empty teacup down on the table next to him, saying, "This has been most pleasant, daroga, but I must be going."

"'Must'?" the Persian echoed, looking more resigned than alarmed. "I had no idea your social calendar was so full."

"I have taken enough of your time," Erik replied. "But now you can be satisfied that I have nothing to do with the murders in the Rue Scribe, and that I want nothing more than a quiet life. Perhaps one day soon I can invite you to tea so I might return the favor."

"I would like that," the daroga said. "You should give me your direction, so I might know where to find you."

Oh, he would certainly not succeed with so transparent a ploy as that. Smiling under his mask—and certain in the knowledge that the corners of the mask's lips would lift at the same time—Erik replied, "Oh, when the time comes, I will send for you, daroga. But meanwhile, have a pleasant afternoon."

He went to the door then and let himself out, knowing that the Persian would not try to stop him.

A plain-faced woman wearing an equally plain dark gray gown opened the door in response to Antoine Saint Denis' knock. "M'sieur?" she said, her tone as uncertain as her expression.

Definitely not Madame Giry. The woman in question was probably a good twenty years older than the specimen who stared up at him now. "I am Monsieur Saint Denis," he replied, sending her a smile that had gained him entrée into far more distinguished homes than this. "I would like to speak to Madame Giry if it is at all possible."

The woman, clearly a maid—probably the only maid, as he doubted the elder Giry's household was fine enough to support more than one —sent a hesitant glance over one shoulder. "She —she has not been feeling well this afternoon—"

"Who is it, Annette?" broke in a woman's voice, one that sounded tired and somehow fretful.

"A gentleman, madame," Annette replied. "He says he wants to speak with you."

A pause, one that Saint Denis thought might have been slightly startled. Then Madame Giry —for he guessed it must be she—said, "Show him in, Annette."

He allowed himself a second or two of relief. There had been no real reason for Madame Giry to refuse him entry...just as there had been no real way he could have gainsaid her if she'd decided to turn him away. Although he might be dogged in his pursuit of a story, he would never stoop so low as to force entry into a woman's home.

Luckily, such measures were not required. Annette led him through a modest foyer decorated with several etchings of the Paris opera house and into a dark sitting room. Although the day outside was fine—glorious, really—the oxblood velvet drapes were pulled almost all the way closed, and a fire burned in the grate. Saint Denis allowed himself a quick look at his surroundings, determined that the furniture and wall coverings were new and in sober but tasteful hues, and then directed his attention to the woman who sat in an easy chair near the hearth.

She appeared to be some fifteen years or so older than he, although he supposed her hair could have been prematurely gray, her face lined with troubles that had aged her beyond her years. Certainly, she looked old to have a daughter who could be no more than twenty-three at the most.

Then again, while Madame Giry's story was not well known, he'd done his best to do his research, and so he knew that her husband had passed away some years earlier, leaving her to support her only daughter with the meager sum she earned while working as an usher at the opera. Once Meg had begun to dance in the *corps de ballet,* their situation improved somewhat, but still, it was nothing short of miraculous that a young woman raised in such circumstances should find herself engaged to a baron.

Hat in hand, Saint Denis approached Madame Giry and bowed slightly. "Good afternoon, madame," he said. "Thank you very much for allowing me to speak to you."

One thick gray eyebrow lifted as she took in his appearance, from the hat in his hand to the blue silk scarf that hung around his neck. "I don't know you," she said, voice still thin and weary, as if simply sitting upright in her chair had tired her beyond all endurance. For the first time, Saint Denis noted the abandoned embroidery hoop that lay on the side table next to her; it appeared she'd attempted to work on the handkerchief that lay within but found she simply didn't have the strength. "Did you attend the opera?"

"No, madame, I fear I am not a devotee," he replied. "There would have been no reason for our paths to cross before this. I work for the Paris *Presse.*"

This confession made her eyes flare open, startled. They were a faded watery brown, possibly dark and sparkling in her youth, but with very little light in them now. "What is it you want?" she asked, now sounding more alarmed than weary.

"Only to speak with you, madame," he said at once. "I was hoping you might provide some illumination on the subject of the Phantom of the Opera."

A spasm passed over her sunken features, although he couldn't say for sure whether it was from fear or surprise. Without responding to him directly, she glanced over at her maid, who had hovered near the fireplace during the previous exchange. "Annette, go fetch us some tea."

"That's not necessary—" Saint Denis began to protest, but she shook her head.

"It is necessary for me, m'sieur," Madame Giry said, with a ferocity he hadn't expected. "Please, sit down while Annette gets us some refreshments."

Since arguing further would be churlish, he retreated to the divan and perched on the edge of the cushion while Madame Giry's maid left the room. Once they were alone, she stirred in her chair and sat up a little straighter, bony hands clenching the heavy black silk of her skirts.

"I thought it would be better if we were alone when discussing such a topic," Madame Giry told him then, her voice brisker than he had expected. "Not, I fear, that there is very much I can tell you. The Opera Ghost has been dead these two years."

Exactly the same thing Christine de Chagny had told him when she came to his offices at the Paris *Presse*. All the same, Saint Denis couldn't quite rid himself of the notion that a secret lurked at the bottom of all this, one which no one involved appeared willing to reveal. At the same time, he knew he needed to tread carefully.

"How is it you know he is dead, madame?" he inquired.

Her pale lips tightened. "Because I saw his body, m'sieur. Indeed, I was the one who buried him."

"You did?" Saint Denis exclaimed, forgetting to moderate his tone.

"Yes, m'sieur. He—he did favors for me, watched out for Meg. In exchange, he asked that I should take care of him if...well, if anything should happen to him."

This extraordinary revelation was enough to make Saint Denis shift backward on the divan as he gazed at Madame Giry in astonishment. Somehow, he was able to recover his composure enough to say, "So, you were friends with the Opera Ghost?"

She shook her head. He noted that her iron-gray hair still appeared quite thick, although it was worn in unfashionable braids crossing her head rather than in a chignon low on her neck, as the current style dictated. "Oh, I couldn't say that, m'sieur. He was not one to invite confidences. I think it was only that he pitied me, pitied my situation, and wanted to do what he could to help me and my daughter."

Oh, so the Phantom of the Opera was a charitable man? Saint Denis couldn't quite reconcile Madame Giry's description of him with the individual who had terrorized the Palais Garnier for weeks and who was responsible for the deaths of Joseph Buquet and the former Comte de Chagny, but he knew better than to contradict her. No, what he wanted was for her to keep talking in the hope that she would let slip even more revelations.

"So, if you buried him…." He let the words trail off there, not sure how to phrase the question without sounding grossly indelicate.

She seemed to understand what he was saying, for her mouth moved in a humorless smile. "He wore a mask, m'sieur. Out of respect for his wishes, I did not remove it. I have no idea what he looked like, or who he truly was."

Damn. Saint Denis supposed he should have expected as much, and yet he'd very much hoped that she would have seen the Opera Ghost's face.

Without waiting for him to speak, she went

on, "And, in accordance with his wishes, I published an announcement in *L'Epoque.*"

"What did it say?"

"'Erik is dead.'"

Erik. "That was his name?"

"Yes, m'sieur."

"What was his surname?"

Madame Giry's shoulders lifted. "I have no idea, m'sieur. He never told me...and I never asked."

And as dogged as Saint Denis knew he could be when in pursuit of a story, even he realized that trying to discover the Opera Ghost's true identity when the man's Christian name was all he had to go on would be an exercise in futility. Still, it seemed that Madame Giry had corroborated what Christine had already told him—that the mysterious Phantom had been dead for two years, and whoever was stalking those prosperous bankers and brokers and merchants on the Rue Scribe, it certainly was not the Opera Ghost.

However, even though it seemed as if this errand had turned out to be a dead end—no jest intended—Saint Denis didn't intend it to be an entire waste of time. "What was this Erik's involvement with Christine Daaé?"

That question took Madame Giry aback. Her complexion was too pale to truly blanch, and yet something seemed to drain from her face, making her appear even more weary than before. "'Involvement'?" she repeated, and then gave a nervous little chuckle that would have fooled no one. "Why, he was a great voice teacher, and so he trained her, recognizing what a pure instrument she had, but that is all."

Voice teacher. Yes, he'd heard a few rumors to that effect—a girl in the *corps de ballet,* a pert individual named Giselle, had told him that Christine had been barely struggling along as a member of the chorus, and then out of nowhere began to sing like one of the heavenly choirs. "She said she had a great teacher, m'sieur," Giselle had said, "but she would never tell any of us who it was."

At the time, Saint Denis had thought the story jealous backstage gossip and nothing more, but it seemed Giselle had the truth of the matter. Christine's teacher had been none other than the Phantom of the Opera.

No wonder she had done her best to keep his identity a secret.

Yet again, he had the feeling he was missing a great deal of the story. However, he knew he could not be too direct in his suspicions. At the same time, he heard the clatter of crockery from the kitchen and guessed he had very little time before Annette made her appearance with the tea service.

"Then perhaps you can help to illuminate the situation, Madame Giry," he said. "For I am trying to understand why a young woman's voice teacher would see the need to kidnap her from the stage in the middle of a performance of *Faust*."

This statement did not go over well with that worthy woman, he could tell. She drew in a breath and looked away from him, pretending to gaze at the door to the kitchen, behind which, no doubt, Annette bustled away with the tea, oblivious to the tense scene in the parlor.

"I—I cannot speak as to his reasons," Madame Giry said after a heavy pause. "As I told you before, he did not confide in me. But perhaps he was not pleased with how the performance was proceeding, and decided to end it before it could become too uncomfortable for anyone."

This feeble explanation did nothing to sway Saint Denis. Indeed, he found it difficult to understand how a situation could be made less uncomfortable by kidnapping the lead performer in an opera under the noses of the entire cast, crew, and audience. However, he also guessed that his own disbelief would not sway Madame Giry; she had closed her mouth tight after making that pronouncement, as if to prove that she had nothing more to say on the subject.

And of course, it was at that moment when Annette returned to the parlor, bustling in with a silver tea tray laden with a very fine porcelain tea set, one so grand, Saint Denis guessed it had been newly purchased with the baron's money, just as everything else in the house must have been.

Surging with disappointment, he made himself sit quietly as Annette placed the tray on the table before him, then made rather a show of pouring for the two of them before retreating to the kitchen. Since there seemed to be nothing he could do except busy himself with adding one cube of sugar and a small dash of cream to his tea, Saint Denis went ahead and performed those tasks, then waited while Madame Giry did much the same thing, although she allowed herself two cubes of sugar.

The tea was too hot to drink, despite the cream he'd used to doctor it, and so he ventured, "Perhaps the Opera Ghost did not confide in you, madame, but possibly Mademoiselle Daaé confided in your daughter? I have heard that they are very good friends."

Unfortunately, this stratagem proved just as futile as his others, for Madame Giry replied, "If she did, Meg did not speak of it to me, and I would not pry. Girls should be allowed some secrets."

Perhaps, if such secrets involved an unexpected admirer or a splurge on a new hat. Having the Phantom of the Opera as one's vocal instructor seemed rather a different matter.

But the set of his hostess's mouth told Saint Denis it would be of no use to pursue the subject further. She was willing to be polite for custom's sake, but neither would she tell him anything of use.

That thought was perhaps rather uncharitable, however. He counted himself a good judge of people, and he had detected nothing false about her reactions when she told him that she herself had buried the Opera Ghost. Perhaps there was a grand and hidden story here, but it involved the events of several years ago, and not what was happening now in the Rue Scribe.

"I suppose everyone should be allowed their secrets," he said, and made himself drink his tea.

After that, he asked a few politely empty questions about Mademoiselle Giry's fiancé, the baron, and watched the young woman's mother expound on Honoré de Castelot-Barbezac's infinite kindnesses, his taste, his wit, and all the sterling qualities that made him vastly superior to any other young man of his generation, even those who might hold a loftier rank.

Somewhere in the midst of this panegyric, she let slip that he was holding a salon at his Paris house to show off some new paintings he'd acquired. Saint Denis wondered that Madame Giry had not been invited, but he knew better than to ask why she was at home rather than at the house of her future son-in-law. Her heart might have been made of the proverbial gold, yet no one would ever accuse Eloise Giry of being fashionable. She would have been terribly out of place at such a gathering.

Eventually, Saint Denis finished his tea. Relieved to have a reason to extricate himself from his hostess's stuffy parlor, he thanked her for the hospitality and took his leave. She seemed somewhat sad to see him go, as if she did not want to bid adieu to her visitor, but she said of course she would not keep him, not when he needed to return to his office.

Back outside in the fresh air, Saint Denis shook his head to clear it, as if to rid himself of the cobwebs he'd felt form whilst inside Madame Giry's comfortable but somehow repressive home. A cool breeze played with the ends of his scarf as he began to walk toward the Place de la Concorde. From there, he could catch a cab to take him to his office at the Paris *Presse,* although the workday was winding down, and there was no real reason for him to return.

Still, he could make some notes, even though Madame Giry hadn't told him much of any great import. Despite feeling as if he had wasted part of his afternoon, he reminded himself that there had been several instances in the past where his notes had revealed something of importance when he went back to revisit them at a later date. He should do the same now, even if he wasn't sure whether he had much of significance to relate.

Only….

His eyes narrowed. He knew something of Honoré de Castelot-Barbezac's salons; they were famous for the eclectic assortments of artists, musicians, writers, poets, and nobility who assembled there. Surely it would be easy enough to gain entrance to such a gathering.

A cab stopped a few feet from him, and Saint Denis looked up at the cabbie and smiled.

"Fifteen Rue d'Artois, please."

CHAPTER 11

Art and Artifice

"So, what do you think of it?" Honoré de Castelo-Barbezac inquired, pausing a little ways behind Christine's shoulder.

She eyed the painting before her with some dismay. Actually, she had just come to the conclusion that she rather liked it, despite the way it only remotely resembled a group of lilies floating on the still waters of a pond. "I like it very much," she said boldly, then looked back at Honoré to see what his response would be.

"You're one of the few, then," he replied. "Why do you like it?"

Christine found herself wondering what Erik

would have said in response to such a question. Tilting her head to one side, she gazed at the painting once more. The salon where the baron had placed his most prized pieces of art was graced with an abundance of natural light; the warm sun of late afternoon glinted through a series of French doors that highlighted the room's southern wall. It was a most unfashionable time for a reception, but Honoré, Christine had begun to discover, cared very little for such things.

"The quality of light," she said at length, staring at the bold yet somehow delicate brushstrokes. "It feels like late afternoon, warm and still. And although perhaps the flowers are not exactly as they look in nature, I knew what they were immediately."

"So would you say that the painting gives a very good *impression* of lilies floating on a pond?"

Honoré's eyebrows were lifted in an amused tilt, but Christine wasn't sure why he should be laughing at her. Feeling out of her depth, she replied, "One could say so."

"Very good, Madame la Comtesse." Whatever his game had been, he appeared to abandon it and went on, "You have a fine eye. I appreciate that you do not appear to be bound by the traditions of the past."

"I know very little about art, monsieur."

"And that is precisely why I trust your judgment far more than I do most of the dilettantes who have come here today." His clear, blue-gray eyes twinkled a bit. "Hidebound, all of them. They don't seem to realize that pieces such as this one are how the art of this era will be remembered one day."

Unsure as to how exactly she should reply to such a comment, Christine managed a weak smile, one that grew more genuine as Meg approached.

"Honoré, I hope you're not boring poor Christine here." The words might have sounded more reproachful if they hadn't been accompanied by an indulgent smile and a playful tap on the arm from Meg's fan.

Christine opened her mouth to protest the baron's innocence, but she was forestalled by the arrival of his grandmother, the Duchess de Montfort.

"I suppose it's no use asking how much of your inheritance you've wasted so far on these ridiculous daubs, Honoré."

Despite the formidable glare that accompanied this statement, Honoré seemed not at all discomfited. "Consider them an investment, grand-mère."

"Meaning that they won't be worth anything

until after we're all dead, I presume?" She raised her lorgnette, stared at the painting upon which Christine had just commented, and gave an audible sniff. Then she transferred her attention to Christine. "You're looking very well, my dear. It relieves me that you had the sense to visit Monsieur Worth as soon as possible, for that gown you wore here last wasn't fit to be seen in polite company."

Once again, Christine found herself at a loss for words. However, she knew that to utter an uneasy laugh or divert the conversation in some other way would not earn her any points with the duchess. Instead, she waved a hand and said in airy tones, "Oh, I know. Wasn't it dreadful? But that, I fear, is the price of languishing in the countryside for so many months. One becomes so terribly out of fashion."

This response earned her a lifted eyebrow and what appeared to be a satisfied nod. "Too true. That is why I put my foot down many years ago and told the duke I had no desire to spend any amount of time at our estate in the country. It is far too easy to miss out on everything important."

"Then I fear I have missed out on a great many things," Christine said. "For this is our first visit to Paris in nearly two years."

"Well, I can understand why the two of you

might have wished to hide yourselves away for a while," the duchess responded. "But even the most sensational scandal dies with enough time, and Paris society has long since moved on. Why, your return here has merited hardly a raised eyebrow."

As to that, Christine hoped the duchess was only relating the simple truth and not attempting to downplay any gossip she might have heard on the subject of the Comte and Comtesse de Chagny. Then again, why should she believe herself to be that important? True, the chaos at the opera house and hers and Raoul's subsequent disappearance—to say nothing of Philippe de Chagny's tragic death—must have left tongues wagging for many weeks or even months, but, as the duchess had said, gossip…even the most titil-lating gossip…could not live forever.

Certainly, no one had seemed to pay her or Raoul any particular attention when they arrived at Honoré's town house, except perhaps to seem surprised that they had come out of seclusion to attend the upcoming nuptials. Perhaps there had been one or two sidelong glances—Christine knew she was not quite so oblivious as to miss the way several of the women present had sent assessing looks in her husband's direction—but no one seemed to have been whispering behind her back, and that was something.

In fact, she would even allow herself some secret amusement over the calculating visual appraisals her husband had received. Raoul, sweet soul that he was, would never think of dishonoring her. The casual affairs of Parisian high society were so anathema to his pure heart that he would be shocked beyond words to discover some of the women who stood in this very room had designs upon his person. If any of those individuals attempted to flirt openly with him, they would be in for quite the disappointment.

As suddenly as it had come, however, that inner amusement evaporated, for she realized she could not be held quite as blameless as Raoul. No, of course nothing had happened between her and Erik, but still, she had hidden the assignation from her husband, had done her best to make sure he knew nothing of her meeting with the man who had once held so much power over her voice…over her very soul.

How long would she be willing to conceal such matters from the one person who should have her utter devotion?

Until the wedding is over and we can return to Chagny, she told herself. *It will be easy enough to stay away from Erik during our time here, after all. I only have to make sure I am never alone. It is not as though he can approach me at our home, or any place I go with Raoul in public.*

Since she realized both the duchess and her grandson were watching her, clearly wondering at her continuing silence, Christine said, "Oh, yes, I suppose all that madness at the opera is very old news. No, I'm sure everyone now is talking about Honoré's upcoming nuptials to Mademoiselle Giry."

The man in question laughed outright at that statement. "Oh, no, I fear a mere wedding is far too tame to occupy the thoughts of this rogue's gallery for very long. Much better to chatter about the Marquis de Caulaincourt running off with an artist's model, and leaving behind a wife and three children. That pretty scandal is much more to their taste."

"How dreadful!" Christine exclaimed. "That poor woman!"

Honoré only shrugged, then paused to snatch a glass of champagne from the tray of a passing waiter. "Oh, she had no love for the marquis, and I have it on good authority that the divorce will leave her a very wealthy woman. Perhaps it is all for the best."

To these shocking pronouncements, Christine had no ready answer. A devout Catholic, she could not support the idea of divorce being "for the best," as Honoré had so blithely put it, but then, she had never been put in the position of being abandoned by a faithless husband.

Nor would she be. Whatever else happened, she knew Raoul loved her with all his heart and would never commit such a terrible act.

She thought she should be a bit more relieved by that knowledge than she actually was. Perhaps it was only that she knew her own heart wasn't quite so pure....

As much as she hated to acknowledge such a truth about herself, she knew she could not deny it. Not completely.

"Christine!" Meg said with some excitement, approaching with Raoul at her side. The two of them had been standing a few feet away, inspecting another of Honoré's new acquisitions, but they came close now, Meg's cheeks tinged with an excited pink that did very well with her claret-colored gown of watered silk. Raoul appeared somewhat more subdued, but he smiled as he came to stand at his wife's side. "I have had the most brilliant idea!" Meg went on.

"What have you cooked up now, my pet?" Honoré inquired, sending his fiancée an indulgent glance. "Are we to push all the furniture out of the way and have an impromptu ball?"

That question made his grandmother raise her lorgnette to her eye and glare reprovingly at her grandson. "That would be *quite* improper, Honoré."

"Oh, pish," he said with a wave of his hand.

He could not go any further, however, for Meg gave an impatient shake of her head, setting her garnet earrings dancing as she said, "No, of course I know more than to suggest a ball at four in the afternoon. What I have in mind is even better."

"Indeed?" he responded. "Then tell me, *ma petite.*"

"Christine should sing for us!" Meg told him, dark eyes aglow. "It has been so long since any of us have heard her, and it would be quite glorious."

This suggestion—offered with loving intentions, Christine reminded herself—made her heart want to sink to the bottom of her new blush kidskin shoes with their buckles of faceted steel. "Oh, no," she said at once. "I doubt anyone would want to hear me, especially when they've come here today to see Honoré's paintings and not to listen to a recital."

"You're too modest, my love," Raoul put in. "I've heard from several people this afternoon who told me that they very much regretted not having the honor to hear a performance by Christine Daaé. And it is not as though you haven't been practicing these past few years."

She wanted to protest that singing a half hour or so a few times a week while limping along with her own unpracticed accompaniment on the pianoforte was not quite the same thing as the rigorous training any performer at the opera was required to complete on a daily basis. In fact, she found the courage to say, "Oh, Raoul, that is not enough to have kept my voice truly limber. I am woefully out of practice."

To her surprise, it was the Duchess de Montfort who spoke next. "Perhaps you see it that way, madame, but most of these dilettantes will not, I am sad to say, be able to tell any difference. I would very much like to hear you sing again. Surely you must know something that is not too taxing, a piece that would be suitable enough for the drawing room, even if it would not be quite the thing to be sung from the stage of the opera."

Feeling fairly trapped, Christine glanced from the duchess to Raoul, but no help there — he was just as eager to see her perform as the rest of them. And while, once upon a time, she could have thought of nothing she wanted more than to sing, to let the music flow through her and become as much a part of her as the very air in her lungs, she certainly did not wish to make a display of herself now, not when she was so terribly unprepared.

"Here," Honoré said, thrusting his untouched glass of champagne into her hand. "A little liquid courage, Madame la Comtesse. You will do very well. I can accompany you."

She might have considered such an offer a jest and nothing more, except that Meg had written more than once about her fiancé's skill on the pianoforte. He might have been a dabbler in many other things, but musically, he was quite gifted.

And perhaps—perhaps it would not be so bad if she had Honoré as her accompanist. At least that way, she might not feel quite so alone as she sang.

Not so exposed.

"Do you know '*Jeu veux vivre*' from Gounod's *Romeo and Juliet?*" she asked, mainly because it was a piece she had practiced recently.

Then again, perhaps Gounod wasn't the best choice. After all, it was during a performance of Gounod's *Faust* that she'd been taken from the stage of the Paris Opera....

But it was too late to take the words back, for Honoré nodded with some enthusiasm and said, "Yes, I do. I think that's a splendid choice." He glanced over at Meg, adding, "Darling, would you like to make the announcement, or should I?"

Color touched her cheeks once again. "Oh, I

think you should, Honoré. This is your house, and your reception, after all."

"Soon to be yours as well, *ma petite.*" He took her hand and kissed it, then let go so he could stride to the center of the salon and announce loudly, "Everyone, if I may have your attention?"

The various conversations around the room stopped abruptly as everyone fixed their attention on their host. Christine thought she would cringe to be the focus of so many staring eyes, but Honoré did not seem to mind at all. With a broad smile, he continued.

"We are to be given a very special treat today. Madame la Comtesse de Chagny has graciously agreed to sing for us this afternoon. Paris has been deprived of her extraordinary voice these two years, and so I know I speak for all of us when I say this is a wonderful gift. Now, if you would—we must all go to the drawing room, where the pianoforte is located."

His speech concluded, he turned toward Christine and extended a hand. She glanced over at Raoul, and he nodded, anticipation bright in his clear blue eyes.

Well, there was nothing for it. She gave Raoul the untouched glass of champagne she held, then stepped forward and laid her hand in

Honoré's, and followed him as he led her from the salon.

Please, dear Father in heaven…let this not be a terrible mistake.

———

The footman had allowed Erik entrance with hardly a blink. "Of course, Monsieur Monet. They are all gathered in the main salon to view your painting."

"*Merci,*" he responded, and hurried away, hoping that the artist in question would not be a tardy guest to the baron's reception. No, Monsieur Monet did not generally attend these sorts of functions, and yet Erik knew it was possible he might yet appear.

Well, in that case, Erik could simply say that the footman had misheard him. At the moment, what mattered most was that he had gained entry to Honoré de Castelot-Barbezac's home. The salon where the paintings were hung appeared to be full almost to capacity, with a variety of well-dressed guests gathered in groups here and there, talking and sipping champagne.

His heart gave a brief, painful thud as Erik caught sight of Christine, standing on the far side of the room in front of a large painting depicting a delicate patch of waterlilies. To one side stood the baron himself, along with an older woman in an impeccably draped gown of black silk. A relative, Erik surmised, seeing something of a resemblance in their determined chins and amused eyebrows.

But he barely had eyes for the other two, wishing nothing more than to drink in the sight of the woman he loved, radiant in the dress he had seen briefly earlier as she climbed into her carriage. Pearls glowed at her ears and her throat, and she smiled as she spoke with Honoré and the older woman. How beautiful she was, his Christine, with a glow in her cheeks that echoed the rosy hue of her gown, her skin smooth as cream, the slanting light from the large windows across the room awakening flickers of russet and gold and warm umber within her chestnut hair.

A passing waiter offered him a glass of champagne, and Erik took it, more to stop himself from continuing to stare at Christine than because he wanted anything to drink. He allowed himself a small sip, feeling the bubbles tickle his nose, the tang of it tart and bright on his tongue. The taste of the champagne pleased him more than he'd thought it would.

As he watched, Meg and Raoul approached Christine and her companions. Although he couldn't quite hear what they were saying—and to sidle closer so he could eavesdrop would be far too obvious—it appeared that both Raoul and Meg were quite enthusiastic about some matter or another, for Meg was gesticulating with her hands, and the comte nodding his agreement.

Christine, on the other hand, did not appear particularly entranced by whatever it was they had suggested. One hand moved toward the pearl choker at her throat, and she shook her head and made what looked like some sort of protest, although he couldn't hear her words. There followed some sort of back and forth, and then Honoré de Castelo-Barbezac stepped forward and announced that Christine would be singing for them in the drawing room.

Those words sent a thrill of shock and anticipation through Erik. More than anything, he wished to hear Christine sing, although he had told himself the chance of his having that particular opportunity was very low. When he had come to this house, all he had hoped for was to catch a glimpse of her, to see her interact with others, to get an idea of what her life as the Comtesse de Chagny might be like. Never had he dared to think he might be able to hear that glorious voice once again.

However, by the looks of it, Christine was not terribly eager to perform. True, she had always been fairly reticent for one who desired to be a diva, had never been the sort to put herself forward. Once she stood on a stage and allowed her magnificent instrument to take over, then she had no peer, but she remained modest for all that.

Because the baron's guests had already begun to move toward the drawing room, Erik allowed himself to be swept along with them, for to hang back would only invite attention. As he went, though, doubt began to enter his mind. Was Christine's reluctance due merely to her humility, or was something else wrong? After all, it had been several years since she last performed. Perhaps she had not kept up with her practice. Perhaps she had suffered some sort of illness which had damaged her voice, although that possibility seemed less likely, since when she spoke, she sounded as sweet and as pure as she ever had.

Well, he would find out soon enough. While he would have preferred to stand closer to the pianoforte so he could study the movements of her throat and body as she sang, he didn't want to risk her seeing him and being thrown off. Better to stand near the rear of the drawing room, partly obscured by a large vase full of hothouse orchids, than to get too close. As far as he was able to tell, the acoustics of the room were quite good; he should have no trouble catching all the nuances of her performance.

Surprisingly, it was the baron himself who sat down on the gilded bench placed in front of the piano's keyboard. He flipped out the tails of his frock coat with a flourish as he sat, earning him a reproving stare from the black-gowned older woman with whom he'd been speaking earlier. Off to one side, Meg Giry flashed him a quick grin, her roguish expression highly at odds with her elegant wine-colored reception dress and modish hairstyle.

Christine moved forward to take her place in the curve of the piano. Although she had appeared reluctant earlier, now her expression was serene, large blue eyes fixed on a place somewhere not too far from where he stood. He knew, however, that she was not looking at anyone in particular, but had only chosen a spot to rest her gaze so she would not be distracted while singing.

Another moment of near-shock as the baron played the opening bars of the piece Christine had chosen. Erik had thought perhaps she would have chosen a sedate recital piece by Bach, or a lively song by Mozart, but instead she had selected Juliet's waltz from *Romeo and Juliet*, "*Je veux vivre*."

Merely a coincidence that she had chosen a

Gounod aria, when her last public performance had been in that same composer's *Faust?* Erik couldn't believe she had been motivated by a desire to send him a subtle message; after all, she could have had no idea that he would infiltrate Honoré de Castelot-Barbezac's party. But still, there had to be some meaning to the selection, when there were so many other songs she could have chosen to sing.

Or was it simply that those words struck him deep within his core, reminding him of the half-life of his existence?

I want to live.

So do I, Christine, he thought then, *so do I.*

He pushed away the ache within his heart and forced himself to focus on her performance. Oh, yes, that bell-like soprano was still uniquely hers, pure as an angel's voice…but he noted the way she breathed, not deeply enough, a faint gasp here and there that the watching crowd probably did not even notice, but which made every muscle in his neck and shoulders tense. She should not be breathing like that, not when he had taught her to pull air in to the very bottom of her lungs so that every note would be floating on a cushion of breath.

And there, too, and again…just the slightest strain to the higher notes, which should have floated out like dandelion fluff on the wind. No, she was not completely out of practice, but she was also nowhere near what she had been at her peak, when she had stepped onto the stage of the Palais Garnier to sing the role of Marguerite in *Faust*. These past two years had not served her any better than they had served him.

Well, he would have to do something about that. It would not take so very much effort to bring her back to top form; only a few weeks of careful tutelage should return Christine Daaé to her former glory. He would remind her of the techniques he had shown her before, would sing with her again to let their voices blend in harmonies not heard since choirs of angels had sung to celebrate a newborn world.

Those pleasant fantasies lived in his thoughts for a moment or two until he realized that was all madness. Her time was not her own, not as the wife of the Comte de Chagny. And even if it were, how on earth could he expect her to bring her silken glory down to his grave of a home beyond the ossuaries?

Then again….

The idea had already begun tickling his mind during his conversation with the Persian, and now Erik saw that he needed to bring it to fruition as quickly as possible. Here at the baron's home, he had walked amongst ordinary men and women, and none of them had given him even a second glance. If he appeared to those around him as a normal man, then he should be able to do the same things a normal man would...including renting a proper house.

His casual pickpocketing had amassed him a good deal of money, since only so much could be spent on food and clothes. The rest he had kept hidden away among his belongings, putting it aside for a future purpose, although at the time, he hadn't known what that purpose might be. Now, however, it seemed simple enough to him. He must rent a house, one with a room that would accommodate a piano, and then he would have Christine come and take lessons from him.

Oh, yes, he mocked himself, *of course she will immediately agree to such an arrangement... and no doubt the comte will have no problem at all with allowing his wife to spend hours in the company of a man who once wanted her more than life itself.*

Still wanted her, if Erik was going to be entirely truthful with himself on the matter. Seeing her today, hearing her sing—even if that singing was not all it should have been—only served to remind him once more of how much space she inhabited in his heart, his soul. With this mask, he realized, he could have easily sought the company of a woman who would sell her body to him, but he had no desire for such a coupling. If he could not have Christine, he would not have anyone.

All around him, the watching audience burst into applause as soon as she finished, having executed the aria's final trill almost flawlessly. Scowling from his vantage point behind the potted orchid, Erik watched as the Comte de Chagny stepped forward and took his wife's hand, bestowing a kiss upon it before he let go so she could curtsy to her admirers. Several of them crowded toward her, no doubt to shower her with praise.

Seeing this, Erik knew it was time to go. Perhaps in the back of his mind, he had entertained the notion of approaching her and offering his own congratulations, but he realized such a fantasy had to remain only that—a fantasy. He might look ordinary enough to a stranger—leaving aside the dark glasses that shielded his golden eyes—and yet Christine would still recognize him right away. Perhaps she would be able to contain her shock; perhaps not. At any rate, he guessed it better to slip away now and decide how next to proceed.

He left the drawing room and hurried out, nodding to the footman, who bowed in return. Nothing so strange about leaving at such a time, for quite often, those who attended such functions had many such gatherings on their calendar in a single day, and would flit from reception to reception as the mood took them.

How he wished he could have been the one to go and kiss Christine's hand, to stand with her as her proud husband while an adoring audience clapped its praise. As it was, better to be far away so he wouldn't have to see the happy couple together.

And yet....

Were they truly so happy? Erik had seen a flicker of something come and go across Christine's lovely features as Raoul approached her, an odd little shadow that most likely no one else had noticed. Perhaps it was only her own disappointment in herself for delivering what was, by her own exacting standards, a subpar performance.

Or perhaps she did not care to share her moment in the limelight with a man who had nothing at all to do with her singular gifts. If anything, it was the comte's doing that Christine was not in as good voice as she should be. No doubt she had to spend her days attending to the needs of the Chagny estate and the people who dwelled there, and not nurturing her extraordinary talents.

If she were with him, she would not have to waste her energy on such petty concerns.

Erik's hands clenched into fists as he paused

on the sidewalk, eyes scanning the street for a cab. One came around the corner, and he unknotted his fingers so he could raise that hand to hail the driver.

First things first. He would find a house and abandon the ossuaries, and then he would have to see. Was it too much to dare hope that Christine might be as much in need of her teacher as he was in need of her?

Very soon, all might be as it once was....

CHAPTER 12

Home and Heart

"*I* am very sorry, m'sieur," the footman said, "but you are not on the list, and I do not recognize you as a friend of the baron."

Of course he didn't, because Antoine Saint Denis had never met Honoré de Castelo-Barbezac in his life, and only knew the man's name because he had become a prominent collector of art, especially modern pieces by men such as Claude Monet and Edgar Degas.

And also because he had gained some notoriety as the fiancé of Meg Giry, erstwhile opera dancer.

For a moment, Saint Denis considered telling

the footman that he was with the Paris *Presse* and it was imperative that he see the baron, but almost at once he abandoned that plan. The man who confronted him, an angular individual with forbidding brows, did not seem the type who would be impressed by such information. If anything, he might regard such credentials as a good excuse to call a gendarme to have the troublesome intruder removed from his master's property.

"I am a friend of his fiancée," Saint Denis said, knowing even as he spoke that this latest gambit probably would also be a futile one. "Or rather, I am a friend of Mademoiselle Giry's mother. Surely you would not turn away someone who is intimately acquainted with Madame Giry?"

For just a second, the footman hesitated, uncertainty clear on his hard features. But then he shook his head. "I am afraid that you are not on the list, m'sieur. If Mademoiselle Giry—or the baron—had desired that you attend their gathering, you would have been sent an invitation. You must understand that I am not at liberty to permit entry to just anyone claiming a relationship with his lordship…or his lordship's fiancée."

Damn. Saint Denis had known coming here was a long shot, but since he'd often been quite successful in talking his way past more formidable guards than the one who now blocked him from entering the Baron de Castelo-Barbezac's town house, he had hoped he might also prevail in this instance.

Well, no matter. There was certainly nothing to be gained by causing a scene, and he would simply have to come up with another plan. After all, Mademoiselle Giry was not in her fiancé's company every hour of the day, and it seemed a simple enough task to determine her movements and decide when would be the best time to approach her. He'd gathered from Madame Giry that her daughter did not live with her in the flat on the Rue de Rivoli, but neither would she have taken up residence at the baron's town house. That would have to wait until they were safely married. Most likely, she was renting a flat of her own somewhere close by, with a modest household to keep up appearances. It should not be too difficult to determine her direction.

This battle was not one worth choosing. Saint Denis smiled and tipped his hat, and said, "I understand. It was an off-hand invitation from Mademoiselle Giry, given at another salon where we met. I have no doubt that she simply forgot to add my name to the list, busy as she is with her wedding preparations."

One would have thought such a magnanimous capitulation would have evoked some softening of the other man's expression, but the footman only inclined his head a fraction of an inch and said, "No doubt. A very good afternoon to you, m'sieur."

As dismissals went, that one was fairly obvious. Saint Denis only nodded in return and made his way down the front walk, past two rows of expertly clipped boxwoods. When he reached the street, he hesitated for a moment, unsure whether he should pause there to hail a cab, or continue to the Rue François, where he probably had a better chance of catching a driver's attention.

While he stood there, weighing his options, a tall man in an elegant charcoal gray frock coat and steel-blue vest moved swiftly past him, the tails of his coat blowing in the brisk breeze. He wore round dark glasses to protect his eyes from the sun, but the spectacles did little to hide the spare, handsome outlines of his face.

Something about the stranger made Saint Denis' eyes narrow, although he couldn't quite say why. He knew he had never seen the man before. And while the dark glasses were a bit odd, it wasn't as though wearing such things was completely unheard of. There must have been at least a dozen times that he had spied an individual sporting shaded spectacles to shield their eyes from the sun.

Even so, he stood and watched as the stranger hailed a cab, then climbed in. After it turned the corner and disappeared from view, Saint Denis found himself remaining as if fixed in that spot, staring down the street long after the cab and its occupant were gone.

Then he shook his head. If he allowed himself to become too obsessed with the story of the erstwhile Opera Ghost, he would be seeing phantoms on every street corner. Besides, the man who'd caught his attention had been ordinary enough in appearance, despite the dark glasses. He certainly wasn't the masked, supposedly disfigured creature who had once haunted the bowels of the Palais Garnier.

Head full of these remonstrances, Saint Denis turned on his heel and walked toward the Rue François. Time to catch a cab and go home, to put all his concerns aside until the following day.

Paris was full enough of ghosts without manufacturing new ones.

"So, m'sieur, you think it will suit you?"

Erik forced his attention back to the woman who stood a few paces away. She was a prosperous, tidy sort, with iron-gray hair drawn into a heavy chignon—a chignon he guessed had been amplified with hair not her own—and an impeccable dove-gray morning gown of fine wool serge.

The house was just one of several she owned and let out to those she deemed suitable. Its previous occupant had passed away recently, and she clearly was in a hurry to rent it again.

Luckily, she seemed to view Erik as someone "suitable." He had worn his best suit for this meeting, had stared at his reflection in the warped mirror in his underground demesne for some time to make sure the mask would pass muster even in the brightest light of day.

And no doubt the way he'd agreed to her terms without blinking an eye had also endeared him to her. The price she was asking seemed somewhat high, but since the house had turned out to be perfect for him in every other way, right down to the pretty little spinet in the parlor, he certainly wasn't going to quibble.

"I think it will do very well," he said. "And I can take occupancy immediately?"

She smiled then. The bright morning light shining through the parlor windows clearly showed every line around her dark eyes. "Of course, m'sieur. And the furniture is all suitable? You will be bringing nothing of your own?"

"Only a few personal items," he told her. "I

have been traveling in the Orient these past few years, and so do not have much to call my own. But it was time for me to return to Paris, which is why I am in need of lodgings."

The story should do well enough to explain why he had only a modest wardrobe and not much else. And if Madame Giroux should surprise him by speaking Mandarin while inquiring about his travels, he could reply in Persian. He had picked up a smattering of several different languages on his travels, but Persian was nearly a mother tongue to him.

However, Madame Giroux proved to be as prosy as she looked, and she offered no such test of his knowledge of the East. Instead, she offered what was almost a simpering smile as she said, "Oh, that is so very fascinating! I always longed to travel, but I never got any further than Frankfurt."

"A worthy town," he replied, even as he wondered a bit at her coy demeanor. Could it be that she was *flirting* with him?

Such a concept was so novel that he couldn't quite force himself to consider it seriously. No, she was being overly friendly because she wanted to get the house rented as quickly as possible. Besides, she had to be at least twenty years older than he, in her middle sixties if she was a day.

Still…he had to admit to himself that he was not used to women smiling up at him. The few who had seen his true face had screamed…or fainted.

"Yes, it was quite a pleasant visit," Madame Giroux said. Her manner became suddenly brisk, as though she had realized he was not inclined to reciprocate her flirtatious words. "That will be two hundred francs, m'sieur, if you wish to let the house."

"I do," he said gravely, then reached into his pocket to remove the necessary bills. He handed them to her, and she efficiently counted them out before placing them in her reticule.

In return, she extracted a key from that same reticule and gave it to him. "This is a quiet, respectable street, m'sieur, and so I would ask you to please refrain from having any loud gatherings."

"I assure you, madame, that I have no intention of hosting any soirées." He paused there, but decided it was better to manage her expectations now, in case some miracle occurred and he was able to coax Christine to come here and continue her vocal lessons. "However, I am a musician and a composer, and also occasionally tutor a select vocal student or two. I trust that will not be too much of a disruption?"

"Oh, no," Madame Giroux said at once. "A composer! How very exciting! I am sure that having a few students here for lessons will not be any trouble at all, as long as there are not too many."

Erik smiled. "I am very selective. It would only be one or two at the most, no more than that."

Of course, he only intended to have Christine here and no one else, but he thought his story would sound more plausible if it included the prospect of more than a single student. This seemed to be the case, for his new landlady nodded and said, "I think that should do very well." A pause as she rather ostentatiously glanced at the pocket watch which hung from her chatelaine. "And now, m'sieur, I fear I must go. I have a luncheon appointment."

"I would not keep you," he said gravely.

"You may bring next month's rent to my house at 20 Rue de Calais," she added. "But in the meantime, enjoy settling into your new home."

He walked her to the foyer and thanked her, and then with some relief, closed the door after she had gone. For a moment, he could only stand there and breathe in the silence of the house, the faint scent of beeswax that arose from the furniture and freshly polished floors.

When was the last time he had stood in a dwelling such as this?

Decades, most likely. He had not had a true home to call his own since he fled his parents' house when he was only a boy.

But he would not think of the house he had left behind so many years ago. The past was a corpse he had long since buried. Now he only wished to look forward to the future...a future that might have Christine in the lovely little parlor with its blue-striped wallpaper and the high ceiling that afforded such wonderful acoustics. It was partly that room which had made him determined to take this house over the others he had viewed. Surely in that charming space, they would be able to revisit the glorious harmonies they had shared only two years earlier.

He went to the parlor, to the spinet that had been placed up against one wall. His fingers trailed over the keys, noting one string that sounded flat, another that was slightly sharp. It would have to be tuned. Luckily, he could manage that task himself. It would be something to keep himself occupied...

...until Christine could be persuaded to come here.

Jeannette entered the sitting room, a small silver tray in one hand. Raoul sat in a rose-upholstered wing chair off to one side, that day's paper spread out on his lap, while Christine occupied one end of the divan, dutifully stitching away at an embroidered handkerchief. Truly, it was quite dull work, but she couldn't sit idle while Raoul read the newspaper. She supposed she could have gotten a book from the shelf and attempted to read as well, but she doubted she would have been able to focus on the words of the story. Better to concentrate on her embroidery, even if doing so allowed her thoughts to run this way and that.

The maid went to Raoul and dropped a quick curtsy. "Telegram for you, m'sieur."

He arched a surprised eyebrow at her. "A what?"

"Telegram. A boy just delivered it."

Still looking rather flummoxed—any message contained in a telegram must by its very nature be urgent and most likely distressing—Raoul lifted the thin sheet of paper from the tray and briefly scanned its contents. As soon as he was done, he muttered an oath under his breath.

"What is it?" asked Christine as she laid her embroidery down on the sofa cushion. To evoke a reaction like that in her husband, the news must have been very bad. He never swore around her — or around anyone else, as far as she had been able to determine.

"Monsieur Fournier sent the wire."

"Is it frost?" she inquired anxiously, for she knew Raoul had been worried about an unexpected cold snap, although the days lately had been quite mild for early spring.

He gave a brief shake of his head. "Worse. Gray rot. They are not sure yet how far it has spread, and Monsieur Fournier is asking if I can come back to Chagny. But…."

Oh, how terrible the relief that spread through her heart at those words. Not the news that their vines were affected by a fungal disease — no, she knew what a tragedy it would be to lose any of the grapevines when they'd been nurtured on the estate's lands for decades. But the thought that Raoul might have to return to the estate, might have to leave her to her own devices here in Paris —

Hating herself for her duplicity, she nonetheless said, "You mustn't worry about me, dearest. It is still almost a week until Meg's wedding, which is plenty of time for you to return to Chagny and do what must be done, then come back to Paris when you feel it's safe. I still have several fittings at Monsieur Worth's atelier, and I know Meg wanted me to consult with her on the menu and the flowers. I will be quite occupied with all that foolishness, so there's no need to worry on my behalf."

The troubled expression lifted from his brow, and he came over to her and pressed a kiss against her forehead. "You are quite sure? I do not like to leave you alone — "

"How can I be alone when I will have Jeannette and Madame and Monsieur Gaston here at the house to look after me? And I am sure Meg and Honoré will also ask me to dinner quite often, so I'll rarely be dining by my lonesome."

Raoul took her hand and squeezed it gently. "I suppose it should be all right, then. And I will do my best to return as soon as I can."

"Do what you must, my love," Christine replied. "I will miss you dreadfully, of course, but you need to take care of your vines."

"Our vines," he corrected her, and she made herself smile. She cared about the vines and the harvest because Raoul cared about them, but she had never thought of them as hers.

To be honest, she had never thought of any of the Chagny estate as hers. Not really. The place was beautiful, and she'd become accustomed to living there, but she still had moments when she thought that someone must surely come striding in at any moment to tell her what an interloper she was, and how she had no business being there. Never had she spoken of these misgivings to Raoul, for she knew he would dismiss her fancies as a woman's foolishness and nothing more...and yet they still lingered in the back of her mind, lending a faint unease to all her days.

"Yes, our vines, dearest," she said. "They need you, and Paris will still be here when you return."

"Thank you for understanding." Another kiss, this one on her cheek, and then he straightened and directed his next words to the maid. "Jeannette, please inform Monsieur Gaston that I will need my valise packed, and that I will need a cab to take me to the train station."

"Of course, m'sieur," Jeannette responded, and hastened from the room, empty silver tray still clutched in one hand.

During that exchange, Christine rose from the sofa. A strange calm had taken hold of her, as if she had to recognize the hand of the universe in these events, and she could do no more than follow where it guided her. She smoothed her skirts, adjusting the drape of her bustled gown, then said, "Is there anything you need me to do, Raoul?"

He reached out to touch one of the long curls that fell over her shoulder. "Only keep yourself safe. I do not much like the idea of leaving you in

Paris whilst there is a madman rampaging about."

When he described the situation in such a way, Christine thought perhaps she did not like it much, either. However, she endeavored to keep her tone light as she replied, "Oh, I do not think I am in much danger. For I have no intention of attending the opera, and that seems to be the only place where these killings happen. Besides, all the victims were older men, were they not? I don't believe I am the sort of prey this murderer seeks."

"Perhaps," Raoul said, although his tone told her he was far from convinced. "Still, it is good that you have no plans to go to the opera with Meg and Honoré. I am sure they would do their best to keep you safe, but — "

"Truly, Raoul, I have no wish to attend. That place holds nothing but unpleasant memories for me."

Yet another lie. For while much occurred in the Palais Garnier that had been dark and dreadful and terrifying, she had also experienced moments of pure beauty under Erik's tutelage, moments she thought she might never experience again. If her impromptu recital at Honoré's reception the day before had taught her anything, it was that only Erik could coax such angelic sounds from her throat.

But Raoul didn't seem to notice anything amiss, for he smiled and touched her hand, and told her he was glad to know she would stay far away from the opera house. And then Monsieur Gaston paused at the door to the sitting room to inform the comte that his bags were packed.

Nothing for it but to give Raoul a farewell kiss and to offer what words of encouragement she could for the recovery of his grapevines. He left then, heading off to the cab Gaston had called for him, and Christine found herself standing in the foyer, staring at the door that had just closed behind her departing husband.

One question throbbed in her mind.

Will Erik discover that I have been left alone?

She was not sure whether she wanted to know the answer.

CHAPTER 13

Back and Forth

*M*ichel, one of the copyboys, ran into Saint Denis' office. "Note for you from Monsieur Aubry, sir!" he said, dark eyes shining with excitement. Although the piece of paper he handed over had been carefully folded, Saint Denis harbored a sneaking suspicion that Michel had peeked at the contents of the note before bringing it to him.

"Thank you, Michel," Saint Denis said, although he only laid the note on his desk and did not open it.

"Yes, sir," Michel responded, disappointment dulling some of the light in his eyes. Clearly, he had hoped to linger while his superior read the missive. But since he knew better than to protest, he only ducked his head and then darted back out to the newsroom.

There probably wasn't much point in looking at the note; Saint Denis had a feeling he already knew what it contained. Still, better to read the thing, just in case his suspicions were wrong.

There has been another, the note read. *We have already cleared the scene, but I will be keeping watch until ten.* —*A*

The hour was just a little past nine in the morning, plenty of time for Saint Denis to get to the scene of the crime while Aubry still lingered there. If it truly had been swept and cleared of any evidence, he wasn't quite sure what his presence there would accomplish. Then again, the errand would get him away from his office for an hour or so, and such a mission might help to clear the cobwebs from his head. He was still annoyed by his failure to get inside Honoré de Castelo-Barbezac's home the afternoon before, especially since he had learned from the paper's society reporter that Madame de Chagny herself had surprised everyone by singing for the baron's guests.

Saint Denis wished very much that he could have been there. Not because he was so much an aficionado of the vocal arts—he did not much care for opera—but because he would have liked to observe Christine de Chagny as she sang, would have given a great deal to also observe the partygoers' reactions to her performance, to hear whether they discerned any differences between how she had sung for them that afternoon and the way she had sung while under the Opera Ghost's tutelage…not that any of them probably any idea who had been her teacher during her time at the Palais Garnier.

But Saint Denis had not been afforded that opportunity, and so he did his best to push his annoyance aside as he got up from his desk and retrieved his overcoat from the rack in the corner of his office. The fine weather of the previous several days had disappeared, replaced by a brooding bank of clouds that hung over the city and dropped a fine, misty rain from time to time.

Since the weather was so inhospitable, he took a cab to the Rue Scribe. As before, Aubry stood on the corner of Rue Scribe and Rue Auber, hands shoved in his pockets. That morning, his hat was pulled low and the collar of his coat was turned up against the thin, needle-like rain, and his expression did not turn noticeably brighter as Saint Denis approached him.

"Once again?" Saint Denis said, and Aubry nodded.

"I'm afraid so. Garroted, like the others."

The paving stones beneath his feet were slick with rain, and therefore even less likely to show any evidence of the crime committed there than they had been the last time he stood in that same spot. Still, Saint Denis stared down at the ground for a long moment, a frown pulling at his brow. Both Christine de Chagny and Madame Giry had stated flatly that the Opera Ghost was dead, and so could not be responsible for these crimes. Very well; he supposed he would have to accept that reality. However, these men were certainly not dead by their own hand, and that meant someone had to be responsible.

What kind of depraved mind would be drawn to this place over and over again, seeking out his victims in such a particular location?

"Perhaps the Sûreté should set a guard here," Saint Denis said, his tone carefully neutral.

Aubry drew himself up, watery brown eyes narrowing with wounded pride. "We *did* have a guard," he returned. "He was on duty starting at dusk, and had orders to keep watch until the last of the opera's patrons had left. He saw nothing."

"Clearly," Saint Denis observed, his tone dry. "And yet, another man is dead. Who was the victim?"

"Giles Parnasse," Aubry replied. "Sixty-two. He was a retired barrister from a wealthy family.

He is survived by four children and seven grand-children."

The severe note in Aubry's tone told Saint Denis that he expected the reporter to show some respect for the loss of such a worthy individual. And indeed, Saint Denis would honor his friend's unspoken wishes. He certainly had no inclination to look on the situation lightly.

"Is there anything that might tie him to the other victims?" he asked, knowing even as he made the inquiry what the likely response would be.

Aubry shook his head, thus confirming Saint Denis' suspicions. "Nothing that we know of. Yes, they were all lovers of the opera and had season tickets, but there are hundreds of such individuals in Paris, and only four have been dispatched in such a way."

Only four. Yes, perhaps that did not seem like so very many in the grand scheme of things, and yet Saint Denis thought that it must seem like a great deal to the men involved...and to their families.

"Who found the victim?"

"Monsieur Langlois, the guard who was on duty here last night. He says the body was still warm, and so the victim must have been killed only moments before he arrived on the scene."

Meaning that the murderer had most likely

known exactly who the guard was and what he was doing, and had only to wait until he was far enough away not to see anything. Fog and rain had rolled in the night before, and so the killer must have taken advantage of those conditions to do his work.

"And Monsieur Langlois saw nothing suspicious?"

Aubry reached up to adjust the collar of his overcoat, probably in a vain attempt to prevent more rain from trickling inside. "No. Neither did he hear anything. Whoever this murderer is, he must be very fast and very silent. No one else who was here saw anything, either. That is, we have done our best to interview some of those who were in attendance at the opera last night, although of course it will be impossible to track down everyone."

Even if the Sûreté had the manpower and the means to interview so many potential witnesses, Saint Denis doubted it would have made any difference. The fiend behind these killings was clearly cunning and fearless, and knew precisely the correct moment to strike.

The only way to catch him would be to discover the thread that connected all these victims, the one thing they all had in common. What that connection might be, Saint Denis couldn't begin to guess. But until someone—

whether he or Aubry or another inspector with the Sûreté—divined what it was that made these men the particular victims of the killer, then he would continue with his rampage, unchecked.

And if there was no connection, if the murderer had committed these heinous acts because of some sort of unholy bloodlust which consumed his black soul, then Saint Denis did not know for sure what any of them could do. Most murders were crimes of passion, acts that could be traced back to a particular motivation, even if such a motivation might appear abhorrent to the rational observer. Every once in a great while, however, there came those who killed simply because they delighted in darkness and death.

If that was what they faced now, then it might be a very long while before the killer was brought to justice...or never.

"I will add his name to the list," Saint Denis said after a lengthy pause. "And I will do my best to discover if there is something we have all overlooked, a commonality so subtle, it has escaped notice so far."

"We have done much the same thing, but to no avail," said Aubry, and Saint Denis clapped an encouraging hand on his friend's shoulder.

"Well, sometimes it is useful to have the

perspective of a third party. A fresh set of eyes is often what a problem needs."

Since that observation was obvious enough, Aubry did not bother to argue, but only nodded. "I hope you are right, Antoine," he said. "For some are beginning to suggest that it is not safe for people to come to the opera, that perhaps it would be wise to end the season now."

"The opera season only has a few weeks left, does it not?" Saint Denis inquired.

"Yes."

"I would not advise doing anything so drastic," he said. "For the time being, I would suggest having at least two policeman keeping watch here...perhaps more, if you can afford to spare them from their other duties. While it might have been too easy for our killer to escape the notice of a single guard, having several of them patrolling the Rue Scribe might be an entirely different circumstance."

Aubry's somber expression lifted slightly. "Yes, that is what I was thinking as well. We will see what we can do."

"Excellent." At this point in the proceedings, Saint Denis might have taken out a cigarette, as smoking helped him to think. But with the way the rain was beginning to fall more heavily, doing so would have been a wasted effort. Better to get indoors before they were both soaked through. "If I think of anything, I will be sure to let you know."

"Thank you, Antoine. Now get inside and out of this miserable weather."

"And you as well."

They made their goodbyes, with Aubry hurrying off toward the Boulevard des Capuchines, while Saint Denis lifted a hand to hail a passing cab. Once he had given the direction of the Paris *Presse* to the cabbie and had settled himself on the worn leather seats inside, he found himself frowning. Yes, of course it was a good idea to have more policemen on duty. They should serve as something of a deterrent, if nothing else.

At the same time, however, he found himself wondering if even the presence of multiple gendarmes would be enough to keep away such a determined killer.

"A letter for you madame," said Jeannette, who entered the sitting room holding the same silver tray she'd used to bring the telegram for Raoul only the day before.

"Thank you, Jeannette," Christine responded. No doubt yet another invitation; all the fine ladies who'd been only too happy to snub her when she was merely a singer in the opera chorus and nothing more seemed to be falling over themselves to invite her to tea or to dinner now that she was the Comtesse de Chagny. Luckily, with Raoul back at the estate, she could easily decline all those invitations, saying she didn't wish to be out in company without her husband. True, that was something of a white lie, since she didn't scruple at spending time with Meg and Honoré, even without Raoul at her side, but if she offended a few of those social-climbing snobs, so be it.

The letter was enclosed in an envelope of heavy cream-colored paper, with the words "Madame la Comtesse de Chagny" inscribed on the front. Christine lifted it from the tray, noting that the inscription was written in an odd, spidery hand, not the elegant copperplate all young ladies of a certain class were taught.

A frown pulled at her brows, even as Jeannette curtsied and then left the chamber. Christine ran a finger under the envelope's flap, not wishing to call her maid back in order to ask for a letter opener.

But the flap lifted easily enough. Inside was a single sheet of paper, cream to match the envelope, although lighter in weight. It held several brief lines in the same oddly crooked hand that had written the address.

My dearest comtesse,

While I was honored to have heard you at the Baron de Castelo-Barbezac's reception the other day, I fear the past few years with no practice have taken their toll on your voice. I look forward to instructing you again. You will come to me today at 22 Rue Saint Germain, where your lessons shall recommence.

Your obedient friend,

O.G.

The paper fluttered to her silk-clad lap, even as Christine's heart began to pound wildly. Her stays, which had not been pulled terribly tight since she had no plans to leave the house that day, suddenly felt as though they stifled her breath. She blinked, but the note remained where she had dropped it. No, she had not imagined the letter…or the man who had written it.

How could Erik have been at Honoré's? She had certainly not seen anyone who looked like the Opera Ghost at the reception—or at least, no one who looked the way the Phantom appeared now, with that counterfeit mask of a face hiding his true countenance.

But perhaps he possessed more than one mask. Or perhaps—in a far simpler explanation —he had arrived long after she and Raoul entered Honoré's house, and had done his best to escape her notice. In a way, that theory only increased her disquiet. She did not like the notion of him creeping around everywhere she traveled, doing his best to catch a glimpse of her as she went about her life.

Worse than that disturbing idea, however, was the knowledge that he'd heard her miserable performance. Oh, everyone had applauded and praised her to the skies, and perhaps they hadn't known any better. In her heart, though, she had known that what she'd offered them all was only a shadow of what she'd once been capable of, barely more than the lackluster performance of a middling student in her second year at the academy.

And Erik had heard every wretched note.

No wonder he wanted to begin teaching her again. His was the sort of soul that would not allow such an affront; he would immediately begin conjuring ways to bring her back to her former glory.

But…how on earth could she accept such an invitation? True, with Raoul gone, she would only have to manufacture excuses for her maid and for the butler and housekeeper, and yet she quailed at having to dissemble even that much.

No, the sensible thing to do would be to reply and tell him that, while she appreciated his generosity in offering lessons to her once again, she was the Comtesse de Chagny now and therefore had no need to burnish her vocal talents. That was definitely the best course of action.

Only….

Could she live with herself if she didn't at least make the effort to restore her voice to what it once had been?

For a few seconds, she wavered, reason and passion warring within her breast. Then she reached for the bell that sat on the table next to the sofa, and rang it briskly.

Almost at once, Jeannette was at the door, expression vaguely confused, as if she couldn't quite discern why her mistress would call her back so quickly. "Yes, madame?"

"How did you get this letter?"

Jeannette's brows lifted, but she answered simply enough, "A boy brought it. He looked to have run through the rain, for he was quite soaked."

Trust Erik to use a street urchin as his delivery boy. Then again, the Opera Ghost was not the sort to trust such an important missive to the ordinary post…and he certainly couldn't have brought the letter himself. The whole situation was utterly ridiculous. She could not go… she *would* not.

And yet….

Her fingers closed on the letter, crumpling it, although Christine made herself say calmly, "Thank you, Jeannette."

"Is something the matter, madame?"

"Oh, no," she replied. And although she had resolved only a moment earlier to ignore the letter—how dare Erik presume that she would come running the second he lifted his finger?—the words spilled, apparently unbidden, from her lips. "It is only that I just remembered I have a fitting at Monsieur Worth's at four, and I dislike the idea of going out in this rain."

"Perhaps you should send him a note to cancel the appointment?"

"No," Christine said hastily. "One does not cancel a fitting with Monsieur Worth. That is an hour off—perhaps the weather will settle by then. However, just in case it does not, I think I will take a cab rather than use the carriage. I don't wish to send our driver out in the rain for such a frivolous errand."

Jeannette nodded. "If you wish, madame. Will you want to change before you go?"

Christine would not allow herself to reflect on the irony of putting on a more formal gown to go to a place where she would only have to remove it to be fitted. However, she wore the lavender half-mourning dress she disliked so much, and had only put it on that morning because she had not seen the point in wearing anything better when she had no plans to leave the house.

Irrational as the notion might seem to an outside observer, she did not want Erik to see her in that dress.

"Yes," she replied. "My new green wool walking gown, since the weather is so unfavorable. And the gray cape with the fox trim."

Jeannette said, "I'll go lay them out for you, madame."

She sketched a quick curtsy and left the room. Alone again, Christine wondered if she had gone completely mad. The best reply to Erik's summons would have been to ignore him completely. Her lack of a response would have told him precisely what she thought of his high-handedness.

However, she knew in her bones that pretending she had never gotten the letter wouldn't have been wise. The Opera Ghost was persistent, after all; very likely, he would have found a way to come to the house and inquire after her in person. That he'd apparently insinuated himself into Meg and Honoré's reception only proved he was now able to move in society without issue. The barrier of his appearance was now no barrier at all.

No, it seemed she must confront him in

person and tell him he needed to leave her severely alone. It was not appropriate for them to maintain any kind of a connection, even if she might be in dire need of his instruction.

But even as she attempted to steel herself for such a declaration, a pang of loss struck her. She had lost her ghost once before. Did she really wish to lose him again?

You must walk away, she thought. *It is not right to think of spending time with a man who once fancied himself in love with you. Not when you are a married woman whose responsibilities lie elsewhere.*

That would be the right thing to do. Only…

…only it felt so very wrong. How she wished Erik's hold on her was something that could be excised, like a tumor from otherwise healthy flesh.

But their connection lived only in her mind and heart, and she would have to use the strength of her own spirit to break the bonds between them.

If only she did not fear that she wasn't quite strong enough to walk away.

CHAPTER 14

Secret Songs

*E*rik did not know why he should be so nervous. This was certainly not the first time he would be alone with Christine; she had come to the house he'd constructed beneath the Paris Opera not once, but many times. It was not even their first meeting after spending two years apart, for of course they had already seen each other on several occasions during her current sojourn in the city.

Perhaps, but this would be the first time he was able to entertain her as a normal man might entertain a lady friend, in a proper house on a respectable street. Madame Giroux had made sure his new home was immaculate, and so there was very little he needed to do to prepare himself for Christine's visit. He had ventured out to the flower market to bring back a bundle of fine red roses, which now graced the marble mantel in the parlor. A fire crackled in the hearth below that mantel, for the day had remained dank and bleak, and it would not do for his guest to strain her vocal chords in too-chilly air. He had also prepared a pot of tea with lemon to help to relax her voice, although he had not laid out any other refreshments. In the larder, there was fresh bread and cheese, but of course, she could not consume those items until the lesson was complete, as they would only serve to thicken her throat.

At a few minutes after four, someone knocked on the front door. Erik hurried to answer it, for of course, he did not dare to hire any servants. His new mask was very effective, true, and yet he still had no desire to share his home with a butler or a footman.

Standing outside on the front step was Christine, the hood of her fur-trimmed cape pulled up to protect her hair from the rain. On the street beyond, he caught a glimpse of a cab drawing away from the curb before it headed down the street.

Good. So at least she'd possessed the discretion to come here in a cab rather than using the Chagny coach with its distinctive crest.

"Thank you for coming," he said, then stepped aside so she might enter the foyer. As he shut the door, she reached up to undo the clasp at her throat and pulled off the fur-trimmed cloak.

Underneath, she wore a dark green walking gown with such a modishly draped bustle and cunning pleated details on the bodice that he guessed it must be a creation of Monsieur Worth. She looked very well in it, and Erik wondered if he should be flattered that she had worn one of her newest dresses for this meeting.

However, when she spoke, the words were not flattering at all. "That was quite the invitation, Erik," she said. "I should say that it felt much more like a command."

"You know I would never command you," he returned smoothly.

Her blue eyes flashed, not meek at all. "Isn't that what you did when you tutored me before?"

Erik allowed himself a smile, knowing that the lips of his mask would move only a fraction. "I never *commanded* you, Christine. I only unlocked the power of the music you held within. If you found yourself compelled to follow that music, that compulsion was born of your own soul."

Something about the lift of her chin faltered, and she glanced away from him. As if glad of the excuse to break their eye contact, she looked down the hallway, appearing to focus on her surroundings.

"And this is where you are living now?"

"Yes," he said, and left it at that. No need for her to know that he was a very recent resident of the place, and that he had spent the previous two years living like a rat underground. "I will admit that it is a bit more prosy than my house under the opera, but it suits me."

An unwilling chuckle escaped her lips. "I suppose it is, when you put it that way. And your neighbors have never noticed anything… unusual…about its inhabitant?"

"What is there to notice?" he inquired. "I live a simple life. I compose, I play the piano or my violin, I go to a market or a café or occasionally the theater. None of those activities would attract any notice."

And really, those weren't lies. Not completely. He had done most of those things while living under the opera house, and he assumed he would do them during his tenure in this new home, if given the opportunity.

Christine gazed back at him for a moment, a strange kind of wonder in her eyes. "You have changed, haven't you, Erik?" she said at last. "That mask…it has changed you."

How could he argue with her statement? Of course it had. He now possessed the kind of freedom he'd once only dreamed of, the freedom to walk through the world as if he were no different from anyone else.

Still, he didn't wish to admit such a truth to Christine. He didn't want to draw her attention to what lay beneath the mask. In his heart, he had hoped that, as she grew more accustomed to his current appearance, she would forget what he once had been. And then….

And then what? he asked himself. *Do you think it will also be enough to make her forget that she is a married woman, is now the Comtesse de Chagny?*

His hands began to curl into fists, but he forced them to relax, lest Christine notice. "Time has moved on," he said lightly. "Time changes all of us, I suppose. Speaking of which," he continued, seeing in his words a way to change the subject without too much awkwardness, "time has not been particularly kind to your voice, has it?"

Rather than take exception to such a comment, she let out a breath and sent him a rueful look. "No, it has not," she replied. "I practiced, Erik…I did try…but of course, it was not the same as training with you, especially when I have no very great skill on the pianoforte."

"Which is why we should get to work immediately," he told her. "Come—there is a fire in the parlor, which is where we will practice. This way."

He led her down the hallway to the room in question. She looked around at the pretty chamber with its striped blue silk on the walls and serene landscape paintings, and a smile touched her lips.

"It's lovely," she said.

"Thank you," he replied, although of course, he'd had little to do with the decor, save the vase of crimson roses on the mantel. "There is tea, if you would like something warm on your throat before we begin."

"Oh, that would be lovely. It is such a raw day outside…especially after all the beautiful weather we've had lately."

"Springtime can be capricious," Erik agreed, then went ahead and poured a cup of tea for her. As she took it from him, he was careful to make sure their fingers never touched. While he would have liked nothing more than to press his hand against hers, to feel the silken perfection of her skin beneath his fingertips, he knew she would not have been pleased by such contact.

She lifted the cup to her lips and took a sip,

and then another. "Yes, that is better," she said. Her head tilted to one side; perhaps in deference to the damp weather, she had put up most of her hair, except for a few thick curls that fell over one shoulder. The style made her look somehow older, more sophisticated, and once again he thought of the years that had passed since she left him beneath the opera.

As much as he would have liked for matters between them to have remained unchanged, he knew such a thing could never happen. Time had marched on for both of them, and he knew he would have to accept the Christine who stood before him now, rather than wish for the one who had broken his heart several years earlier.

Which would not be a problem, he told himself. He had loved her then as a frightened ingenue, and he still loved her now as the elegant Comtesse de Chagny.

Speaking of which….

"What did you tell the comte to get yourself away this afternoon?" Erik inquired.

The hand holding the teacup shook slightly, but Christine sounded composed enough as she replied, "I did not have to tell him anything. An emergency at the vineyards called him back to Chagny. I am not sure when he will return, although of course, he will be back in Paris for Meg's wedding."

A surge of mingled relief and triumph swept through Erik, so strong that for a second or two, it made him nearly dizzy. He had never been one to call the universe his friend, but it seemed in this matter—if no other—the gods had decided to smile upon him. The hated Raoul de Chagny gone for an indeterminate time, and Christine left alone in Paris. Truly, it was a miracle.

But Erik knew better than to allow her to see anything of what he was thinking. In measured tones, he said, "That is a pity about the vines. I hope the problem can be rectified."

"I am sure Raoul will sort it out," Christine responded. "Or rather, I believe that he, working with Monsieur Fournier, the estate manager, will be able to manage well enough." Her head tilted then, and the glance she sent him was almost sly. "That is all, Erik? You do not wish to show me how happy you are that my husband has left the city?"

"Nothing of the sort," he said, knowing he needed to do his best to disabuse her of the belief that he wanted Raoul out of the way. "Or rather, I suppose it is a good thing, if only that you will not have to invent excuses to come and practice here with me."

A dimple showed in her cheek as she lifted the teacup toward her mouth. "Oh, how little you know of a noblewoman's life if you think it so very easy for me to get away. I told my lady's maid that I had an appointment at Monsieur Worth's atelier, but I cannot overuse such an excuse, or she will begin to wonder why I do not have trunks full of clothing appearing at the house after so many fittings."

A good point. Well, Erik supposed they would manage one way or another. The very fact that she hadn't protested that this would be her only visit, that she had only come here to tell him they must have no further meetings, heartened him very much. And in the meantime....

"I see," he said dryly. "Since you have used up one of your excuses to come here this afternoon, we should make the best use of your time. Are you ready to begin?"

The half-amused smile she'd worn up until that moment disappeared, replaced by a wariness he found troubling. Was she so very concerned about singing in front of him?

Perhaps. After her performance at the baron's home, Erik could see why. And yet, he knew it wasn't that her abilities had disappeared over the past two years, only that her voice, like any other muscle, had grown somewhat atrophied from lack of use.

She made rather a show of setting down her teacup and saucer on a side table. However, it seemed that brief moment was all she needed to compose herself, for when she looked back over at him, her expression appeared steady enough, with no trace of the worry he'd seen there just a few seconds earlier.

"Yes, I think so," she said. "What would you like to work on?"

"Some scales to begin," he replied. "After that…we will see."

A flicker came and went in her clear blue eyes at that statement, but she only nodded and made her way over to the spinet, standing a pace or two away while he settled himself on the bench. Although he would have preferred a grand piano, there certainly wasn't room enough for one in this house, and the spinet at least was a finer instrument than he'd had any right to expect, obviously kept in decent repair even when it wasn't being used regularly.

He began with a major scale in C, thinking they might as well start at the beginning. Christine pulled in a breath—one more controlled than those she'd employed while singing that Gounod aria a few days earlier—and sang along, voice pure and true, its crystalline perfection awakening an ache he'd thought he would never experience again, an ache of longing…but more than that, a need to know that such beauty truly did exist, that it wasn't merely a dream which had haunted his soul for as long as he'd been alive.

Tears stung his eyes, but he blinked and shifted into a minor scale in D, praying Christine would be so focused on her breathing and her technique that she wouldn't notice the way his eyes glistened. He hadn't been wearing the dark glasses, for he'd seen no need to hide behind them while in his own home.

His eyes were the one thing the mask couldn't conceal….

Up again, this time to a scale in E-minor. Christine's voice soared along with the piano's clear, sharp notes, reverberating off the room's high ceilings and shining, polished wood floors. Yes, the acoustics in here were very good, indeed.

Erik stopped there, lifting his hands from the keys, and sent her a searching look. "You are not as out of practice as I thought," he said. "If you had sung that well on Sunday afternoon, I would not have seen the need to summon you here for a lesson. What happened?"

Pink tinged her cheeks, and her fingers fussed with the pleated edging of her overskirt. "I—I am not sure. Perhaps it was nothing more than being asked to perform when I hadn't expected anyone to make such a request. I—it took me off guard, I suppose. I thought of how I hadn't practiced enough, and how I did not know whether my voice was truly up to the task, and…."

The words trailed off there as she gave a helpless little shrug.

"And you created a self-fulfilling prophecy for yourself," he said, finishing the thought for her.

"I suppose I did."

"Well, there is no audience here," he told her. "Only you and I, and we have practiced together many times before. You have already proven yourself to me, so there is no need for any nervousness."

One graceful eyebrow lifted. "You make it sound so simple."

"It is," Erik said. "I am not here to judge, only to help. Although perhaps you are not as much in need of help as I thought."

"A few more minutes of warm-up," she suggested. "Then I should be ready to move on."

Which was wise of her. Before performing at the opera, she would have run through at least twenty minutes or so of vocal exercises to make sure her voice was up to the demands of singing for two hours or more. Not that he believed she would stay nearly so long today—his knowledge of dress fittings was perhaps not what it might have been, but he guessed they did not consume hours and hours—but he also wanted to make sure she ran no risk of damaging her voice. That could have been part of the problem at the baron's reception...she would have had to go into it cold, so to speak, which was never a good thing.

After they spent five minutes or so working through some simple exercises, he played the opening chords of Juliet's waltz, the aria Christine had sung at the baron's house. Erik had debated with himself which song to work on, but had decided that one was the safest choice—it was not a role Christine had sung at the opera, and so could have no connection to the events which had taken place there two years earlier. Also, because she had made such a poor showing with the piece so recently, it was the one she probably would expect him to use in their practice.

This time, she was in much better voice. In fact, she was so improved that he lifted his hands from the keyboard when she was done and applauded. At once, another flush rose in her cheeks, and she fidgeted again with the pleats of her skirt.

"I am not sure that performance was worthy of applause," she protested, and he shook his head, even as he rose from the piano bench and came toward her.

"Since I am the teacher, that will be for me to determine," he said.

Her mouth pursed, and for a moment, he thought she was going to offer another objection. However, she only said demurely, "Of course, m'sieur."

The glint in her blue eyes told him she was not quite as meek as she pretended to be. Once again, he found himself pleased by the newfound spirit he had seen in her these recent days. "You did much better this time, but that does not mean there is not still room for improvement. In the last cadenza, I was able to hear a very slight break as you shifted registers. Those transitions must be smooth as glass. Let us start again, at *douce flamme, reste don mon âme.*"

Her head tilted. "A cappella?"

"If you please. I wish to stand closer so I might observe your posture and your breathing."

He wondered if she would object to that request, although he stood a respectable distance away, with nearly an arm's length separating them. But although he thought he saw her shoulders tense slightly, she merely replied, "Of course, Erik."

"Now…proceed."

She sang the final cadenza of the aria once again. This time, the notes were less fluid than they had been during her first run-through, no doubt because of the way she had stiffened when he drew near.

Disappointment surged in him, but he told himself that it was natural for her to be tense. Once upon a time, she had let him stand very near her, had allowed him to touch her hand, her cheek.

But time had passed on since then, and clearly she was not yet ready to return to such intimacies. Not that he had even intended to take those sorts of liberties today.

She finished and fell silent. The downward droop of her mouth told him she knew very well that this performance had shown no improvement…rather, quite the opposite.

"You are carrying too much tension in your neck and shoulders," he said. "You know that everything should be fluid, weightless."

Should he leave it there, or should he utter the words they had both been thinking?

No point in dancing around the problem, he supposed.

"Once, you were not so troubled by my presence," he murmured, and her forget-me-not eyes flared with alarm…and guilt.

"You are very much changed from who you once were," she replied, her voice barely above a whisper.

"Am I?" Erik responded. "For you know I am still your Opera Ghost."

Those words forced an unwilling chuckle from her lips. "Are you certain you can even still call yourself that? For now you live in a fine house, and you wear a face that allows you to walk amongst men without fear. That does not much sound like the Opera Ghost I knew."

Her tone was almost rueful. Did it bother her so very much, this alteration he had made in himself? He had done so because he thought she would be more comfortable in his presence if he looked like other men, but now he began to wonder. Surely she could not prefer the hideous being he had once been.

Who you still are, he reminded himself. *The mask only conceals...it does not transform what lies beneath.*

"We all change as time carries us along," he said lightly. "But if you would prefer for me to return to my old mask, I can do so for you."

"No," Christine replied at once. "I know you are enjoying the freedom your current appearance has given you. It is only that I have not had the time to become accustomed to this new mask." She drew in a breath and straightened, chin lifting. "I will do better this time. Let me try again."

This request awoke a cautious hope in his

heart. Despite everything, she still wanted to please him.

"Of course, Christine," said Erik. "Once again, if you will."

She lifted her voice and sang, and this time, there was no nervousness, no tension, nothing but the glory of her voice echoing off the walls and the ceiling, seeming to reverberate in his very bones. The beauty of that voice was rivaled only by the glory of her face, fine skin flushed, cerulean eyes gleaming, her very hair seeming to glow from within as those perfect lips parted and sent into the world a sound worthy of an angel.

He watched her, and knew that he loved her…would always love her. It did not matter that she was another man's wife, or that she could never be his. In those few transcendent seconds, he thought it enough that he could hear her, be in her presence, be able to breathe the same air that she breathed. He would drink in every stolen moment, every word they exchanged, every note she sang. This idyll could not last; Erik knew that. Sooner or later, the Comte de Chagny would return to Paris, and these "lessons" would end.

In the meantime, though…in the meantime, Erik would let himself love Christine.

And it would have to be enough.

CHAPTER 15

Everything Fitting

"You are quite preoccupied, Christine," Meg said, her tone faintly accusing. "Whatever are you thinking of?"

With some effort, Christine dragged her thoughts away from the hour she had spent at Erik's home the previous afternoon. Oh, what glory it had been to sing again—to *truly* sing, to let her voice float free and wild, to know that however much he challenged her, she would rise to that challenge, would make herself recall the time when she had first fallen under his spell and allowed her voice to become what it was meant to be. All the supposed "practice" she had made herself dutifully perform seemed like wasted time in contrast to the sounds the Opera Ghost had been able to coax from her throat.

But of course, she could say nothing of the experience to Meg. No one could know that the Phantom of the Opera yet lived, and that she, his erstwhile muse, was slipping off to see him while her husband was away. Stated in those terms, the situation did seem truly awful.

And yet...nothing terrible had happened. He had accompanied her as she sang, or stood nearby to scrutinize her technique. She had sung the final cadenza from Juliet's waltz over and over again until at last it met his exacting standards. Afterward, he had brought out some bread and butter and cheese, and made another pot of tea for the two of them. Truly, it had been almost a prosy experience, with certainly nothing passing between them that anyone could have viewed as exceptional.

Only she knew better. She had told him she was having a difficult time getting used to his new mask, but she knew the situation was far more complicated than that. As before, she had come to the uncomfortable realization that the mask changed so much between them. Now, she could almost view him as an ordinary man...an attractive man whose musical talents and passion for the arts made him a far more compatible partner than the man she had married.

Oh, no, she could certainly say nothing of the sort to Meg. She could barely admit such a terrible truth to herself.

Because Christine delayed so long in replying, Meg went on, her eyes sharpening, "Why, you are almost glowing! What has happened?" And her gaze went to her friend's midsection, as if looking for evidence of the happy event that had produced such an inner glow.

"Nothing of that sort," Christine said quickly, trying not to sound annoyed. Was even her closest friend going to subject her to those unwelcome expectations? "I suppose—well, that is, I had a telegram from Raoul this morning, and he said that the new treatments he and our vineyard manager are using on the vines seem to be working, and that perhaps he will be able to return to Paris sooner than he thought."

All this was a complete fabrication; she had received a telegram from Raoul once he reached Tours, just to let her know he had arrived safely and that the Chagny carriage had been dispatched to take him the remainder of his journey, but she had not heard from him since. Nor had she thought she would, since she guessed that his labors in the vineyards would keep him occupied, and he would not reach out to her again until he knew with some certainty when he would be able to leave.

But Meg did not seem to find anything amiss in her reply, for she said, "Oh, that is good news. And I am glad that I could give you something to occupy a few hours during his absence."

They currently sat on a divan in the front parlor of the charming flat Meg was occupying until the fateful day when she would become the Baroness de Castelo-Barbezac. Christine assumed that Honoré was paying for the apartment, just as he was paying for the house where Madame Giry now lived, but of course, she would never mention the arrangement to her friend, as doing so would be horribly crass.

Meg had asked her to come over and view the sketches the florist and the baker had provided of the flowers and the planned cake, and naturally, Christine had agreed, even though she knew she did not have much expertise to offer on either topic. Her and Raoul's marriage had been a hasty affair, with strangers for witnesses and a small bouquet of pink roses purchased from a street vendor as the only flowers. No wedding cake, although they had shared a plate of pastries at the restaurant where they had dined afterward.

"I am not sure how much help I can be," Christine said, gesturing toward the sketches that were scattered on top of the low table in front of them. "Perhaps it is a dreadful *faux pas* to have orchids at this time of year, and perhaps an orange marmalade layer in the cake is not at all the thing for a spring wedding."

These self-deprecating comments were dismissed with an airy wave of one hand. "Oh, if I decide on anything that is utterly beyond the pale, Honoré will simply fix it…or rather, his grandmother will. But I have looked at so many sketches and tasted so many samples that my head is fairly spinning. I needed another opinion, even if, as you say, you do not have much experience with such things." Meg's expression sobered as she went on, "And—and if it troubles you to look at all of this, when I know your own wedding was very small and simple, please tell me, and I will put it all away."

"Oh, no," Christine said quickly. "I certainly do not begrudge you any of it. In fact, seeing how complicated all this can be, I am more glad than ever that Raoul and I eloped."

A twinkle entered Meg's dark eyes, and she reached over and gave Christine's hand a grateful squeeze. "I am glad to hear that…and I believe you are right. An elopement would have been much easier to manage. Then again, I can only imagine the duchess's reaction if her grandson should do anything so scandalous."

Having met that formidable lady, Christine thought she would definitely not want to witness the Duchess de Montfort's response to such an unthinkable proposition. Yes, the duchess had been kind to her...but she had also made it quite obvious that she expected the world to be ordered a certain way, and woe betide anyone who did not adhere to that order. Luckily, Christine had not been forced to contend with anyone quite so intimidating in Raoul's family, although his older sisters...especially Louise...had not been pleased by the alliance, and had made their disapproval known by a series of cool answers and elegantly lifted brows than by any outright attacks.

"No, better to do things the proper way," Christine agreed. "And I think that the affair will be utterly enchanting when all these elements come together. In a way, it's rather like mounting a stage production, is it not? We can hear the music and see the costumes and the choreography, but it's when everything is combined that the magic happens."

Meg appeared pleased by that analogy, a smile lifting the corners of her lips. "Yes, I hadn't thought of it that way, but you are right. All the same, I doubt I will tell the duchess that of course I have everything in hand, thanks to my experience dancing at the opera." She paused then as her expression sobered. "I have a favor to ask of you, Christine."

"Another one?" Christine responded, mouth curving slightly so her friend would know she was teasing her just a little.

"Yes. You see, I need to take Maman to Monsieur Worth's for her final fitting, and she is very reluctant to go. She says there's no reason for her to be gotten up so fine when everyone already knows how common she is."

"Your mother is not 'common,'" Christine said. "She is a very worthy woman."

Meg fidgeted with the diamond on her left hand, not meeting Christine's gaze. "Yes, we both know that, but I cannot seem to convince her that she is as worthy as anyone else who will be attending the wedding. I honestly think that if there were some way for her to avoid the event altogether, she would. But I suppose in her mind, she sees the act of not attending as even worse than having to be there when everyone around her is her superior."

"They are not her 'superiors,'" Christine retorted. Several years of being in company with the nobility of the Loire Valley had removed the scales from her eyes when it came to weighing the relative merits of the aristocracy. "They were luckier in birth, that is all."

"Perhaps you can tell her that. She does not want to listen to me."

Christine had her doubts as to whether Madame Giry would heed her counsel, but she supposed she should at least try. Since Meg's mother was clearly preoccupied with matters of rank, it seemed plausible that she might listen to a comtesse, even if said comtesse had achieved that rank by marriage rather than birth.

But if nothing else, Christine had nearly two years of experience mingling with the upper crust of society, and she had learned quickly enough that they were people like anyone else. Their high birth and their wealth did not make them better, only luckier. If anything, they seemed more prone to behavior she found ugly —indulging their prejudices, gossiping, drinking and eating and spending too much, participating in quite open affairs with the spouses of their neighbors and friends. Was it any wonder that she preferred to keep to Chagny and not socialize with the men and women Raoul had known all his life? Perhaps he could overlook their foibles, but she found it far less easy to do so, for she did not have the familiarity of long acquaintance to smooth those associations.

But are you so blameless? she asked herself then. *For while you are not unfaithful to Raoul in body, can you honestly say that you have been entirely faithful in spirit?*

She did not think she wished to answer that question.

"Of course I will come with you to visit your mother," she said. "I would very much like to see Madame Giry, since it has been years since we were last in company."

"Wonderful," Meg replied, relief clear in her expression. "Then let us go, for her appointment with Monsieur Worth is in an hour and a half, and we will need to fetch her first."

This plan was amenable to Christine; she nodded and rose from the divan, with Meg following so they could both fetch their mantles. The rain of the day before had moved on, and the day was sunny and bright, but with a bite to the wind that necessitated an outer wrap of some kind.

They descended the stairs and hailed a cab. "Honoré would have lent me his carriage," Meg confided as they began to move down the street in the direction of the Rue de Rivoli, "but I know Maman does not care for anything so fine, and so a cab seems a safer choice."

"Which is certainly not a problem for me," Christine said, "as I often use cabs myself. Truly, I am not sure why we even need to keep a carriage and driver at the Paris house, when we are here so seldom and could use other means of transportation when we are in town."

As she spoke, Christine wanted to shake her head at herself. Oh, what a very fine lady she had become, to speak so dismissively of having a private driver. The Christine of several years earlier might not have even recognized her.

However, Meg did not seem to notice anything amiss about her friend's statement, for she nodded knowingly. "Yes, I suppose it does seem something of an extravagance, but appearances are everything, are they not? Or at least, that is what my mother seems to think."

Yes, appearance did make quite a difference. Christine thought once again of the mask Erik had fashioned for himself, one that made him look like any other man. Any other *handsome* man, she corrected herself. Different from Raoul, dark where he was fair, those manufactured features sharper drawn, more angular. She supposed it would have been foolish for Erik to create a mask that gave him a less than attractive face. Why make a different kind of ugliness when that very ugliness was the thing he desperately wanted to escape?

Still, she wished the mask were a little less handsome. Perhaps then she would not have such a war within herself.

Voice musing, she said to Meg, "I suppose

for some, appearances are everything. But perhaps they shouldn't be."

Her friend regarded her carefully for a moment, as if she guessed that Christine's comment was not only about Madame Giry's preoccupation with her standing in society. Whatever crossed her mind then, she appeared reluctant to give it voice, for she merely shrugged and said, "I have tried to tell Maman that she shouldn't worry about such things, but she does not want to listen to me. To be quite honest, I simply want to get through this wedding with as little fuss as possible."

"And I will do whatever I can to help," Christine replied, leaning over so she could give Meg's glove-encased hand a gentle squeeze. "I know she is happy for you, Meg—it is only that she has been thrust into a situation very outside her usual experience."

A nod, and Meg managed a tremulous smile. "I know that. And I am very glad to have you here. It will make everything easier."

They fell silent after that exchange, and the women watched the streets pass by outside the carriage windows, each occupied with her own thoughts. Eventually, the cab stopped in front of the house on the Rue de Rivoli that was now Madame Giry's. Christine had no idea what the Girys' lodgings had been like before Meg became engaged to Honoré de Castelo-Barbezac, but she doubted they could have been anything so fine as this. The home stood three stories tall, with wrought iron framing the balconies. Fresh spring flowers bloomed in pots in the courtyard out front, and everything appeared neat and clean and well-kept.

A woman with a narrow, plain face looked out from the door in response to Meg's knock. Seeing the visitors, the woman said, "Good day, Mademoiselle Giry. Your mother is expecting you."

"Thank you, Annette," Meg replied. "This is my friend, Madame la Comtesse de Chagny."

At once, Annette curtsied. By that point, Christine had grown used enough to such gestures that she no longer had the impulse to tell the maid there was no need for her to make obeisances, even though she still found being the recipient of such honors horribly awkward. Instead, she smiled at the other woman, then followed Meg into the house.

Because of the brisk temperatures outside, a fire burned in the hearth. Madame Giry sat in a chair that had been drawn close to the grate, but she also had a shawl draped around her shoulders, as if even the fire and the high-necked wool gown she wore were still not enough to keep her warm.

She rose from her chair when the two younger women approached, eyebrows lifting slightly as she took in Christine's presence. "Madame la Comtesse," she said. "I was not expecting you as a guest."

"'Christine,' please, Madame Giry," Christine protested. "We have known each other too long for you to be so formal. And I thought it would be more amusing for all of us to have a group of three when we go to visit Monsieur Worth's atelier. I hope you do not mind that I have invited myself along."

Meg's lips pursed slightly, but she said nothing, not bothering to protest Christine's version of events. Most likely, she had determined that her mother would be more pliable if she thought that the comtesse had decided to include herself in the outing, rather than have the idea originate with her daughter.

"Oh, well," said Madame Giry. "I am not certain how 'amusing' it will be to watch Monsieur Worth try to stuff me into a gown I will end up wearing only once, but of course, I cannot object to having you there." Her gaze shifted to Annette, who had been hovering a few feet away, as if she wasn't quite sure whether she might be called to bring refreshments or perform some other task for the comfort of her mistress's guests. "Annette, fetch my wrap. I suppose we should all be going, or we shall be late."

The maid ducked her head and hurried upstairs, heels clacking on the wooden steps.

"It's odd, actually," Madame Giry went on. "I was only talking about you with Monsieur Saint Denis the other day, and here you are on my doorstep."

At that name, Christine went cold. What on earth had Antoine Saint Denis been doing in Madame Giry's home?

What do you think? she reproached herself. *He was on the trail of the Phantom of the Opera, a trail that brought him to Madame Giry's door. God only knows what all they discussed.*

Still, she realized she couldn't betray to the Girys that she'd even heard of Saint Denis, let alone met him and confronted him in his office over his slander of the Opera Ghost. Doing so would only invite far too many questions.

"Who on earth is Monsieur Saint Denis?" she asked, praying she had injected the correct amount of astonished curiosity into her tone. "And why in the world would he be discussing me?"

"Oh, he is a reporter, you know," Madame Giry replied. "Such a dashing man, actually."

Christine supposed that a neutral party might consider him dashing. He was a rather fine figure of a man, after all. Unfortunately, that dashing figure of a man had an uncomfortable obsession with the Phantom of the Opera.

Annette chose that moment to reappear and drape the requested mantle on Madame Giry's shoulders, so any further questions would have to wait. Indeed, it was not until Christine and the two Girys were seated in a cab and making their way toward the Rue de la Paix that she had the opportunity to speak.

"Why would a reporter want to talk to you about me?"

Madame Giry fussed with the bronze chain of her reticule, then said, "Oh, he wanted to know about the Opera Ghost. It was something to do with those terrible murders that are happening in the Rue Scribe."

Christine found her fingers digging into the rough horsehair upholstery as anger pulsed through her. What right did Antoine Saint Denis have to continue pursuing that subject when she'd told him Erik was dead, that there was no chance the Phantom of the Opera could be involved in these current killings? Of course, it had turned out she'd been quite wrong in part of that assumption, but still. Monsieur Saint Denis had given her his word that he would no longer sensationalize the gruesome events by hinting the Opera Ghost might be the culprit.

266 | CHRISTINE POPE

To be fair, she hadn't seen the reporter publish any further articles making those claims. Even so, it seemed quite clear to her that although he was no longer writing such sensational allegations, he had decided he was not quite ready to put the matter of the Opera Ghost aside. Most likely, he had determined that Madame Giry was the best person to speak to, as Christine had made it quite obvious what she thought of him and his works, and approaching Meg while she was in a flurry of wedding preparations wouldn't be proper.

"But the Opera Ghost is dead, Maman," Meg said then, looking more mystified by such revelations than anything else. "You yourself told me that."

"Yes," Madame Giry replied. Her own expression was one of melancholy, as if she had mourned the dead man when no one else would. Perhaps she had grieved a good deal; Erik had done quite a lot to look after Madame Giry and her daughter, had made sure that Meg was promoted to principal dancer. If she had not occupied such a lofty place in the *corps de ballet,* she might not have attracted Honoré's attention in the first place. And besides, Erik always left a handsome tip for the elder Giry to thank her for looking after Box Five at the opera. "And I told Monsieur Saint Denis the very same thing. He seemed disappointed, but he did not attempt to contradict me. I only thought of the conversation because of seeing Madame—of seeing Christine today. Nothing came of it. He thanked me for my hospitality, and left."

From her aspect, it appeared that Madame Giry did not think there was anything odd about the conversation. On the surface, perhaps there wasn't. After all, it had been fairly common knowledge at the opera that she had something of a special relationship with the Palais Garnier's resident ghost. No doubt someone had passed that information along to Antoine Saint Denis.

It is only that you know Erik is still alive, Christine told herself. *For you, that puts a very different complexion on these inquiries. Everyone else would believe it is a harmless enough line of questioning.*

"Well, I hope that is the end of it," she said. "For, as you said, the Opera Ghost has been dead these two years. I will be the first to admit that these current murders are quite horrific, but they are certainly none of his doing."

Both of the Girys looked at her in some surprise, as if startled she should be so emphatic on the subject. Inwardly, Christine winced, even as she told herself that she could not take the words back now.

Should she attempt to explain herself?

No, that would only make matters worse. She had never been good at prevaricating; having to keep Erik's secret was challenge enough without going into long explanations regarding her motivations.

To her relief, the cab stopped in front of Monsieur Worth's atelier, and the conversation was abandoned in the complicated dance of getting three women in large bustles extricated from the cab's interior. Eventually, however, they were all free of its confines, and made their way into the shop.

They did not have to wait so long that day, and Monsieur Worth was once again effusive in his greeting to Christine, exclaiming how lovely she looked in her blue walking dress. She did her best to smile and accept the compliments with good grace...but she also couldn't help but note that, while he was gracious enough to Meg and her mother, he did not appear inclined to heap praise on either of them, even though she guessed they both wore his creations as well.

Eventually, though, the fitting commenced, and Christine was able to sit in her chair and sip from the tea Monsieur Worth's assistant had offered her while she watched Madame Giry's elegant reception gown of dark gray silk be pinned and draped as she stood on a dais a few feet away, trying to look engaged by the process.

Meg observed from a much closer vantage point, and seemed to have no difficulty arguing the finer points with the designer, whether the issue at hand was having elbow sleeves or full-length ones, and whether the intricately ruched trim should be black or a deep wine color.

Through all this back-and-forth, Christine's thoughts drifted. She wondered what Erik was doing at that moment, and whether he would send her a summons for another lesson. When they'd parted the day before, he had been vague as to his plans, saying only that he would send another note when he deemed the time was right.

She hadn't much liked the sound of that, especially since she had no clear idea when Raoul would return to Paris. Shouldn't they have been taking advantage of their current freedom by doing their best to see one another at every opportunity?

Of course, as soon as that thought passed through her head, Christine wanted to scold herself. She sounded like an adulterous wife sneaking off to see her lover, which was ridiculous. There was nothing between her and Erik, nothing except music.

Which to both of them was everything.

She clutched her reticule and pulled in a breath, hoping that doing so would help to calm some of the torment which raged in her breast.

How had she allowed Erik to put her in such a terrible position? If only he had left her alone. Then she could have blissfully continued as Raoul's wife, with no thought of the Opera Ghost to rouse these disturbing sensations within her.

"What do you think, Christine?" Meg asked then, and she blinked, forcing herself to tear her mind away from Erik so she might focus on the scene before her.

Attempting to bluff her way through an answer did not seem feasible, since she had absolutely no idea what Meg's question was even in reference to. "I am so sorry," she said. "I fear I was woolgathering. What were you asking?"

Meg's brows drew together, and she gave her friend a measuring glance, as if trying to determine what had actually been occupying Christine's thoughts. "Monsieur Worth has suggested pleated trim rather than ruffles. I was wondering what you thought."

Behind her shoulder, the gentleman himself frowned as well. Clearly, he did not think his clients should be deferring to a friend's advice rather than his own expertise, but he would not jeopardize their business by saying so out loud.

Thank God that Meg had already stated Monsieur Worth's preference in the matter, so it was not terribly difficult to decide whose advice should be followed. "I think pleats should do very well," Christine said. "They will present a more tailored silhouette, which I think will be more elegant in the end."

The couturier's expression relaxed. In fact, he even sent her a smile. "Madame la Comtesse de Chagny has excellent taste," he stated. "But of course, it is up to the bride and her mother to decide."

Madame Giry waved a hand. "It does not matter so much to me, but I also prefer the pleats."

That seemed to settle the matter. After a bit more discussion, Monsieur Worth proclaimed the fitting was over, as he had everything he needed to finish the gown. Looking relieved, Madame Giry retired to the dressing room in the company of Worth's assistant so she might be helped back into her dress, and in less than a quarter-hour, they were back in a cab as they returned to her flat in the Rue de Rivoli.

"Less than a week left," Meg said. "Goodness, there is so much to be done in those few days!"

"It sounds as if you have it all very well in hand," Christine replied, which was only the truth. True, there were a great many details to keep track of, but it did not seem as though Meg intended to allow any of them to escape her attention.

"I suppose." Her friend's expression seemed distracted, however. Perhaps she was still sorting through all those details and making sure that none of them had slipped her mind. "And you are quite sure the comte will be back in time for the ceremony?"

"I am certain of it." Or at least, she had Raoul's assurances that he would return for the wedding even if his business at Chagny was not yet concluded, and she could not see how he would go back on his word.

This clarification seemed to be a source of some relief, for Meg nodded and allowed herself to lean back against the worn leather upholstery inside the cab. Madame Giry appeared disinclined to comment on the matter, which was just as well.

For while Christine told herself she should be eagerly awaiting her husband's return, she knew her feelings on the matter were not quite as unmixed as they should be.

And she did not know what to think about that.

CHAPTER 16

Shifting Stratagems

*S*aint Denis sat at his desk and brooded over the welter of papers scattered there, a mess even more out of control than usual. He had spent the day gathering as much information as he could about the victims of the Rue Scribe killer, but he feared that all he had done was waste his time. As far as he could tell, he had discovered nothing that would lead to new insights, nothing which might lead him to the thread that connected them all.

All prosperous, all in their fifties or sixties, settled, with families. No one of the nobility, unless one could count Marcel Saint Michel, the first victim, whose maternal grandfather had been a baron. Still, these were men with some standing in society, men who would be missed. No known enemies, except possibly a few who had dealt past business partners a bad blow. Even so, the petty financial squabbles he had uncovered were certainly not enough to have provoked someone to murder. A crime of passion in the heat of the moment, perhaps, but not anything that would have led to the sorts of calculated, brutal killings which were occurring in the Rue Scribe.

No, the motive had to be something else entirely. Not for the first time, he wished he had the ability to peer into the victims' banking records and private correspondence so he might see whether the answers were buried somewhere within. If given enough time, he might be able to find solicitors and bank clerks who would be willing to let slip that sort of information...if he made it worth their while...but Saint Denis had the uncomfortable suspicion that time was a luxury he couldn't afford. The killings didn't happen on a perfectly ordered schedule, of course, but neither did more than a week elapse before yet another body was discovered by the Sûreté. If the murderer was trying to be careful, surely he would give himself more of an interval between crimes.

That he had not—and that the latest victim had been discovered only two days after the previous one—seemed to indicate that the killer could not quite restrain himself, and had sought his next victim just as soon as he thought it would be safe. Such a rapid pace must mean that he had his own timetable to follow, even if no one else could yet discern what it was.

And if that timetable was accelerating somehow....

The ticking of the clock on the table across from his desk only seemed to be a further irritant. Saint Denis scowled at it, even as he told himself that there would be no murders tonight, for the opera was dark. A small breathing space, but better than nothing.

He ran a hand through his hair, not caring how mussed it might appear. By that hour, past six o'clock, most of the *Presse's* reporters had gone home to their wives and families. In the past, he had always enjoyed the solitude of that time of day, how it allowed him to sit alone with his thoughts without the tumult of the newsroom to distract him, but in that moment, he found himself wondering if his pursuit of the truth, of the story, had prevented him from participating in an aspect of life which might have brought him its own fulfillment.

You are letting this case affect you far too

much if you are now going to be melancholy about all your missed opportunities, he thought. And yet he found himself thinking about the women who had come and gone from his life, the ones who had realized soon enough that for him, the work would always come first. He had never before regretted his choice, and yet....

His thoughts kept circling around to the story of Christine Daaé and the Opera Ghost. There was far more to the tale than Madame Giry had let on, echoes of passion and obsession that still reverberated to this day. It would have been so much easier for everyone involved if it truly were the Phantom who was responsible for these killings, although it seemed that must be impossible.

Still, even if the Opera Ghost was no longer in the world and incapable of murdering four men in cold blood, that did not mean the opera might not still be the connection amongst the victims. They were all season ticket holders, but that seemed to be the only trait they shared in common. As far as Saint Denis had been able to tell, they had not known one another, except perhaps in the general sense of being members of a class of men who might have had box seats near one another or who had perhaps met at certain parties and receptions.

His head ached slightly, and he told himself

that he might as well go home for the evening. Certainly there was nothing to be gained by sitting here and staring at the scattered papers on his desk. They might as well have been written in ancient hieroglyphs for all the meaning they currently held for him.

Yes, time to leave. Not home, however. He had no desire to sit alone in his house and think of the voices it might have contained, if only he had chosen differently. No, he would go to one of the restaurants on the Boulevard des Capuchines, where the noise and the light and the chatter of the other patrons might serve to distract him from these crimes he had yet to solve.

Who knows? Perhaps being in such proximity to the opera might provide some of the insights he so desperately sought.

At the very least, he would have a decent meal and a glass of wine…or two.

He let himself out of the office, giving a brief farewell to Louis, the sole reporter who remained on duty during the overnight hours, in case any important news should break. For just a moment, Saint Denis considered offering to take over for the other man. It was not as if he had anything better to do with his time.

But no, there was not much point in that. Better to get away and hope his mind would refresh itself. What else was there for him to do?

More opium for these nights when the opera was shuttered, when the diva and the chorus and the orchestra and the dancers were all given a brief respite. The need to kill ached in his veins even more than the need for the drug, but he could do nothing about it that evening.

No, he sat in the wretched flat that was his current home and attempted to find some measure of peace as he sat with the pipe and smoked some of the precious drug, letting its alluring, insidious touch move through him, quieting the ache within…but not eradicating it altogether.

The only thing that would calm his soul would be accomplishing his goal. Now there were four black lines drawn through the names on the list. Four gone, but two still remained, and he could do nothing about that while he sat here.

He knew where they all lived. Such information had not been terribly difficult to gather, and he held those addresses in his heart, not daring to write them down. Even possessing the list of their names was a danger, although he kept it with him at all times and never left it behind when he ventured out. His landlady was not an inquiring soul, and only cared that the rent was paid on time, but still, he knew he could not run the risk of anyone discovering the shabby piece of paper and making a connection between the names written there and the men who had been killed on the Rue Scribe.

Perhaps it was time to go hunting outside the place he had made his killing grounds. Just two nights before, he had spied the man who had paced up and down the Rue Scribe, clearly keeping watch. Of course, it had not been so difficult to elude him and still manage to harvest the soul who had been his target that night. The next evening, though, two men watched that same area, men he knew must be with the Sûreté, although they wore no uniforms. Striking at his remaining victims would be far more difficult going forward.

Except, of course, he did not have to kill them on the Rue Scribe. Doing so had merely been his way of dragging the opera into yet another scandal. The connection was truly right there for anyone to see, but so far, no one had yet determined why those men had been made his targets.

Which was perfect. He would shift his killings to these men's home ground, would catch them coming and going from their homes. Or, even better, slip into their fancy houses and make his way to the beds where they slept, and have the garrote steal the life from them even as they lay next to their wives.

Yes, that sounded like a very good plan. His mouth curved in a smile, and he thought of the horror of those women as they awoke to find their husbands dead...the consternation of the Sûreté as they discovered that the killer had moved on to hunt these men in their very beds.

Perhaps it was time to begin a new reign of terror in the City of Light....

———

Erik stared down at the blank piece of notepaper that lay on his desk. He had gone a whole day without summoning Christine to his side, and had thought his forbearance quite noble. Besides, he knew that she was supporting Meg Giry in these last few days before the wedding, and had thought it better to allow the two women some time together.

This morning, though, he had arisen knowing that he could not allow another day to pass without seeing her, not when he ached so much to gaze upon her face, to hear her voice. And surely there was not anything so terrible about spending an hour or so working on her technique, of reminding her again of how it felt when the music flowed through her, became part of her, rather than some external entity she only visited occasionally.

He picked up the pen.

Christine,

I hope you are well. If your schedule permits, perhaps another lesson this afternoon between three and four?

I remain,

Your obedient friend,

E

He stared down at the note for a moment. Was that too timid? In the first missive he had sent her, he had been quite the opposite, attempting to make it seem as if she had no real way to refuse. Today, however, he did not wish to seem overbearing. He had seen something in her eyes during their previous meeting, a startled acknowledgment that perhaps matters between them had shifted and she did not quite know what to do about the situation.

Well, he reflected with grim humor, that made two of them. There was no longer any use denying that his feelings for her had not disap-peared over the past few years, but had only grown deeper and stronger. He had loved the girl she was, but he wanted the woman she had become.

The woman he couldn't have.

Face twisting beneath the mask, he picked up the note he had just written, balled it up, and threw it into the wastepaper bin next to his desk. For a moment, he contemplated doing the same thing to the mask he wore. All he had wanted was to make an appearance for himself that allowed him to live as other men. He had not thought wearing such a face might be the one thing that finally allowed Christine to love him.

Perhaps he should be annoyed with her for such shallowness, for such concern for surface appearances, but he could find within himself no anger, only a deep weariness. The face he had worn as he was brought screaming into this world was something that could inspire only revulsion. Long ago, he had become, if not resigned, at least cognizant that he could never expect any woman to see past it to look into his soul.

And really, he thought then, *my soul is no bargain—crabbed, angry, full of spite for my fellow man, with their perfect faces and their perfect lives. It is probably a good thing that no one has attempted to peer into its depths.*

Only...Christine had. Not completely, of

course, but she had heard his music, heard his voice. Had bent to press her pure, perfect lips against the horror of his face, to whisper, "Poor Erik."

He didn't want to be her "poor Erik." He only wanted to be her Erik…simply that and nothing more.

Fevered imaginings filled his mind. She had accepted him with the mask, and that should be enough. He could tell she was not happy as the Comtesse de Chagny…and how could she be? She had not been born to that life, had grown up in a world of music and fairy stories, and she would get precious little of either at the comte's estate outside Tours.

He could convince her to leave Raoul. Surely she must realize that she had made a mistake in choosing such a callow boy. They could go away together…to Italy, perhaps. Yes, someplace warm and sun-drenched, where they could leave behind the shadows that had haunted them here in Paris. They could go to the opera there. Perhaps she could perform. Yes, that would do very well. She could be Rome's newest diva, and he could compose, and….

Erik stopped himself there. What a pleasant fantasy he had constructed…but it was a fantasy and nothing more. Even if her heart was not as completely Raoul's as she pretended it to be,

Christine would never leave her husband. She would not subject him to that kind of scandal, would not break the poor boy's heart.

For a long moment, Erik sat in his chair, his own heart beating painfully in his chest. He was acutely aware of the silence in the house, the way the faintest echoes of carriages passing in the street and people speaking as they made their way along the sidewalks drifted up to the second-floor office where he sat. Hard to believe that just a few days earlier, these rooms had reverberated with the ringing purity of Christine's voice, how every inch of the place echoed with the scent of her rose perfume once she was gone.

Even when she was not there, the house seemed to breathe of her essence.

Slowly, he reached for another piece of paper, then picked up his pen and dipped it into the inkwell. Still moving with exaggerated care, he began to scratch out another note...one that would signal something of his intentions, one that would allow her to demur if she so desired.

If she did not...well, they would both have to see what happened next.

Christine,

It is time for another session. I would like to sing together the duet from Act V of Faust.

Come to the house at four o'clock.

E.

Christine stared down at the note — brought once again by a street boy, according to Jeannette — and wondered what on earth Erik was playing at. How could he possibly expect her to sing a piece from *Faust?* And not just any selection, but the climax, where a dying Marguerite is visited by Faust, and he proclaims his love for her?

Was this a test? Was Erik attempting to determine whether her feelings toward him had changed?

Or did he already know…or at least suspect?

She rose from her chair and went to the window so she might gaze down at the gardens below. The day was fresh and bright, with buds beginning to appear on the rosebushes, giving just the faintest hint of the colors they would reveal when they reached their full glory, pink and red and yellow, and the ones she loved the most, pale cream with edgings of blush along the edges of their fragile petals.

Coward that she was, Christine wished Raoul would come back to this house. With him present, she would not have to struggle with her terrible attraction to the Opera Ghost. She could pretend to be a good wife—in appearance at least, if not in her heart.

But she had heard nothing from her husband, except a quick note to say they were making progress but he did not yet feel comfortable returning to Paris, and so she realized that cruel fate had left her to manage this dilemma on her own. She must look within and decide what to do.

You know what you must do, she told herself. *There is no easy way out, but there is the right way.*

True enough. She must tell Erik she would not sing that duet with him. No, she would not allow him to tell her that he loved her, even if he intended to use the words of the song rather than his own to make such a declaration.

But then, he had once done that very thing, had told her he was dying of love for her...which turned out to be false. His heart had not struck him down; actually, he appeared to be quite hale and hearty.

For a moment, she considered writing him a note in reply to the one he had sent her, and refusing him that way. However, while doing so would save her from the inevitable confrontation, she would still have to find some means of getting the note to Erik. Oddly, she had a better chance of escaping detection if she went herself, for she could simply tell Jeannette that Meg had asked her the day before if she would return to her apartment for some last-minute wedding planning.

Did she have the courage to do such a thing, though? Could she face Erik and tell him she would no longer play his games?

She knew she must...or she would never be free of him.

For some reason, once she had made that inner decision, she found herself much calmer. It was easier than she'd thought to ring for Jeannette and inform her she'd forgotten about her promise to visit Mademoiselle Giry that afternoon, and that she needed her morning gown changed out for a visiting toilette.

That involved procedure took the better part of an hour. By the time she was arrayed to her maid's satisfaction, the hour had slipped past three-thirty, and Christine needed to be on her way. To her relief, Jeannette did not offer to come along, and soon enough, Christine was sitting in a cab as it headed into the Marais, where Erik's rented home was located.

Traffic was thicker than she expected, and so she was nearly ten minutes late, according to the silver pocket watch she carried in her reticule. Not a very auspicious way to begin a meeting that she feared would end in acrimony, but there was no help for it.

When Erik answered the door, she saw no hint of irritation in his expression — not that she had expected to see any. The mask he had constructed for himself was uncanny in the way it mirrored the features of a normal man, but its one failing was that it did not convey emotion very well. The mouth lifted slightly when he smiled, and the brows would raise and lower as well, but it was still not the same as watching a regular person's reactions.

Then again, why would he be annoyed? He had sent her a note that was something of an ultimatum, and she had come in response to that summons. He could have no idea of what she planned to say to him.

"Tea?" he asked, once she had divested herself of her shawl and hung it on the hall tree in the foyer.

Christine thought to demur, but she realized her throat was quite dry. Some tea might give her the strength she needed for the coming confrontation. "Yes, please."

"I already had some prepared. Come along."

They made their way into the pretty blue-hung sitting room where she had sung a few days earlier. The same porcelain tea set waited for them on the low table in front of the divan, and Erik lifted one of the cups and handed it to her as she stood off to one side.

"I apologize for my tardiness," she said, deciding that seemed a safe way to begin their conversation. "The traffic was terribly thick today."

"I thought it might be something like that," he replied. "You are usually quite prompt."

Those commonplaces, uttered in Erik's spell-binding tenor, did nothing to put Christine at ease. When she was away from him, it became easier to forget the effect he had on her, how that voice of his could almost always coax her into doing his bidding.

Not this time, however. She swallowed a mouthful of fragrant lemon tea, hoping it would give her the necessary courage to deliver her own ultimatum. "Still," she said, "I should have taken that into account. But that is not what I wanted to discuss." Lifting her chin, she went on, "I came here to tell you I will not sing that duet with you."

Nothing in those still, perfect features changed…not that she had really expected it to. Perhaps a flicker of his amber eyes, come and gone in an instant. Voice bland, he replied, "Should I be honored that you traveled halfway across town to deliver such a message in person?"

"That is up to you to determine, I suppose," she said. "But the message needed to be delivered one way or another, and it was just as easy for me to come here myself. I will not ask what you were thinking, Erik, in making such a request of me, but I will tell you that I find it entirely inappropriate."

"Inappropriate in what way?" he inquired, his tone silky.

Did he want her to write it on the side of the house in letters ten feet high? Frowning, she set down her teacup and turned back toward him, hands on her hips. "You know the lyrics to that piece as well as I do. It would be inappropriate for you to be singing such things to me, considering our current situation."

Several long seconds passed as he stood there and gazed at her. Finally, the lips of his mask quirked, and he said, "Tell me, Christine—did you have such scruples when you sang the role of Marguerite with Monsieur Fauré as your Faust? I have a feeling you did not."

"That was entirely different," she protested.

"How? Has the role changed between now and then?"

Oh, she should have known he would try to talk rings around her. This time, however, she would not allow him to have all the advantage. "No, of course not," she said. "But neither had

Monsieur Fauré ever told me that he was dying of love for me."

Again, Erik was silent. He stared at her with those catlike eyes, and she made herself gaze back as unflinchingly as possible. When he spoke, his voice was barely a murmur. "Yes, I did say that to you once. Perhaps I even meant it. But here we are."

"Yes, here we are," Christine returned. "In a situation that is impossible. I fear I must ask you to respect me as the wife of the Comte de Chagny, which means not demanding that I sing a duet with you which is entirely too fraught."

Beneath the mask, Erik's mouth must have twisted fearfully, for those perfectly sculpted lips somehow bent themselves into a scowl. "I will respect you as who you are, Christine *Daaé*, and not because you made the mistake of harnessing yourself to a pretty nobleman who has no more idea of who you truly are than he does of the mathematical formulas necessary to determine the span of an arch."

Hearing those words, her heart began to beat fiercely within her breast, but she told herself to stand her ground. "Oh, and I suppose *you* know who I am?" she retorted.

"Far more than Raoul de Chagny," Erik said. Strangely, he seemed calmer now, as if something in her words or her expression had told him he'd struck more of a blow than she thought. "What does he know of music, of passion, of beauty? Except, perhaps, to steal what he can of them from you, the only thing of true beauty in his life. Does it serve you well, Christine, being relegated to the role of a wife who must play hostess at his dull parties, who must manage his house, who must one day bear an heir to the Chagny name? Does not the very ordinariness of such an existence drive you mad?"

Each of those questions was a nail being driven deeper into her heart. She gasped, knowing the truth of what Erik had said, and at the same time wanting to flee from it, wanting to run far, far away so she would not have to face all the mistakes she had made.

"You must not say such things of Raoul," she whispered.

"Oh, I will say them," Erik replied, his tone fierce. "What's more, I will say the words of that song you refused to sing with me. *Oui, c'ést toi je t'aime.* Yes, it's you I love, Christine. I have loved you from the first moment I heard your voice, and more so once I came to know your sweet soul. Do you not think I have suffered torments because of this? I, a monster, to look upon such perfection and think that he could share even a single moment of its beauty?"

His voice shook as he spoke. Christine

wanted to raise her hands to her ears, but it was too late—he had spoken the fateful words to her, and she knew there was nothing she could ever do to erase them from her memory.

"You are not—" she began, and he lifted a hand, cutting off the sentence before she could complete it.

"Oh, I am a monster," he said. "Long ago, I accepted that truth about myself. But even monsters have hearts, even monsters can love. And all you must do, Christine, to rid yourself of me forever is to tell me you are indifferent. For you know that indifference is the true opposite of love. Not hate, for hate is its own passion. But to not care one way or another—that is the death of love. Tell me you don't care, and I will trouble you no more."

Her heart thudded painfully against her ribcage, against the constricting whalebone of her stays. It would be so easy to say those words, to tell him she didn't care.

But that would be a lie...and he knew it as well as she did.

"I—I must go," she said. Without waiting for a response, she turned on the heel of her kidskin boot and fled for the front door, quite forgetting her shawl in her haste. Down the steps and on to the sidewalk, slowing her headlong dash when a comfortable-looking couple walking down the street from the other direction gave her an askance look.

Christine risked a glance over her shoulder, wondering what on earth she would do if she saw Erik following her, the tails of his frock coat flapping behind him like the billowing cloak of a vengeful god.

But he was not there, and she did not know whether to sob with relief…or loss.

Instead, she raised her hand to hail a cab passing by and then climbed inside. Only once she was safely locked within did she allow a sound, halfway between a gasp and a sob, to escape her lips, although she knew she couldn't break down into tears, not there, not when she would be home soon enough, and Jeannette would see her reddened eyes and wonder what on earth was the matter.

Christine leaned her head back and closed her eyes, willing herself to be calm.

He has broken himself against me like a ship on the rocks, she thought. *And I do not know how to fix this.*

Perhaps she never could.

CHAPTER 17

Cover of Darkness

Someone was pounding on the front door. Antoine Saint Denis opened one eyelid and determined that yes, it was very dark, obviously the middle of the night. Why on earth would someone be knocking? Was the house on fire?

A quick glance around the room told him that everything appeared to be in order. With a slight groan, he pushed himself up from the bed, then winced as his bare feet touched the cold wooden floor. The fire in the bedroom hearth had died down to barely embers, and the air was uncomfortably chill as he hurried over to gather his dressing gown from where he'd flung it across a chair the day before. He had no servants who lived on the premises, only a woman who came to clean once a week and another who showed up every evening to cook his dinner whether he planned to be home or not, and so he knew he would have to answer the door himself.

When he reached the ground floor and flung open the front door, he saw Monsieur Aubry standing there, his round face pale and sheened with perspiration.

"There's been another one!" he exclaimed.

Saint Denis didn't bother to ask what he meant by "another one." Yet another murder, yet another soul lost mere steps from the opera house. A tragedy, yes, but did it warrant waking him up in the middle of the night?

"What has made this murder so much more urgent than the others?" he asked, not bothering to hide his frown.

The detective shook his head in impatience. "This man was murdered in his bed."

That declaration made Saint Denis' eyes flare open in shock. "What the devil?"

"As I said, m'sieur. We are still trying to determine how it could have happened, but the murderer somehow crept inside the house and killed the man as he slept. His wife heard nothing. But then she awoke sometime later to get herself a drink of water, and she…found him."

Good God. Saint Denis ran a hand through his hair as he attempted to digest this alarming piece of information. "And you're certain it is the same killer?"

"This man was garroted, just like the others. I suppose it could be another murderer imitating the first, but that explanation seems somewhat far-fetched."

Yes, it did. Or rather, his studies of similar crimes had taught him that murderers did not tend to change their methodology midstream, as it were. Possibly, a slight change of location here and there—Saint Denis would not have been terribly shocked to learn that this latest killing had taken place on the Boulevard des Capuchines or the Rue Auber rather than the Rue Scribe itself—but to alter his pattern so greatly that he was now attacking his victims in their very beds?

"This is…alarming," he said slowly, and Aubry nodded.

"Yes, it is. I was hoping you would come with me and speak to the widow."

"Now?" Saint Denis demanded, wondering if he'd heard the other man correctly. "Surely this can wait until morning."

"The inspectors have come and gone. The

298 | CHRISTINE POPE

woman has no family in Paris. I asked her if she would like to speak to the man who has been working on the Rue Scribe killings with me, and she said yes." Aubry paused there before adding, "I think it would be better if you spoke to her while matters are still fresh in her mind."

And what, Saint Denis thought sourly, *will she have to tell me, if she slept through the entire incident?*

But then he softened. What a terrible thing, to fall asleep next to the person you loved, only to awake some hours later and discover he had been killed in his sleep!

A shiver went through him. "I will need a few minutes to get dressed," he said. "I very much doubt the widow would appreciate me showing up on her doorstep in my dressing gown."

Relief shone in Aubry's weary face. "Thank you, m'sieur. I will wait here."

It was on Saint Denis' lips to invite the detective in—surely that would be the polite thing to do—but he could tell the other man was reluctant, no doubt thinking of the great social gap which existed between the two of them.

Arguing would only waste breath and time. He inclined his head slightly and said, "And I will be as quick as I can."

He hastened back upstairs and flung off the

dressing gown as soon as he entered the bedroom, then hurried to divest himself of his pajamas, exchanging them for wool trousers and a shirt, waistcoat, and frock coat. His fingers slipped as he attempted to knot a cravat at his throat, and with a mumbled curse, he flung it down on the dresser. Perhaps the widow would forgive him for his disarray, considering the very late hour.

If she noticed at all. Certainly she would have far more important—and distressing—matters to occupy her thoughts.

In less than five minutes, he was back downstairs. After locking the door behind him, he followed Aubry to a carriage that waited on the street. They were on their way in no time, the clopping of the horse's hooves sounding unnaturally loud on the cobblestones as they drove through the empty boulevards.

Perhaps Saint Denis had been out this late during his boisterous college days, when he and some of his fellow students would carouse until almost dawn, but that had been many years ago.

Nearly twenty, he thought with some surprise, wondering how the ripe age of thirty-seven could have crept up on him without him even seeming to notice.

But he was distracted from those brooding realizations by the arrival of the carriage at a large house just off the Rue de l'Université. It had a low wall surrounding it—something that could have been easily scaled—and well-groomed gardens on all sides. In the darkness, a faint shimmer caught his gaze, and Saint Denis realized that shimmer must have been the waning moon reflecting in the still waters of a fishpond.

Clearly, this victim, like all the others, had been a man of means. Expression sober, Saint Denis followed Aubry to the front door and waited while the detective lifted the knocker and let it fall.

A moment later, the door opened and a stern-faced older woman with reddened eyes looked out at them. "Monsieur Aubry," she said, her immediate recognition signaling that he must have been one of those who'd first responded to the tragedy. "And this is Monsieur Saint Denis?"

"Yes, madame," the detective replied.

She nodded and stood out of the way so they might enter. The house appeared to be of First Empire vintage, with clean neoclassical lines and a minimum of the fuss that had taken over interior decoration during the last few decades. "I am Madame Gaspard, the housekeeper. I will take you to see Madame Manigault. She is waiting in the parlor."

So, this formidable-looking woman was not

the widow. Saint Denis supposed he should have realized that; a home as fine as this one would of course have its household staff, especially since not everyone was as careless in their domestic management as he was.

When they entered the parlor, he received another surprise, for the woman sitting on the graceful divan with its curved back was far younger than he'd been expecting, probably no more than thirty. She wore a high-necked black gown, probably left over from mourning another family member, and although her thick reddish-brown hair hung in its nighttime plait over one shoulder rather than put up in a more formal style, she appeared remarkably composed.

She was also, he realized, strikingly lovely, with a graceful oval face and wide hazel eyes that were probably bright and lively when they weren't reddened by tears.

"Madame Manigault," Saint Denis said. "I am Antoine Saint Denis. I am so very saddened by your loss."

She glanced from him to Aubry, then back again. "Detective Aubry said you had been working with him on these terrible killings, and that possibly you would be able to offer some help."

Her voice was lower-pitched than he had expected, forthright when most women were trained to speak in soft, submissive tones. "Like cooing doves," his sister had joked to him once many years earlier, before their parents had begun subjecting her to a variety of "suitable" suitors.

This Madame Manigault certainly was no cooing dove.

"I have assisted the Sûreté on this case and several others, true," he said cautiously.

"And yet you still have no idea who this animal is who has been killing all these men?"

Aubry took a step forward. "We have several theories, but—"

"No," Saint Denis said simply, cutting him off. "I fear we do not. So far, we have not been able to determine what the connection is between the victims, if one exists at all." He paused and took in the woman's pale, composed face, the forthright way her gaze met his. "I was hoping that perhaps you might provide some illumination. Was your husband a devotee of the opera?"

"Yes," Madame Manigault replied. "He has held season tickets for many years, long before we were married. I believe his first wife was the one who introduced him to the opera."

Her comment seemed to confirm Saint Denis' suspicions that the current Madame Manigault must be a much younger second wife, since all of the victims had been quite a bit older than she, in their late fifties or early sixties. Such alliances weren't as common as they once had been, but it still wasn't terribly rare to see a couple where the husband was several decades older than his wife.

"Did you know Monsieur Saint Michel?" he asked next. "Or Monsieur Bertrand, or Monsieur Valois?"

She shook her head. "No, I am afraid not. But then, I did not go out in company with my husband all that often. He had his club, which he preferred to attend, and although he took me with him to the opera if he thought the production being offered was suitable, I did not accompany him all the time, however. He preferred that I stay at home."

Her words were accompanied by a fleeting flash in those long-lashed hazel eyes—what Saint Denis guessed was a flicker of anger, one she probably wished to keep hidden. So, there had been no love lost between her and her husband. Well, that would explain why she was so remarkably composed. Most women in a similar situation would have been in hysterics, but although she appeared upset, she also seemed to be completely in control.

"I see," he said, doing his best to contain his disappointment. While it would have been a boon to have her in possession of information the other widows did not, he supposed that was asking a bit much. "Well, then, can you try to tell me what happened?"

She folded her hands in her lap. A gold band glinted from the ring finger of her left hand, although the rest were bare. Of course, they would be. She had been awakened from her sleep to find a most hideous surprise waiting for her. She would not have been wearing any jewelry other than her wedding ring.

"I wish I could," Madame Manigault replied. "I was very deeply asleep. I heard nothing, saw nothing. Or rather, I was dreaming, and in my dream, it seemed as if there came an echo of a sound that should not have been. That was when I awoke, thinking I would get myself some water...and then I saw Frederick. There is quite a fine moon tonight, and it was shining through the window. I"—she paused there to pull in a breath, and reached up with a shaking hand to smooth the heavy braid that lay over one shoulder—"I saw the marks on his throat. Still, I tried to rouse him, but of course, he was already gone."

Good lord. Saint Denis had imagined the scene in his mind, and yet it seemed far more terrible now as recounted by the man's widow, her voice almost preternaturally calm. He realized then that she most likely was exerting such rigid self-control because otherwise, she would fly apart.

"Was there any easy way for an intruder to get in or out of the house?" Aubry asked then, notepad in hand.

"I don't believe so," Madame Manigault replied. "Although I think Madame Gaspard would know better than I."

The two men glanced over at the housekeeper. She was pale, but seemed to have taken her cues from her mistress, for her voice was steady enough as she responded, "The house was locked up tight, m'sieurs. I checked all the doors and windows, and none of them seem to have been disturbed."

Was this killer a new kind of phantom, one who could come and go like a ghost? Saint Denis frowned, pondering this perplexing conundrum, even as Madame Manigault spoke again.

"I fear this might be my fault," she said, then continued quickly, seeing both her visitors open their mouths to protest. "That is, I stepped out on the balcony before I went to sleep, so I might look at the moon. I should have locked the door behind me, but I cannot recall whether I did or not."

"That balcony is nearly twenty feet from the ground," the housekeeper put in at once, as if eager to defend her mistress. "I cannot see how an intruder could have come in that way, even if the door to the bedroom had been left unlocked."

Without bothering to respond, Saint Denis went over to the door in question and opened it so he might look on the balcony Madame Manigault had mentioned. It was larger than he had expected, with a wrought-iron set of chairs and a small table in between, and several pots filled with flowers he thought were begonias. Yes, the balcony was quite high off the ground, with a precipitous drop to the garden below...but it also had a large and well-established trellis of roses up against the wall to the right.

He peered at the trellis and its vining roses. Although the moon had moved on toward the west, its light was still bright enough that he thought he could detect several broken branches and buds here and there, as well as pieces of the trellis itself snapped in two. It seemed plausible enough to think the intruder had made his way into the house by that route.

No ghost at all, but a clever and resourceful killer.

Saint Denis rejoined the group inside. "I believe the intruder came up the trellis. That is why there would be no sign of him attempting to break in anywhere else in the house."

If possible, Madame Manigault went even paler. "So, it is my fault."

"Of course not," Saint Denis told her. "A simple oversight is certainly not enough to assign any blame. Even with the door left unlocked, you should have been perfectly safe. It is not your fault that a madman targeted your husband."

She did not protest, but the droop of her full mouth seemed to tell him she was still inwardly assigning blame to herself, even if she had decided it was not worth her energy to debate him.

"We will go down and inspect the trellis," Aubry said then. "For now, madame, it is probably better if you rest. There is no reason to think that the killer would return here, but I will have a gendarme sent over to guard the house so you will know you are safe even after Monsieur Saint Denis and I have gone. And if you can think of anything else, please contact me at once."

"I will, m'sieur," she replied, although her gaze strayed toward Saint Denis as she spoke, as if she wondered whether she would do better to reach out to him instead.

Well, he could not say he would mind if that turned out to be the case.

Before he could speak, she went on, "You

must find this villain. It is not right that one man can cause so much terror."

"We will do everything we can, madame," he said, and bowed. "But for now, let us continue our inspection. You have another room where you can sleep, I assume?"

A flush of color tinged her cheekbones, but she only nodded. "Yes, I will use one of the children's bedrooms. Frederick's children," she added. "They are all grown and married, but of course, their rooms are still here. Madame Gaspard will help me move my things."

Immediately, the question entered his mind — had she no children of her own with her late husband? — but Saint Denis knew better than to ask. Instead, he said that sounded like a very good idea, and then took his leave of her, Aubry trailing along as they went downstairs and outside to inspect the rose trellis.

Down on the ground, the damage was even more obvious. Several cross-pieces had been broken, as though the murderer had tried his weight on them and had them splinter under his feet before he determined the best way to ascend without causing further damage.

"So, we know the killer is agile enough to climb this trellis," Saint Denis observed as Aubry scribbled away on his notepad. "And he must be a fairly slender man, or he would have caused even more damage than this."

"But would a man with such a slim build be able to throttle his victims so effectively?" Aubry asked, his dubious expression obvious even in the moonlight. "Several of them were rather portly, and so their weights would have been quite at variance."

"Maniacs are often capable of feats of strength," Saint Denis replied. He recalled several such cases he had come across before, crimes that seemed implausible on paper but were successful because of the sheer frenzied strength of the murderer. "Perhaps this man is under the influence of some kind of drug—I have read that hashish can sometimes render its users quite maniacal."

This theory appeared to alarm Aubry, whose eyes widened, owlish, in the moonlight. "So, now we are contending with a drug-crazed madman?"

"I am only theorizing," Saint Denis said. "Still, we should not ignore any possibilities, no matter how outlandish they might seem." He stopped there and stared up at the trellis, eyes narrowed. Yes, it was all too easy to imagine the killer climbing up the wooden framework, grinding rosebuds under his feet as he went.

But how had he known that the door to the

balcony would be unlocked? Had he hidden himself on the property, watching and waiting until he saw the opportunity present itself? This prospect seemed the most likely, but he did not much like the idea of such a fiend lurking in the shadows, watching Madame Manigault as she stood there clad in her dressing robe.

Of course, now he was embellishing the situation. He could not know for sure that she had not been wearing her dinner gown when she stepped out to look at the moon, but from the way she had spoken, it sounded to him as if she had gone outside just before retiring for the night.

Either way, it was immaterial. Yes, the killer had probably watched her as she went outside, but clearly, she was of no concern to him, since he had left her sleeping peacefully while he committed the murder in silence. There certainly had been nothing in his past acts to indicate he intended to expand his repertoire of gruesome crimes by preying on helpless women.

A gentlemanly murderer, he thought with an inner chuckle. *I suppose it could be worse.*

"Well, now we definitely know how he gained entrance," Aubry said, although he didn't sound terribly cheery about acquiring that particular piece of information. "But I am not sure if we know much of anything else—in particular, why he would suddenly decide to start killing these men in their homes."

"Because he knew he was being observed in his hunting grounds at the opera," Saint Denis answered calmly. "You had the two gendarmes watching there last night, did you not? So, perforce, he must find a new way to eliminate his victims."

"Oh," said Aubry, looking more dejected than ever. "Which means we have accomplished little, save to terrorize a helpless woman in addition to losing yet another citizen."

Saint Denis supposed they could look at it that way—although he rather thought Madame Manigault was far from "helpless." And yes, it was frustrating to once again be called to the scene of the crime and still not be any closer to an answer as to how all these victims were connected.

But his was by nature an optimistic personality, and he told himself that this latest development, rather than a setback, was only another means to gaining greater understanding of their killer. He had been driven to come here because his usual hunting grounds were no longer safe. A driven man was often a reckless man.

And a reckless man made mistakes.

312 | CHRISTINE POPE

Erik glared down at the Paris *Presse.* Yet another killing, this one even more sensational than the former murders, as this crime appeared to have taken place in the man's own home.

Well, he thought sourly, *at least they are not trying to blame these killings on me anymore. The Opera Ghost was many things, but even he was not the sort to creep into a man's house and throttle him in his own bed.*

Still, something about the report unsettled him, and he tossed the paper aside and stood, going to the window so he could look out onto the small front garden. The day was bright and clear, showing no sign of the dark deeds that had been committed within the city limits the night before. Carriages passed by on the street, and a pair of pigeons strutted down the front walk, looking very self-important with their puffed-out chests.

He knew the real reason for his current disquiet had nothing to do with the news reports, and everything to do with the woman who had stalked down that same walkway only the day before. It had been foolish and mad of him to present such an ultimatum, but at the time, he had only been thinking that this impasse between him and Christine must end, that matters could not continue indefinitely in such a way.

Now, of course, he knew that it would have been far better to go on as they were, neither person choosing to acknowledge the tension building between them. Yes, better to have her in his life, uncomfortable as the situation had been, rather than to know she was gone forever.

Did it have to be forever, though? Yes, she was angry, and he knew better than to approach her at the Chagny town home and attempt to smooth matters between them, but Christine's was not the sort of soul to bear a grudge. Surely she would forgive him if he was contrite enough.

And yet, he did not know how he could possibly get close to her. Meg's wedding was now only two days hence, and he knew Christine would be much occupied with assisting her friend. Also, Erik had lost his little spy, the scullery maid Lise, and so he had no idea whether the comte was due to return in the immediate future. He must be, though; Christine had made it quite clear that her husband would be back in Paris in time to attend the Giry/Castelo-Barbezac nuptials, and so, even if he were not yet home, he would be very soon.

No, the whole situation seemed quite impossible. He would have to sit back, helpless, and wait while Raoul de Chagny returned to his wife's side, and they attended their friends' wedding…and then they went back to their home in the Loire Valley, far away from Paris and the Opera Ghost who had once haunted their lives.

His hands clenched into fists at his side. He was not used to feeling so impotent, and he found he did not like it much.

Quite the Opera Ghost you are, he mocked himself. *Once, you had the entire company of the Palais Garnier quaking at your every movement, and now you are to be flummoxed by that ridiculous fop of a count?*

There must be something he could do. Perhaps this was already a losing battle, and yet Erik vowed he would not go down without a fight. Because Christine was worth fighting for. If the end result of all this was only that she ended up telling him she could never care for him and would be nothing but a faithful wife to her husband to the end of her days, then at least it would all be well and truly over.

He would have his answer.

But how to see her, when the Chagny town home might as well be hidden behind a moat for how accessible it was?

He frowned. Better to approach Christine in public, in a place where there would be so many people crowding about that his presence there wouldn't be exceptional. A place where Raoul might be distracted, and perhaps would not even notice his wife speaking to a man who was a stranger to both of them....

At once, his frown reversed itself into a crooked smile beneath the mask. Why had he not thought of it before? After all, it was not as though he hadn't already gained entry to the place. Doing so again would not be terribly difficult.

Yes, it seemed that Meg Giry and Honoré de Castelo-Barbezac would soon have a very unexpected wedding guest!

CHAPTER 18

Many Returns of the Day

*T*ruly, Meg couldn't have been granted a more sublime day for her wedding than if she had interceded directly with the Divine to have things ordered perfectly. The sun shone in a clear blue sky only lightly dotted with clouds, the air had warmed to a point where shawls and cloaks certainly were not needed, and even the birds singing in the trees seemed to have modulated their songs so they would be that much sweeter.

The ceremony itself took place in Notre Dame, where the ancient cathedral was thronged with family and friends and well-wishers. When she entered the cathedral, a frisson of unease passed over Christine, for she could not forget her meeting there with the Opera Ghost, how she had seen for the first time the uncannily realistic mask he had created for himself. Indeed, she gave a quick, uneasy glance around her, as if thinking that he would be there, but of course she didn't catch even a single glimpse of that handsome, sharp-edged face.

After that first uneasy moment, she allowed herself to relax—but not too much, not so she would commit some sort of gaffe in front of all those watching people. And really, everything went quite smoothly, with a glowing Meg becoming the Baronesse de Castelo-Barbezac while Christine stood to one side, holding her friend's lavish bouquet of orchids and creamy-pale roses. In that moment, she thought again of her hasty wedding with Raoul, how not a single person who cared about them had been there to witness their joining. At the time, she had told herself it didn't matter, that she was with the man she loved and nothing else was of any true import.

But then she saw the doughty dowager Duchess de Montfort dabbing an eye as she watched her grandson from the front pew, and an equally misty-eyed Madame Giry sniffing into a handkerchief from the other side of the aisle, and Christine realized that these rituals were often as much for the people watching as they were for the two intimately involved in the ceremony. No, she had no mother to watch over her at her wedding, and no father, either, but Raoul had his sisters and his cousins and many, many friends who would most likely have preferred to be present for their joining.

Well, there was little either of them could do about it now. All the same, Christine found herself relieved when the ceremony was over and all the well-wishers had gathered at Honoré's home—now a home that would be shared by the happy couple—and the celebrations could commence. Truly, it seemed as if there were even more people present at the reception than there had been at the wedding itself, which she supposed shouldn't have surprised her all that much. Honoré had invited musicians and artists and actors to the festivities, and some of them might not have been terribly comfortable within the cathedral's grandeur and had instead chosen to appear once that part of the day was over.

There were those she recognized, of course —many of the members of the *corps de ballet,* as well as several who had been members of the company when she was a performer at the Opera. Their greetings to her were friendly enough, but she caught the sidelong glances and whispers, the murmurs which seemed to inform her that she was no longer considered one of them, not when she was now the wife of a comte with a glittering diamond on her finger and wearing a gown on her back that had probably cost more than most of them earned in a month.

Christine did her best to shrug off their reactions. After all, she had known, once she and Raoul had decided they must return to France, that it was very likely she would never again be able to mingle with the same people who had been her friends when she was a member of the opera chorus. The only reason why no one saw anything exceptional about her continuing friendship with Meg Giry was that the young woman in question had also elevated her standing in society, and so it was perfectly natural for the wife of a baron and the wife of a count to socialize.

Still, it was with some relief that Christine approached her friend, resplendent in her Worth gown, the more modest elbow-sleeved bodice she had worn for the cathedral ceremony now traded for a ballgown bodice that showed off the creamy curves of her shoulders, as well as the glinting diamond necklace around her throat. A gift from Meg's new husband, Christine guessed, since she knew she had never seen the extravagant piece before.

Christine had made a similar change in her attire, since the bridesmaids' gowns had also been created with a second bodice for evening wear. However, Honoré's two sisters had taken advantage of the gap between the ceremony and the reception to wear completely different gowns in darker shades that showed their coloring a bit more to their advantage, one in claret-colored silk, the other in a deep teal. It was clear that they were none too happy about the hues Meg had selected for the bridesmaids' gowns, although they had both claimed that they simply didn't think it would look well for all three women to be wearing identical dresses at the reception.

A man Christine didn't recognize stood next to Meg and her new husband. He was of middle height, with gray-flecked brown hair and brown eyes, and he seemed to be gesticulating about something, although precisely what, Christine couldn't be sure.

However, the stranger's eyes lit up when he caught sight of her, and he said, "Ah, the lady in question! What timing!"

Confused, she looked from the stranger to Meg, who smiled and appeared to take pity on her puzzlement, saying, "Christine, this is

Monsieur Gailhard, who has been the owner of the Opera for the past few years. He has a favor to ask of you."

"'A favor'?" Christine echoed, hoping she didn't sound as unenthusiastic as she felt. Not that she didn't like performing favors for people when she could, but she also didn't like to make promises until she knew what she was promising. She glanced around, wishing Raoul would come to her rescue. He had gone to fetch her some water, since the waiters circulating with their silver trays only offered champagne, but she had begun to wonder if he'd been waylaid by some acquaintance or another, since he was taking so long to return to her side.

Monsieur Gailhard bowed. "Madame la Comtesse, know that I would not ask such a thing if I were not in such a predicament. I know that you have been absent from the stage these past several years, but it is my hope that you will agree to sing at a charity performance the Opera is hosting two days from now. Mademoiselle Lamont, our reigning diva, is in bed with a sore throat, and it seems she will not be well enough to perform. Would you do me the honor of taking her place?"

Oh, no. Christine's hand went to her throat, fingers touching the cool surface of the choker of pink pearls and diamonds that rested at the base of her neck. How in the world could Meg have thought she would be willing to do such a thing? Bad enough to be pressured into performing at a private reception, but to have to stand upon the stage of the Paris Opera once again and show the world how woefully out of practice she was?

"I—I am not certain," she faltered. "That is, surely you have understudies who could take Mademoiselle Lamont's place?"

Monsieur Gailhard waved a dismissive hand. "An understudy will not bring in the audience we need to make the benefit a success. But to have the Comtesse de Chagny—the woman who left the stage in such a spectacular fashion only two years earlier—*that* will be quite the draw. Everyone will wish to hear you sing."

Not if they knew my voice is not what it once was, she thought then, although she realized she was being a bit disingenuous. Perhaps her form was not quite the same as it had been when her voice was at its peak, but her practice session with Erik only a few days earlier had proved to her that she was not as clumsy as she feared. *And if you had not had that row with him, then you could have asked him to work with you for the next several days, so you might be as polished as possible.*

Alas, that was not to be. She moistened her

lips, desperately thinking of the best way to respond.

"I know this is a great deal to ask of you, Madame la Comtesse," Monsieur Gailhard said. "And I do not do it lightly. But the recital is for the benefit of the Orphanage of Saint Vincent-de-Paul, and I do not like to think of those poor children suffering because we were not able to have a full house."

Oh, clever man. How had he known the precise way to pierce through her protests, to produce the one piece of persuasion most likely to sway her? For she was herself an orphan, even if she had been nearly an adult when her father passed. Still, she knew the heartbreak of losing both parents, of wondering what her place in the world would be without them to guide her. How could she say no when she had the power to make those children's lives even a little better?

She met Monsieur Gailhard's gaze and said, "I do not like to think of such a thing, monsieur, and yet I fear that my voice is not quite what it once was."

"Pish," said Meg, hands planted on her slender hips. "I heard you the other day at Honoré's reception, and you were wonderful. You've always been your own worst critic, Christine."

"And it is for the children," Honoré put in,

appearing at his bride's side with a glass of champagne in either hand. He gave one to Meg and then, looking a bit wistful, offered the other one to Christine.

She shook her head. "No, thank you, m'sieur. My husband has gone somewhere to fetch me some water, but he seems to have quite disappeared."

Relief spread over Honoré's features, and Christine had to hold back a chuckle. Clearly, he had no desire to relinquish his drink, and who could blame him? This was his reception, after all—he deserved that champagne.

"But yes," he went on, "I think it would be a wonderful thing if you were to perform at the charity gala. You must give us one last chance to hear your voice before you disappear into the wilds of the Loire once more."

From the way he smiled, blue-gray eyes glinting, Christine had the impression this wasn't his first glass of champagne. She said, her tone gentle, "The Loire Valley isn't quite as wild as you think, m'sieur."

He gestured with his champagne glass, barely avoiding slopping some of it onto his hand. "It is not Paris, madame la comtesse, and that is wild enough for me."

Meg sent him an indulgent look. "My Honoré likes to exaggerate. But truly, Christine

—it would be wonderful if you sang. Surely no one could object to you helping the orphans!"

By "no one," Christine assumed her friend meant Raoul. And no, he would not be likely to forbid her to sing, not when it was for such a worthy cause.

But then he had his chance to chime in, for he approached then, relief clear on his features upon seeing her standing there and speaking with their friends. "I am so sorry to abandon you for so long, my dear," he said as he handed her one of the glasses he held. "They had to send someone to the kitchen to fetch this water for us."

"That is because no self-respecting wedding guest should be drinking water at a reception," Honoré said reprovingly. But his smile didn't falter as he spoke, and Christine knew he was teasing them.

"Champagne doesn't agree with me," she said mildly. "Or at least, not any great amount of it. I am holding off so I may have some for the toast."

"Ah, well, that is a good enough reason for abstinence, I suppose." He tilted his head to one side, considering her, then Monsieur Gail-hard, who had been waiting patiently throughout their exchange. "Do say yes, madame. It would do such good for so many people."

"Say yes to what?" Raoul asked, now looking somewhat concerned.

"Monsieur Gailhard has asked me to sing at a charity gala at the Opera two nights hence, as their diva is ill," Christine replied. "I was not sure, since I am so out of practice, but — "

"Oh, no, you must do it," her husband broke in. "You sounded wonderful the other day, and not out of practice at all."

Those words should have reassured her, but they only awoke a stir of impatience. Raoul had never been anything but supportive of her singing, and yet his also wasn't the most discerning ear. He tended to praise everything he heard because he didn't want her to be discouraged. So unlike Erik, who appreciated her voice but also didn't scruple to tell her everything she had done wrong if a performance fell short of his exacting standards.

It seemed she had little choice in the matter. And if she ended up embarrassing herself, well… as Honoré had said, she would be back in the wilds of the Loire Valley soon enough. It wasn't as though she would have to show her face at any receptions or salons in Paris in the near future.

"Very well," she said, and Monsieur Gailhard's expression cleared, the frown disappearing from his brow.

"Excellent," he said. "You may choose the piece you wish to sing, madame, for it is your presence that will be the draw, and not any particular aria."

She smiled back at him, a bit relieved to hear those words. At least she could select something that she had practiced recently, and not a song she would be forced into because it was already on the program.

That matter settled, Monsieur Gailhard excused himself after saying he would send more information on the gala to the Chagny town house. From there, the conversation moved to a discussion of Meg and Honoré's honeymoon, which they planned to spend in Italy—"we shall have a whole month there!" her friend exclaimed in some excitement—and then to an exhibit by Degas that Honoré was very much looking forward to when they returned. Christine had no doubt that more paintings would soon adorn the walls of the house where she now stood, and she smiled to herself, just a little.

At the same time, however, she could not help but feel a bit melancholy. Meg and Honoré's busy social life would continue here in the capital —the receptions and exhibits, the outings to the opera and the theater and the ballet. They would host parties and balls, would occasionally venture out to the Bois de Boulogne so they might catch some fresh air and pretend to rusticate, if only for the day.

Christine could not help but contrast such a social whirl with the quiet life she and Raoul led on the Chagny estate. Oh, she had never been one to live a wild existence, going from party to party with nary a thought of anything more important, and yet she knew she missed the culture of Paris, all the myriad opportunities for music and art it offered. Things would be very different for her once she and Raoul returned to his ancestral lands.

Still, she managed to hide her doubts, and smile, and say the appropriate words at the appropriate times. Eventually, they were seated for dinner, a sumptuous feast of such surpassing variety and excellence that she wondered if she would be able to eat even a tenth of what was offered. Champagne after the meal and before the cake was served, and then at last, it was time for Meg and Honoré's guests to move on to the ballroom.

Christine danced the opening promenade with Raoul, and the quadrille that followed with Honoré, and several more with men she didn't know but recognized as friends of the happy couple. Although she had drunk only a very modest amount of champagne, she still felt half dizzy and strangely carefree and light on her feet at the same time, as if the bubbly liquor had the power to take her far beyond her worries and into a place where nothing mattered too terribly much.

A man approached her, tall and dark-haired, elegant in his tailcoat and white watered-silk vest. Something about him seemed familiar, but she couldn't say exactly what.

"Good evening, Christine," he said, and her eyes widened in shock even as he took her hand and led her to the dance floor, where couples were already assembling for the next waltz.

She would have known that voice anywhere. "Erik," she whispered, "what on earth are you doing here?"

The orchestra played the first chord of "The Blue Danube," and Erik bowed. There was nothing for her to do except curtsy in return, and then allow him to take her by her fingertips and place his hand on her waist as the music began. To do anything else would have been to cause a scene, and she hadn't forgotten herself enough to take that kind of risk.

As they began to twirl to the intoxicating music, he replied, "Why, I wished to attend the wedding of Mademoiselle Giry. She does look very beautiful, does she not?"

Christine could not argue with that statement. "Yes, she does," she agreed. "And she is very happy, which is even more important. But I cannot believe — "

"Cannot believe that I would show my face here?" Erik cut in, smiling.

And he was smiling. She realized that she had not recognized him at first because he had done something more to that oddly human-seeming mask, must have performed some sort of refinements to make it even more lifelike. The ballroom was lit by hundreds of candles, shimmering from both the crystal chandelier overhead and the sconces on the walls, and even in that warm, bright light, she could detect nothing about his visage that seemed at all unnatural. Before, he had been just slightly too pale, too expressionless, but now….

"An altered face, it seems," she observed, and he continued to smile.

"Yes, I used my time this past day or so to make a few adjustments. How do you like it?"

All the spinning around was making her dizzy…or perhaps it was only her nearness to Erik, her realization that he had never held her like this, his hand strong and heavy on her waist, the other holding her fingers with some firmness, but not enough to be uncomfortable.

Or rather, she was uncomfortable for a whole host of other reasons.

"It is…quite an accomplishment," she managed.

"An 'accomplishment,'" he echoed, his tone mocking. "I will admit that I was rather hoping for a stronger reaction than that."

Because of the way he held her as they danced, she couldn't precisely shrug. However, she said, "Well, what exactly did you expect of me, Erik, especially after how we parted the other day?"

His face went still. "I fear I must apologize for that. I should not have asked such a thing of you."

Of all the reactions she had expected from him, an apology was certainly the last. Unsure how to respond, she remained silent for a moment, then replied, "Perhaps I was somewhat harsh with you as well. Can we agree to be friends?"

"Of course," he said smoothly.

Relieved, she danced in silence with him for a few moments. As she spun around, she caught a glimpse of Raoul standing off to one side, the dowager Duchess de Montfort at his side, although it seemed his attention was focused solely on the dancers. On Christine and her partner, she realized with some discomfort, although she told herself there was no way in the world he could possibly recognize the man

she was dancing with as the Phantom of the
Opera.

Worry tightened her midsection, but she
made herself say, "I had no idea you could dance
so well. Wherever did you learn?"

"I didn't," he said, and his tone sounded
almost abrupt, as if he had also seen Raoul
watching them and did not know precisely how
to react. "Or rather," Erik went on, "I observed
others, and learned by watching. It was nothing
terribly difficult."

Not for a man who was a musical genius, to
whom music was the very air he breathed, the
water he drank. A thought struck her. Dangerous, perhaps, but now that they appeared to be
reconciled….

"Do you know, I have just agreed to sing at a
charity gala at the Opera in two days," she said,
doing her best to sound light and unconcerned
about the whole affair. "Something of a leap, and
nothing I would have agreed to if it were not to
benefit the orphans. But now I think it best if I
do whatever I must to be in the very best voice I
can be when I sing."

"Is that your way of asking if I will tutor
you?"

His voice was amused, and the false face he
wore appeared amused as well, if the way his
brows and a corner of his mouth lifted was any

indication. Christine chose to take his shift in expression as a sign that he was willing to entertain her request. "Yes," she said simply. "If you have the time."

"If I—" He stopped there and chuckled, as if amused by her comment, then continued in a lower voice. "And you will not have any difficulty meeting me for such tutoring sessions, with the comte now in town?"

True, Raoul's presence might present some impediment to such an arrangement, but she did not think they were insurmountable. "No, because I will tell him the truth. Not," she went on quickly, as Erik stared down at her in obvious surprise, "that I am meeting with the Opera Ghost, but that I am having a few sessions with Mademoiselle Lamont's voice teacher. Surely, Raoul will find nothing exceptional about that. Indeed, since you are so far altered from your usual self, and since you are living in an utterly respectable house, he could even follow me to discover where I have gone and would still not find anything amiss."

"It seems you have thought of everything."

"Not really," Christine replied. "I am not as clever as you, after all. But I think this plan should work."

For a moment, Erik continued to gaze down into her face. She could not begin to guess what he might have seen there, but he offered no protest, only said, "Very well. Shall we say two o'clock tomorrow afternoon for your lesson?"

"That would be excellent," she said. "My calendar is quite open, now that Meg's wedding is all but over. Indeed, we would have already been making plans to return to Chagny, if it were not that we now need to stay in Paris through Wednesday for the concert."

"Then, thank goodness for Mademoiselle Lamont's laryngitis," Erik observed.

Christine shot him a narrow glance tinged with suspicion. "How did you know that is what she is suffering from?" For she realized she would not have put it past him to do something that would affect the diva's throat so she would not be able to sing, and a replacement would have to be found. He had done something not so different to La Carlotta back in the day.

But he chuckled and said, "No, I had no hand in Mademoiselle Lamont's current illness. Only, even if I no longer have Box Five for my personal use, I still attend the opera on occasion, and pay some attention to the doings of its stars. That is how I know she has been ill."

This explanation sounded reasonable enough. Christine hoped it was true. Even if it were not, however, she had already told Monsieur Gailhard that she would sing, and had already asked for Erik's assistance. There was little she could do now except continue on her current course.

The waltz was reaching its conclusion, and so, now that they had made a plan, it seemed better to stay silent for the remainder of the dance. Erik spun her in one final, graceful twirl, and then they stopped. For one breathless moment, their eyes met, and a tremor went through her. It had been so easy to pretend when they were apart, but now….

He bowed and said, "I will see you tomorrow afternoon at two," then escorted her from the dance floor—not to the place where Raoul had been standing and watching with narrowed eyes, but to the opposite side of the room.

Another bow, and the Opera Ghost was gone.

CHAPTER 19

Concerts and Confidences

*H*e had paced back and forth so many times, it was a wonder he had not worn a hole in the carpet beneath his feet. The clock ticked heedlessly away on the mantel, indifferent to his impatience. Two o'clock was almost here, but not quite.

Not soon enough.

Erik still couldn't quite believe that Christine had agreed to this. After their exchange several days earlier, he had honestly thought he would never see her again—or at least, never see her in an intimate setting such as this. Perhaps there might have been a chance encounter on the street the next time she came to town, although he guessed the odds of such a thing happening would have been very low.

It is only her desperation, he told himself. *She does not wish to make a fool of herself in front of such a crowd.*

And perhaps he would have believed such a thing, once upon a time...only he had seen the look in her eyes as they finished their waltz. Longing...and confusion. Her soul had begun to recognize what it truly wanted, and she had no idea what to do about it.

Because he had experienced much the same inner torment, he could sympathize with her current predicament. Indeed, some part of him pitied her, pitied the impossible circumstances in which she found herself. At least he was not torn in two, his soul and heart pulled in opposite directions by those he cared about. His entire being was consumed by longing for Christine Daaé, and he did not wish to know how difficult it must be to feel that same emotion for two individuals at the same time.

Although...

He knew he flattered himself, but he had a notion that perhaps—just perhaps—she was beginning to wonder if she had made the wrong choice. Very possibly, his new mask had something to do with such a sea change. Some might ridicule her for feeling that way, for being so shallow that an alteration in appearance would be all which was required to initiate such a shift in perspective, but Erik was not one of them. He knew exactly what he looked like without the mask. No woman could be expected to love such a face. But if that face had a proper covering, then it would not distract from an understanding of the soul which lay beneath.

A knock came at the door, and he hurried to answer it. Outside stood Christine, radiant in a walking gown of heavy blue-gray faille. Her cheeks flushed with pink as she met his gaze. "Good morning, monsieur," she said politely, but in a voice that also would carry to anyone listening nearby. "I am here for my lesson."

Expression grave, he replied, "Good afternoon, Madame la Comtesse. Please, do come inside."

These conventions satisfied, he stepped aside so she might enter, then closed the door behind her.

"This way," he went on, and led her into the parlor. She followed, silken skirts rustling on the wooden floors. Even though she walked behind him, he couldn't help but be acutely aware of her presence, of the faint perfume of roses that seemed to accompany her everywhere she went, the faint *click-click* of her heels, the soft, whispery sound of her silk gown. Once they had entered the parlor and he'd gone to take his place at the spinet, he asked, "Did you have any problem getting away?"

Her cheeks flushed even pinker, if that were possible. "None at all," she said, her tone almost too airy. "I told Raoul that I needed some intensive practice for the next two days so I might be in my best voice for the gala, and he said that sounded like a very good idea, and that it was very kind of Mademoiselle Lamont's voice instructor to offer to assist me."

"Well, then," Erik responded, "I suppose we should get to work. Have you chosen a piece?"

"I thought I would stay with Juliet's waltz. Yes, quite a few people heard it at the baron's recital, but it is the piece I have sung most recently, and I thought I might as well polish something I am familiar with rather than having to start over from scratch."

This seemed like a practical enough plan, but Erik couldn't help saying, "Why not Marguerite's 'Jewel Song' from *Faust?* You know that one very well…and no one has heard you sing it recently."

A faint frown formed in the fine skin between Christine's brows. "You seem to be quite obsessed with *Faust,* Erik."

"'Obsessed' is, I think, too strong a word," he

told her, hoping he was correct in that assessment. "Rather, I know you sang it brilliantly several years ago...and I know that you know it. Would you not rather sing something at the gala that most people have not heard from you recently?"

This question made her frown deepen, and she appeared to ponder it for a few moments before she gave him a reluctant nod. "I suppose you are right," she said.

"Excellent." He went ahead and sat down on the piano bench; whatever he might have envisioned from this meeting, he knew that first and foremost, Christine must practice. There would be no repeats of her lackluster performance at the Baron de Castelo-Barbezac's reception the previous Sunday afternoon.

Because she knew the song so well, there was no need to do more than a quick run-through for both of them to refamiliarize themselves with the piece. After that, it was all about tightening her pitch here, working on her breathing there, making it so the song felt as though it was bubbling up from a deep inner well of joy.

Indeed, as she stood there in the middle of the rug, the blue of her dress reflecting the blue striped fabric panels on the walls, Erik could well imagine her as Marguerite, eyes glowing as she selected first one jewel from the coffer

Mephistopheles had left behind for her, and then another. Unfortunate that this was only a recital concert and not a full production of the opera, for he knew he would very much like to see her again gowned in the fashions of a time long gone, golden headdress and earrings and necklaces adorning her fair form.

"Very good," he said, when she had completed her third run-through. "It is almost there. I thought I detected the faintest hint of breathiness in the '*Marguerite, ce n'est plus toi*' phrase, so let us begin a few bars before that section and see if we can work on that."

She nodded, gaze intent. He thought he loved her the most when she was like this, her entire being focused on the music, on burnishing it so that it became just as perfect as she was.

Which was why, of course, she should be with him, and not that insipid comte.

No time to focus on that particular thorn in his side, however. Or rather, Erik would have the luxury of such brooding once Christine returned to the Chagny town house. For the moment, it was the music, and only the music.

They ran through the questionable section three more times, and then returned to the beginning of the piece. This time, it sounded flawless from start to end, the notes ringing through the room as if they had drifted down from heaven above.

When she finished, Christine gave him a halfway questioning glance, as if she thought she had done very well but wanted his corroboration before she spoke.

"You have lost nothing in these two years," he said. "In fact, I believe your voice may even be stronger for having lain fallow during that time. I do not think you should have any worry of embarrassing yourself tomorrow evening… quite the opposite, actually."

She smiled, but he detected some anxiety in her clear blue eyes. "And so you do not think I should come for another lesson tomorrow?"

In a way, her worry pleased him. It meant that, like him, she wished to spend as much time in his presence as she could before she was whisked away to the Chagny estate. "That is not what I said," he replied evenly, making sure his inner eagerness for such a meeting did not reveal itself in his tone. "I think more practice can only help. If nothing else, it will serve to limber your voice so it is in peak form for the gala performance. Perhaps we should meet a little later in the afternoon. Would four o'clock be suitable?"

"Very suitable," she said. "That is, the gala is at eight, and Monsieur Gailhard sent me a note

344 | CHRISTINE POPE

this morning informing me that I should be at the opera no later than seven."

"Which will give you enough time to be ready, and to eat a light meal beforehand. Lean meat, and greens, and water. No alcohol, or anything with sugar."

That fetching dimple appeared next to her rosy mouth. "I know, Erik. This is not my first performance."

"I realize that, but I thought it better to remind you, since it has been several years since you were on the stage." He paused there, then said quietly, "And what will you be doing after the performance?"

Her fingers played with a fold of her elegantly draped overskirt. "Oh, Monsieur Gailhard said there would be a reception at the Opera, so I suppose Raoul and I will attend that. And afterward...." A breath that was not quite a sigh escaped her lips. "We will return to Chagny the next morning. There is still much to be done with the vines, and Raoul is anxious to return."

Of course he is, Erik thought savagely. *For it must always be about what he wants, what he needs. Has the bastard ever stopped to ask Christine what it is she wants?*

But he was not given a chance to speak — probably a good thing — for she went on, "And

that will be the end, I think, for I do not antici-
pate us returning to Paris any time soon."

His heart wrenched. When confronted with
the reality of losing her forever—again—he
found he could not be quite so dispassionate as
he had been a few minutes earlier when he was
alone. Perhaps it was only being with her,
hearing her speak, hearing her sing, that made
the sense of loss so much more profound.

Perhaps she had an inkling of what had
passed through his mind, for she said quietly,
"Really, Erik, what did you think was going to
happen? My life is far away from here. I cannot
change what it is."

The words escaped his lips before he could
stop them. "You could tell Raoul that his over-
seers should manage the vines, and that you
want to remain in Paris."

No protest, only a sad smile as she crossed
the distance that separated them and laid a
gentle hand on his arm. "And what would such
an ultimatum do, except torture us both
further?"

"So, you admit this is torture for you as well."

For a few painful seconds, she remained
silent, those forget-me-not eyes fixed on his face.
"It is…difficult," she said at last. "I had thought
I'd left you well and truly behind me when I
departed Paris two years ago. I thought…I

suppose I thought many things. But no matter what I may be thinking, it does not change the fact that I am the Comtesse de Chagny, and that I have duties and responsibilities I cannot shirk."

Was she admitting she felt a sense of duty toward Raoul de Chagny, and nothing more? No, Erik guessed that she loved the man and did not wish to hurt him. He could not have expected anything else from her. Had he not admitted to himself only a few days earlier that he would not care for her so much if he knew she was capable of being untrue to the man she had married?

He supposed he had. In that moment, he experienced a sense of great weariness, as if the weight of the world had suddenly doubled itself upon his shoulders.

"I understand," he said. How he wished he could reach out for her, could pull her close and kiss those lovely pursed lips. He would not be able to feel them precisely, for the mask would not allow him to experience much in the way of physical sensation, but it would still be enough to hold her in his arms, to breathe in her beauty and let it fill his soul.

But he would not do such a thing, for it would destroy the fragile trust she had in him. She knew what was in his heart, but she also knew he would never force the issue, would never betray her trust.

No, he would go listen to her sing at the gala the next night, would pay homage to her beauty and her brilliance…and then he would let her go. To do anything else would not be worthy of her.

She must have glimpsed the shifting emotions in his expression, for she said quietly, "I will see you tomorrow at four," and left the room. A moment later, the front door shut with a soft *thud*.

One more day, he told himself fiercely. *You will be able to see her, to hear her, for one more day. It is not quite over.*

But it would be soon enough…and he had no idea what he would do after that.

"Lady to see you, sir," said Jean-Louis, in an echo of his introduction of the Comtesse de Chagny the week before.

However, the woman who entered Saint Denis' office was definitely not Christine, but Madame Manigault. She wore black from head to toe, as befitted a woman who had lost her husband so recently in tragic circumstances, but she did not appear all that bereaved. Now there was color in her cheeks, her auburn hair was styled simply but elegantly, and her hazel eyes met his directly as he stared at her in some astonishment.

Remembering his manners, he got up from the chair behind his desk and went toward her, even as he inclined his head toward Jean-Louis, dismissing the boy. "Madame Manigault," Saint Denis said. "What an unexpected pleasure."

"It is very irregular, I know," she replied. In one kid-gloved hand, she held a leather folder. She extended it to him, saying, "I was going through my husband's papers, and I found some items that perhaps you might find of some relevance."

Startled, he took the folder from her. "Please, do sit down," he said, indicating the chair in front of his desk, still resting there from the time the Comtesse de Chagny had used it.

Madame Manigault nodded and sat down, black silk skirts spreading around her. "I thought I might as well begin to go through Frederick's papers," she went on. "The funeral is tomorrow, and once that is over with and the will is read, I know I will need to start packing my things."

"I beg your pardon?" Saint Denis asked. "Surely no one would expect you to move from your house so soon after such a tragedy."

An ironic smile touched her full mouth. "Oh, but you have not met my stepson. He will wish to take possession of the house as soon as possible, so I thought I might as well sort through the items that I know Charles will have no wish to handle. There are a great many papers having to do with the house and his father's finances, and of course, I will leave those behind. However, I also found some correspondence and other items from the time that Frederick was a patron of the Opera, and so I thought you might be interested in those, since some of your articles seemed to indicate that you thought the Opera Ghost might be connected to these terrible killings."

"I was not aware your husband was so intimately connected with the Palais Garnier," Saint Denis said, interest sparking within him. He longed to open the folder and immediately begin rifling through its contents, but he knew to do so would be rude while Madame Manigault remained in his office.

"Oh, he is—was—not any longer," she replied. "I believe he stopped his patronage when the Opera changed hands. At least, that is the impression I had, although Frederick did not discuss all his business dealings with me."

"I see." And because the promise he had made to the Comtesse de Chagny still weighed heavily on his mind, Saint Denis found himself saying, "And it turns out there is no connection to the Opera Ghost. The man in question passed away several years ago, in fact."

This new information seemed to disappoint Madame Manigault, for her mouth drooped slightly and she said, "Then perhaps these papers I have brought have no significance at all."

"Do not be so certain of that," he told her. "I have often found that the most unlikely pieces of information can have the greatest bearing on the solution of a mystery. Have no fear that I will study them very carefully. And also, the Opera must have some importance to the killer, or he would not have committed so many of his murders so nearby."

For a moment or two, she did not respond, only seemed to study him, as if she wished to confirm something to herself of his character. The faintest amused glint appeared in her hazel eyes as she remarked, "I find it interesting that you are not a detective, Monsieur Saint Denis, since you seem so dedicated to solving crimes."

He allowed himself a chuckle. "Oh, I just barely remain respectable by being a newspaperman. I fear my family would disown me entirely if I went to work for the Sûreté."

Her mouth curved. "Ah, I see now. You are a gentleman only playing at being a reporter."

"No, madame, I assure you that I am not 'playing' at all." Their gazes met, and he found himself wondering what circumstances had led her to marry a man so much her elder, whether she had ever dreamed of a different life for herself.

Whether she wondered what her future would hold…now that she was free.

Faint color touched her cheeks. "I am sorry, monsieur," she said. "I did not mean to offend you."

"I am not offended," he replied, still watching her directly. "But I thought I should clear the air."

"Of course." She sat there for a moment, oddly irresolute. But then she seemed to come to a decision, for she stood and said, "I will not keep you any longer. I do hope you will find something of worth in those papers."

"I'm sure I shall," he said. "Thank you very much for thinking of me, Madame Manigault."

Her eyes met his, steady and unblinking. "You may call me Elise."

And then she was gone, leaving a faint trace of lavender behind her.

Saint Denis stared at the door to his office, mind humming with possibilities he might not have considered even a half hour before.

No matter what, he knew he would find a way to let her know exactly how his investigation ended.

Tonight, he thought. *It will all end tonight.*

The announcement in the paper had brought him the unexpected but joyous news. A gala concert at the Palais Garnier, starring Madame la Comtesse de Chagny, the former Christine Daaé. Everyone who was anyone would be attending...among them the quarry he had sought for so long, finally within his reach.

He had almost given up hope, almost decided that a complete revenge would be utterly out of reach. Now, though, he had only a few hours left before he achieved the peace he'd thought he would be forever denied.

His eyes closed as he imagined the garrote slipping around his final victim's unsuspecting neck, the futile gasping breaths that would follow...the man's eyes finally shutting as his useless life drained away.

Yes, as a wise man had once said, that was a consummation devoutly to be wished.

But first, to prepare. Whiskers trimmed, hair combed and slicked back with pomade, his evening clothes brushed and free of any distracting specks of lint. He had held on to the garments all this time, as if some instinct had told him that he might need to pass among his former peers again one day.

When he inspected himself in the mirror, he thought he had done very well. Thinner than he used to be, true, so the shoulders of the tailcoat drooped slightly and the hems of his trousers pooled upon his newly blacked shoes, but still respectable enough. If anything, the loss of those pounds had altered his face enough that even those who had known him once upon a time might not recognize him at first glance…and he intended to be stealthy enough that none of them would get more than a single glimpse.

He coiled the garrote tightly and placed it inside the inner breast pocket of his tailcoat. For a moment, his gaze lingered on the pipe and the block of hashish that sat upon it, but decided it would be better not to indulge. His wits needed to be sharp. Dulling them with narcotics was not a good idea.

A whistle escaped his lips as he went out the door and locked it behind him. Dusk had already fallen, and a bruised-looking twilight lingered over the city. He breathed deeply of the cool night air, letting it flow through him. Yes, he was ready.

Time to kill.

CHAPTER 20

The Point of No Return

*A*ntoine Saint Denis stared down at the muddle of papers before him and let out an exasperated breath. It had been his every intention to go through the file Elise Manigault had given him as soon as she left his office, but he had been called out to cover a house fire in Belleville, and then there had been a shockingly brazen robbery at a jewelry store on the Champs Elysées, and between one thing and another, he had not been given the opportunity to truly sit down and begin reading through Frederick Manigault's papers until very late in the day.

In fact, it was already so late that most

everyone had gone home, and the clock ticking on the mantel told him the hour was nearly eight o'clock. No wonder he was so hungry. At another time, he would have gotten up from his desk and gone to the café at the end of the street to order something he could bring back to the office, but he found himself disinclined to such a plan. The thought of eating alone at his desk once again felt intolerable.

He wondered what Elise Manigault was doing. Perhaps finishing her own solitary meal, or perhaps she had eaten much earlier. Had she gone back to packing up her late husband's belongings, or had she abandoned the enterprise, knowing she needed to save her strength for the ordeal of the funeral the next day?

Thinking of her alone in that large, coldly elegant house only served to increase Saint Denis' dissatisfaction with his current situation. It would be much better, he thought, to take her to dinner somewhere, to see if he could once again awaken that amused glint in her smoky hazel eyes.

Of course, even imagining such a situation was completely absurd. Elise would be in deep mourning for at least six months, and certainly not in a position where she could go out to restaurants or do much of anything except attend church services and perhaps allow herself quiet visits to the homes of friends and family.

And yet…he could not quite let go of the memory of her smile.

Annoyed with himself, he opened the leather folder she had given him and began sorting through the papers inside. As she had said, it seemed to be paperwork from the time Frederick Manigault had been a patron of the Opera. He had paid handsome sums each year for the past fifteen, stopping two years earlier, when the Comte de Chagny was killed by the Opera Ghost and the managers were forced out, to be replaced by Monsieur Clement Gailhard. There were quite a few letters exchanged between Monsieur Manigault and Monsieurs Richard and Moncharmin, the former managers, mostly about trifles such as upgrading Manigault's box seat and attendance at various dinner parties the managers had hosted.

In fact, one of those letters had a list of the patrons invited to that winter's New Year's soirée. Saint Denis stared down at it for a moment, wondering why those names should sound so familiar.

His body seemed to comprehend for a second or two before his brain caught up, for his heart began to pound irrationally in his chest at the sight of those names.

Dear God.

They were all victims of the Rue Scribe killer. Or at least, all but the last name on the list.

He was here in Paris now. Which meant....

Which meant it was only a matter of time.

Saint Denis ran a hand through his hair, mind working furiously. He must go and warn the man, that much was clear. But warn him of whom?

Who would hold such a grudge against those former Opera patrons that he would wish them dead in a gruesome and very public fashion?

Perhaps it would be wise to get in contact with the previous managers. Monsieur Moncharmin now lived in the countryside near Chartres, and Monsieur Richard....

Saint Denis' thoughts came to an abrupt, hideous stop. The gentleman in question had suffered a nervous collapse after the scandal at the Opera, had been sent to a sanatorium in Basel. Presumably, that was where he still resided to this day...but what if he didn't?

What if he had returned to Paris to wreak his revenge on those he viewed as destroying the life he had once lived? For once the scandal broke, the patrons had all withdrawn their support, and the managers had been forced to sell the Opera at a terrible loss.

The simplest way to determine if his hunch

was anywhere close to the truth of the matter would be to find out exactly which sanatorium had been chosen as Monsieur Richard's place of rest and recovery, and then to send them a telegram to discover if he in fact still resided there.

But that plan would take some time. It was very unlikely that Saint Denis would be able to get at the truth before the next day. And in the meantime...

...in the meantime, Monsieur Richard—if he truly was the killer—could strike again, attacking his final victim.

No, better to follow his hunch and look a fool if he should be proved wrong.

Saint Denis got up from his desk, drew on his coat, and hurried out.

He only hoped he wasn't already too late.

———

Erik had just finished knotting his tie to his satisfaction when a knock came at the front door. He turned at once away from the mirror, frowning. His tenure in the house hadn't extended for even a fortnight yet, and in all that time, the only people who had come to his home —besides Christine—had been the delivery boys from the butcher and the baker, or from the local cafés when he was not inclined to cook his own meals.

But all those delivery people had come to the back entrance off the kitchen, not the front door.

Frown deepening, he wondered if he should ignore the knock. Then it came again, sharper this time, four knocks instead of three. The decisiveness of those knocks told him that whoever was out there did not intend to go away soon.

He muttered a curse under his breath and went downstairs, gathering up his evening cloak as he went. The feel of the heavy wool draped over his arm reminded him of the cloak he had worn when he first took Christine to his home beneath the opera house, and a pang went through him. So many years of effort had gone into building that place, so many stratagems had been involved in transporting his furniture down there stick by stick.

And now it was all gone, burned to ash.

The taste of bitterness was strong in his mouth. As much as he wanted to see Christine sing tonight, he knew it would be the end between them. A spark had been rekindled—or perhaps had really kindled for the first time—but he knew they could not allow it to grow into a true flame.

When he flung open the front door, shock flared in him. Standing on the front step was none other than the Persian, green eyes level under the gray brows, brows nearly the same color as the hat of curly lamb he wore upon his head.

"Good evening," said the Persian, calm as if he had been invited rather than appearing out of nowhere. "I was hoping I might speak with you."

"I was just on my way out," Erik replied, not bothering to hide the sharpness of his tone.

The daroga inclined his head, as if he had been expecting such an answer. "To the Opera?"

Erik might have asked how the other man had known such a thing, but where else would he be headed at that time of night, wearing evening attire and carrying an opera cloak?

"Yes," he said. "And I do not wish to be late."

The Persian did not even blink. "You have plenty of time. And this will not take very long."

Once again, curses bubbled to Erik's lips, but he knew that arguing would only waste more precious minutes. Better to let the man have his say and be done with it.

He stepped aside, allowing the daroga to enter the house. Since it did not seem appropriate to hold their conversation in the foyer, he went into the parlor, where the Persian took a quick, appraising look around, as if to familiarize himself with his surroundings.

"You have done very well for yourself,"

observed the daroga, to which comment Erik only shrugged.

"It is comfortable enough. What do you want?"

"You are going to see Madame de Chagny sing tonight, are you not?"

"Yes. What of it?"

The Persian did not reply at once. Instead, he stood there for a long moment, gaze intent, clearly taking in the further refinement of the mask Erik wore. At last the daroga said, with a gesture toward the false face that covered his friend's true features, "Do you think that is going to change anything?"

Oh, but it has, Erik thought. *It has changed a great deal…only not quite enough.*

"If you are referring to my friendship with Madame de Chagny," he said coldly, "then no. If you are speaking of how I comport myself in the world, then yes, it has changed everything. As you see, I can now live as a normal man. I can rent a house, I can go to a café, I can walk down the street without worrying that I will send women screaming and risk imprisonment yet again."

Pity stirred in the other man's face, and he said, "Yes, I can see how all that might make a great deal of difference to you. But as for this other thing…what do you hope to accomplish by going to the charity gala at the Opera this evening?"

In that moment, Erik realized the daroga had come to his house tonight out of concern for a man he had once counted as a friend, worried that the erstwhile Opera Ghost might attempt some kind of spectacular stunt like the one he had pulled off two years earlier. The anger within him cooled, and he knew then that all he had to do was give the Persian the simple truth. And because the man had once been a chief of police back in his home country, and possessed very good instincts when it came to knowing whether someone was lying or not, he would recognize that truth for what it was.

"I am going to say goodbye," he said, the sadness in those words clear. "It will be my last chance to hear Madame de Chagny sing, for she travels tomorrow to her husband's estate near Tours, and I have no belief that she will ever return to Paris. It is a way to put an end to this thing."

Several moments passed, during which the ticking of the clock on the mantel seemed preternaturally loud, like the awful *click* of a death-watch beetle, counting down the seconds until the only love he had ever known died an ignominious death.

At last the Persian said, "I am very sorry, Erik."

"Do not be sorry," he replied at once. "Just let me go, and make an end of it."

"Of course." The other man turned, as if to make his way to the door, then looked back at Erik, jade-hued eyes piercing. "And what will you do after that?"

Erik shrugged. "Learn how to live like an ordinary man."

Christine stood backstage, willing herself to remain calm, to not allow her heart to begin speeding up, to tell her mouth it could not turn dry. After all, she had done this sort of thing many times before. As part of a full production, true, with the support of her fellow cast mates and the knowledge that she would not be alone on the stage, but still.

The opera chorus had just finished singing Handel's "Zadok the Priest." Now Monsieur Gailhard was approaching the stage, making another speech about the orphanage and how he hoped that all who had already donated so generously by attending that evening would open their hearts and their purses once again.

Christine ran a nervous hand over her skirt,

smoothing the fabric. Thank God that she had allowed Meg and Monsieur Worth to talk her into commissioning another evening gown, although at the time, she hadn't thought she would need yet another one, not when she planned to retire to the country very soon.

But even if she didn't feel as though she was ready for this moment, she knew she appeared the part in her elaborately draped gown of midnight blue silk with its jet trim. At least no one observing her would think she looked like an impostor.

Which you are not, she told herself severely. *You are here at Monsieur Gailhard's express request, and Erik himself told you this afternoon that he had never heard you in finer voice.*

She did not want to think of that session, however. Raoul had suspected nothing, had wished her well as she left the house and took a carriage to Erik's home in the Marais. And truly, there had been nothing exceptional in their meeting, as if both she and Erik had come to an agreement that everything which needed to be said had been spoken already, and now they needed only to focus on her performance that evening.

"You look absolutely stunning, my darling," Raoul said, and she started, then turned to give him a belated smile.

"Thank you, Raoul," she replied. He had given her much the same compliment before they left the house earlier, but perhaps he had detected her nervousness and wanted to make sure she had his praise ringing in her ears as she stepped out onto the stage. She went on, "I think I had forgotten how grand the Palais Garnier is, and just how many people are sitting out there, watching."

He came close and placed a kiss on her cheek —but gently, so he would not disturb the powder and rouge she wore for her performance. "It is nothing you have not done before," he told her. "You must remind yourself of that."

In response, she reached over so she might take his hand in hers and give it a gentle, appreciative squeeze. How dear he was, really, how thoughtful...most of the time. It was not his fault she wanted something from this life that he could not possibly provide.

"And remember," he went on, "I will be standing here in the wings, listening and watching. You will do splendidly."

For he had decided, because he knew she was worried about this performance, that he would forego the box Monsieur Gailhard had reserved for him and instead remain off to one side backstage so he might be close to his wife. Christine had told him that such a sacrifice was not necessary, but Raoul had insisted, saying he would have a better vantage point from his spot in the wings than he would stuck in a box far away from the stage.

"I hope so," was all she said, but she hoped he could see from her expression that she was grateful for the support he'd provided.

Then Monsieur Gailhard said, "And now is the moment you have been waiting for. Here is Madame Christine de Chagny, who will sing the 'Jewel Song' from *Faust* for us."

There was her cue. Christine sent Raoul a smile, and he smiled and nodded in return. She stepped onto the stage, her long trained skirt rustling behind her, and tried not to blink at the brilliant lights illuminating the stage. Had they always been that bright? She couldn't recall.

In a way, the lights shining into her eyes helped to allay some of her nervousness, because she couldn't see the audience clearly, could only make out a dark, moving blur, a blur from which a thunderous sound of applause emerged. Should they be clapping so loudly when they hadn't even heard her sing yet?

No matter. Monsieur Gailhard came up to her and thanked her for graciously agreeing to perform, and she dipped a small curtsy in reply, to the sound of more applause. Then he stepped away, and she was left alone on the stage, those bright lights seeming to burn into her eyes.

The orchestra launched into the lively opening bars of the aria, and she took in a breath. This was the moment where she had to leave everything behind except the music, to think of nothing else but the notes and the way her voice would shape them.

The first trill of the aria emerged from her throat, clear and ringing to the very rafters of the auditorium. She found herself smiling as she sang, *"Ah! je rit, de me voir…."*

And she knew all would be well.

What madness was this? Why was the Comte de Chagny not in the box that had been given him?

It should have been so simple. He should have been able to slip in, drop the garrote around the unsuspecting man's neck, and then be on his way long before anyone discovered the body.

But the box was empty, with no sign that anybody had occupied it at all that evening—no program left behind, no discarded gloves or coat.

Damn it, where was the man?

He had learned of the location of the comte's seat from one of the ushers, a woman who had clearly been hired after he left the Opera, for he did not recognize her. Such a simple ploy—he had told the woman he was an old friend of the comte and wished to stop by his box and offer his congratulations on the comtesse's return to the Opera, and the unsuspecting usher had told him exactly which box to visit.

Only the comte was nowhere to be found.

Scowling, he exited the box and stood outside, irresolute. It seemed inconceivable to him that Raoul de Chagny would not be present to hear his wife sing, so he must be somewhere within the opera house.

His own seat was far back on the orchestra level. Certainly not an optimal placement, but since he had acquired the ticket by the simple means of attacking the man who carried it and stealing it from his pocket before he hid the body in an alleyway off the Rue Scribe, he realized he couldn't be too choosy. He'd needed that ticket to gain entrance to the auditorium, since he dared not create any kind of disturbance before he was safely inside.

He made his way to his seat as Christine began to sing. In the part of his mind which was still capable of rational thought, he found himself somewhat surprised that she should be in such good voice after two years of rusticating. Had she retained the services of a coach or teacher whilst in Paris? That seemed the most plausible explanation for the artistry he heard now.

But her performance was immaterial. She could have sung with the voices of men and angels, and it would have done nothing to shake his resolve.

No, he wanted to know what the devil had happened to her husband.

Just as he was about to take his seat—since he did not know what else to do—he caught a glimpse of movement at the far left of the stage. A glimmer of something pale.

His gaze sharpened, and he realized that glimmer had been a white shirt front and white waistcoat. Someone was standing off in the wings, watching as Christine sang.

Not merely "someone," however. The Comte de Chagny.

Triumph surged in his heart, and he headed away from his seat, moving quickly toward the front of the hall. From there, he made his way backstage. No one stopped him, for he walked with such purpose that any stagehands who saw him thought he must have permission to be there.

The garrote leapt into his fingers, coiled, ready to be used for its final, wonderful purpose.

He approached the man from behind, and cleared his throat. The comte turned toward him, expression puzzled...until recognition began to dawn in his eyes.

"Hello, Monsieur le Comte," said Monsieur Richard.

The only seat Erik had been able to procure for the gala performance was off to the side, toward the front of the orchestra level. No longer could he make any claim to his beloved Box Five, and the thought that he would have to be sitting down there cheek by jowl with all the other concert-goers rankled.

And yet, at the same time, there was something oddly satisfying to be seated there in the thick of things, to not have anyone in the audience give him a second glance as he sat down... save, perhaps, the handsome woman of around his own age, who gave him an appreciative glance before she returned her attention to the program she held.

The new mask was serving him very well, it seemed.

The preamble to Christine's performance was tedious at best—several pieces performed by the *corps de ballet,* their quality definitely not what it was when Meg Giry had been among the company. Songs from the chorus, who were in fine voice but who also seemed to be quite aware that they were not the main event.

But then Christine walked on stage after an unctuous introduction by Monsieur Gailhard, the current opera manager, and Erik had to prevent himself from moving forward so he would be perched on the edge of his seat. Doing so would be very bad form, and so he sat there, expression neutral—easy enough to accomplish while he wore the mask—as he attempted to ignore the need within him. Oh, but she was beautiful in that dark blue gown with its jet beaded trim, sapphires gleaming around her white throat, jet combs shimmering from within the masses of her warm chestnut hair.

He thought he glimpsed a certain sadness in her eyes, although perhaps he was only fooling himself. And indeed, as the orchestra crashed its way through the lively opening bars of the piece, her blue eyes seemed to light up from within, and she smiled, dimples showing in her cheeks. He guessed that she was imagining herself as Marguerite, adorned with the gold and jewels that Mephistopheles had left behind to tempt her.

And oh, how magnificent her voice as she lifted it in the trill that began the aria, how sure and strong and clear. He had hoped she would sound like this—her practice earlier that afternoon had seemed to indicate her performance would be an utter triumph—but he hadn't known for sure. Her doubt and worry could have returned, and she could have sabotaged herself despite all their preparations.

But it seemed his fears had been for naught. As he listened, he wondered if this was also her way of saying goodbye, of giving him one last gift of her voice before she left his life forever. Tears started to his eyes, but he forced them back, knowing that weeping could damage his mask.

An odd sound came to his ears then, beyond Christine's voice and the swell of the orchestra. Something like feet scuffling, a man's tortured groans. It seemed to be coming from the wings.

As Erik stared, two men staggered out from behind the curtains. One of them was Raoul de Chagny, while the other —

Was it? Yes, haggard and thin and with a terrible, feverish light in his eyes, but the man was still recognizable as Firmin Richard, one of the former opera managers. He was tugging on something.

A garrote. A garrote around the comte's neck.

In the next moment, Christine let out a piercing shriek, stopping just before the aria's final triumphant notes. She ran toward the two men, hands reaching out to pull Richard away from her husband.

The erstwhile opera manager dealt her a backhanded blow and she staggered away, falling to her knees as the horrified audience gasped. Rage pounded in Erik's ears, blind red fury.

Without thinking, he pushed himself up from his seat and ran toward the stage, not caring who he shoved out of the way in his headlong flight. He scrambled up onto the platform and went immediately to Richard, who had pulled the garrote tight around the gasping, groaning comte's throat.

No, Erik did not have the Punjab lasso with him, but there were many other ways of killing a man. He caught hold of Richard's chin and the back of his head, and gave his skull one quick, sharp twist to the side. A satisfying *crack* told him he had succeeded in snapping the opera manager's neck, and indeed, the man immediately released his hold on the garrote and slumped to the stage, lifeless eyes staring up at nothing.

A sobbing Christine approached as Erik carefully lifted the garrote from around Raoul's neck. The man's tortured breathing told him that his windpipe had been crushed; already the comte's eyes were beginning to shut.

Christine sank to her knees and took her husband in her arms, tears dropping onto his slack features. Her gaze met Erik's with terrible hope.

Hating to crush that hope, he paused. But then he shook his head, knowing there was no consolation he could give her that wouldn't be a lie, and she let out a sob so wretched, it sounded as if it had been torn from her slender throat.

Oh, how he wished he could take her in his arms, offer her what comfort he could! There would already be far too many questions in the aftermath of such a tragedy, however, and so he slowly backed away as Monsieur Gailhard and several of the stagehands rushed over to where Christine clung to the body of her dead husband.

Like the ghost he had once been, Erik vanished from the scene.

EPILOGUE

Seven months later...

A shadow filled the doorway of Antoine
Saint Denis' office, and he looked up
from the scattered papers on his desk to see Elise
Manigault standing there, a faint smile on her
full lips.

"You haven't forgotten our appointment,
have you?" she asked.

"Of course not," he replied as he laid down
his pen. "It is just that I wanted to set down
some more notes before I sent the book off to the
publisher."

"It is tremendously exciting," she said. "I
don't think I know anyone who has written a
book."

It was his turn to smile. He rose from his

chair and said, "Well, now you do."

The volume had been written as quickly as he could, for he had not wanted the scandal to die down utterly before the story was published. At the same time, it had been the work of several months to retrace Firmin Richard's steps, to interview the woman who had rented him his flat, the nurses and the doctors at the sanatorium in Basel who had released him, thinking him cured…even his erstwhile business partner, Armand Moncharmin, who had not been happy to be sought out for his opinion of the man who had turned out to be a rage-maddened killer.

"I assure you, he never behaved in such a way when *I* knew him," Moncharmin had asserted over and over again.

But now the book was done, and would be published on the seven-month anniversary of Raoul de Chagny's death. One mystery still haunted Saint Denis, however.

"You still do not know who it was that tried to save the comte, who pulled Monsieur Richard away?" asked Elise, who had clearly seen the distracted expression on her companion's face.

"No," Saint Denis replied. "The Comtesse de Chagny told the detectives on the case that she had never seen the man before, and no one he had been sitting near in the audience knew anything of him, either." He studied Elise, realizing for the first time that she had at last abandoned the mourning gowns she'd been wearing for the past six months and more, was now radiant in a dark green walking dress that suited her autumn-hued coloring.

How very beautiful she was.

"Perhaps the stranger was the Opera Ghost," Elise suggested, still wearing a smile, one that brought an appealing curve to her lovely lips.

But Saint Denis shook his head. "No. I don't know who he was, but he was definitely a man. I have it on good authority that the Opera Ghost is dead."

"Oh," she said, now looking disappointed. "That is too bad. I rather liked the idea of the Opera having its own ghost."

He went to her and looped his arm in hers, feeling a bit daring. Over the past seven months, they had performed a complicated dance around one another, knowing they wanted to grow closer…knowing they needed to remain apart until the world would not raise an eyebrow at their connection.

To his relief, her gloved fingers tightened on his forearm, and that little glint he loved so much appeared in her hazel-green eyes.

Because it seemed clear to him that she didn't want to linger on such a melancholy subject, he didn't tell her what he'd just been thinking.

The Opera Ghost might be no more, but the Palais Garnier would always be haunted by the violence done there.

Christine set down the letter and turned to see Erik watching her from the place where he stood near the window. Once again, she had to marvel at how natural his features appeared, even in the bright southern sunlight flooding through the glass.

"Well?" he said.

"I'm afraid Meg and Honoré have had to cancel their trip to visit us," she replied. "She just discovered that she is in a delicate condition, and so they think it better not to travel."

He gave an understanding nod. "I'd say that it is a pity, but I'm sure they don't feel that way. We must send them our congratulations."

"Yes," Christine said, "I will write her and tell her we are both very happy for them."

And she was, even if that happiness was tinged with disappointment at not being able to see her dear friend. It would have been good to have a familiar face about, although Christine had to admit that she and Erik had been very warmly welcomed in Rome. He had already begun to develop quite a reputation as a voice teacher of great talent and intuition, and she had already given several well-received recitals, although she was not sure whether she ever wanted to set foot on the opera stage again.

In this warm, sunlit place, she had begun to heal. She knew she would never forget the agony in Raoul's face as she held him and his life slipped away, but time had a way of smoothing over such painful recollections, of reminding one that it was possible to move on.

Of course, she understood such things were easier when you had the assistance of someone who loved you with every ounce of their being.

It had not come easily, of course. Months and months had passed before she would even entertain the thought of escaping, of allowing Erik to take her away from the city that had been the site of so much pain. In the immediate aftermath of Raoul's death, she discovered that her place in the world was far more precarious than she'd thought; there had been an inheritance, but a small one, as she had not borne him an heir, and the estate had passed to his eldest cousin. Strangely, though, knowing she had no more ties to Chagny had made it easier for her to at last turn her back on France. Meg and Honoré had given her a place to live for a time, and eventually Christine had told her friend everything of what had passed between her and Erik.

Meg, dear heart that she was, had somehow understood, and when Erik once again broached the subject of leaving, of starting over in a place where no one knew them, she had thrown in her own support.

"I will miss you dreadfully," she had said to Christine as they sat in Meg's pretty rose-hung sitting room one afternoon. "For I must confess that I have quite enjoyed having you here with us. It was like having a sister at last—a *real* sister, not those spiteful sisters of Honoré's. But I also know that there is far too much tragedy here for you. It is all right to want to escape."

Christine had embraced her friend, and then went to Erik's house in the Marais to let him know that she would be ready to leave whenever he deemed it to be a suitable time. And he had drawn her to him, and kissed her, and said he would take her to Rome...but only as his wife, as he would not dishonor her.

In some ways, that wedding had been much like her wedding with Raoul, small and with no real ceremony. However, this time, she had her friends Meg and Honoré as witnesses, and the four of them went out to dinner at a restaurant afterward, and toasted one another with champagne...although not too much, because it still did not quite agree with her.

Christine knew she was not the innocent she

had been when she first went to her marriage bed. That is, she had thought she knew what to expect, but Erik's embraces brought her alive in a way Raoul's never had, and she finally understood what it was to have another's soul echo yours in every way possible.

Their only disagreement had been over the mask. She had told him there was no need for him to wear it when they were alone together, that she knew who he was and did not care.

But he had only shaken his head and kissed her again, those counterfeit lips of his feeling so much like those of flesh and blood that she had to wonder at the talent which could create such artifice. "I know that," he'd told her, his voice thick with emotion. "I do not wear it for you, Christine. I wear it for myself. I want to be the man who stands before you now, not the monster I once was. If I can be this person, then I am no longer a ghost, a creature who hides his face from the light. Do you understand?"

And she'd told him that of course she did, and he embraced her once more, and made love to her in a way that assured her no woman on earth had ever been adored as she was.

Then they had gone to Rome and bought a house on the Piazza Piombino, and enjoyed their days in the sun. The plan to have Meg and Honoré visit had been hatched around that time, since they had both thought it would be good for their friends to come to Italy and enjoy more weeks of warmth just as northern France slipped toward winter.

But it was not to be. Christine told herself that was all right, for they had made friends here in Rome as well, and of course she could not be anything but happy that Meg and Honoré would soon be adding to their little family.

Erik came to her and took her hand in his, then raised it to his lips. A warm flush moved through her at his touch, and she smiled despite her disappointment.

"Are you sorry that we have waited?" he said then.

She did not bother to ask him what he was talking about. Early on, he had told her that there were ways to prevent a woman from conceiving, herbal concoctions he would brew for her if she wished, and she had agreed. Not because she feared bearing a child who looked like him, but because she wanted them to have this time together to truly know one another first before they moved on to starting a family.

Now, though, she thought of what it might be like to have a son with Erik's brilliance and fire, someone who would, she hoped, have his same almost mystical affinity for music. It would be quite something to have a child like that.

Perhaps such a day would never come. It was entirely possible, after all, that she was unable to bear a child. However, something inside, some deep, hidden instinct she hadn't even known she possessed, told her that wasn't the truth, that if there had been any lack, it had been Raoul's, not hers.

She looked up at Erik, at the finely molded planes of the face he had created for himself—a face he informed her had been modeled upon that of his late father—and told herself it was time. The love they shared was so deep, so expansive and profound, that she knew an addition to their family could do nothing to change it, would instead only make their connection grow that much greater.

Her fingers tightened on his. "No, I am not sorry," she said. "But I also think our time for waiting is done."

He stared down at her for a long moment, then pulled her into his arms, kissing her again and again.

And yes, now she could acknowledge to herself that she had never wanted anything more than his embrace, his love...that now at last in Erik's arms, she had come home.

The End

AUTHOR'S NOTE

It's always a daunting task to take on a project like this, a book that builds on what another author has created. I've been haunted by Erik's story for more than twenty-five years, and I made several false starts to this novel, only to lay it aside to pursue other projects. However, I never forgot what I'd imagined could be a continuation of the Opera Ghost's tale, one that might give it the ending I'd always secretly hoped for.

This book was written with loving respect for Gaston Leroux's original novel. I know there are some who probably won't care for the ending I've provided, and I understand. For others, though, those who always wanted Erik and Christine to find a way through all their travails so they might finally share one another's lives…I hope you've enjoyed this book and understand the few liberties I've taken with the primary story. It does feel wonderful to have completed something that's been waiting, unfinished, for so many years.

Christine Pope
October 2020

ALSO BY CHRISTINE POPE

HEDGEWITCH FOR HIRE

(Mystery/Paranormal romance)

Grave Mistake (January 2021)

Social Medium (March 2021)

———

THE WITCHES OF WHEELER PARK

(Paranormal romance)

Storm Born

Thunder Road

Winds of Change

Mind Games

A Wheeler Park Christmas (November 2020)

Blood Ties (February 2021)

———

PROJECT DEMON HUNTERS*

(Paranormal Romance)

Unquiet Souls

Unbound Spirits

Unholy Ground

Unseen Voices

Unmarked Graves

Unbroken Vows

THE DEVIL YOU KNOW*

(Paranormal Romance)

Sympathy for the Devil

Charmed, I'm Sure

A Wing and a Prayer

THE WITCHES OF CANYON ROAD*

(Paranormal Romance)

Hidden Gifts

Darker Paths

Mysterious Ways

A Canyon Road Christmas

Demon Born

An Ill Wind

Higher Ground

Haunted Hearts

THE WITCHES OF CLEOPATRA HILL*

(Paranormal Romance)

Darkangel

Darknight

Darkmoon

Sympathetic Magic

Protector

Spellbound

A Cleopatra Hill Christmas

Impractical Magic

Strange Magic

The Arrangement

Defender

Bad Blood

Deep Magic

Darktide

THE DJINN WARS*

(Paranormal Romance)

Chosen

Taken

Fallen

Broken

Forsaken

Forbidden

Awoken

Illuminated

Stolen

Forgotten

Driven

Unspoken

THE WATCHERS TRILOGY*

(Paranormal Romance)

Falling Dark

Dead of Night

Rising Dawn

THE SEDONA FILES*

(Paranormal Romance)

Bad Vibrations

Desert Hearts

Angel Fire

Star Crossed

Falling Angels

Enemy Mine

TALES OF THE LATTER KINGDOMS*

(Fantasy Romance)

All Fall Down

Dragon Rose

Binding Spell

Ashes of Roses

One Thousand Nights

Threads of Gold

The Wolf of Harrow Hall

Moon Dance

The Song of the Thrush

THE GAIAN CONSORTIUM SERIES*

(Science Fiction Romance)

Beast (free prequel novella)

Blood Will Tell

Breath of Life

The Gaia Gambit

The Mandala Maneuver

The Titan Trap

The Zhore Deception

The Refugee Ruse

STANDALONE TITLES

Hearts on Fire

Taking Dictation

Night Music

Golden Heart

* Indicates a completed series

ABOUT THE AUTHOR

USA Today bestselling author Christine Pope has been writing stories ever since she commandeered her family's Smith-Corona typewriter back in grade school. Her work includes paranormal romance, fantasy romance, and science fiction/space opera romance. She makes her home in Arizona's beautiful Verde Valley.

Christine Pope on the Web:
www.christinepope.com

f facebook.com/ChristinePopeAuthor

🐦 twitter.com/ChristineJPope

📌 pinterest.com/ChristineJPope

Made in the USA
Columbia, SC
20 January 2023

10803133R00238